*The Most Lovable Detective
You'll Ever Meet . . .*

Heron Carvic's
MISS SEETON

Don't miss a single misadventure of
the marvellous mistress of mystery!

### PICTURE MISS SEETON
A night at the opera strikes a chord of danger when Miss
Seeton witnesses a murder . . . and paints a portrait of the
killer.

### WITCH MISS SEETON
Double, double, toil and trouble sweep through the village
when Miss Seeton goes undercover . . . to investigate a local
witches' coven!

### MISS SEETON DRAWS THE LINE
Miss Seeton is enlisted by Scotland Yard when her paintings of a little girl turn the young subject into a model for
murder.

### MISS SEETON SINGS
Miss Seeton boards the wrong plane and lands amidst a
gang of European counterfeiters. One false note, and her
new destination is deadly indeed.

*Continued . . .*

## ODDS ON MISS SEETON

Miss Seeton in diamonds and furs at the roulette table? It's all a clever disguise for the high-rolling spinster . . . but the game of money and murder is all too real.

## ADVANTAGE, MISS SEETON

Miss Seeton's summer outing to a tennis match serves up more than expected when Britain's up-and-coming female tennis star is hounded by mysterious death threats.

## MISS SEETON, BY APPOINTMENT

Miss Seeton is off to Buckingham Palace on a secret mission—but to foil a jewel heist, she must risk losing the Queen's head . . . and her own neck!

## MISS SEETON AT THE HELM

Miss Seeton takes a whirlwind cruise to the Mediterranean—bound for disaster. A murder on board leads the seafaring sleuth into some very stormy waters.

## MISS SEETON CRACKS THE CASE

It's highway robbery for the innocent passengers of a motor coach tour. When Miss Seeton sketches the roadside bandits, she becomes a moving target herself.

## MISS SEETON PAINTS THE TOWN

The Best Kept Village Competition inspires Miss Seeton's most unusual artwork—a burning cottage—and clears the smoke of suspicion in a series of local fires.

## HANDS UP, MISS SEETON

The gentle Miss Seeton? A thief? A preposterous notion—until she's accused of helping a pickpocket . . . and stumbles into a nest of crime.

## MISS SEETON BY MOONLIGHT

Scotland Yard borrows one of Miss Seeton's paintings to bait an art thief . . . when suddenly a *second* thief strikes.

## MISS SEETON ROCKS THE CRADLE

Miss Seeton returns a kidnapped infant to her royal home—and happens on a plot to topple the British crown.

## MISS SEETON GOES TO BAT

Miss Seeton's in on the action when a cricket game leads to mayhem in the village of Plummergen . . . and gives her a shot at smashing Britain's most baffling burglary ring.

*Available from Berkley Books*

# MORE MYSTERIES FROM THE
# BERKLEY PUBLISHING GROUP...

**THE HERON CARVIC MISS SEETON MYSTERIES:** Retired art teacher Miss Seeton steps in where Scotland Yard stumbles. "A most beguiling protagonist!" —*New York Times*

*by Heron Carvic*
MISS SEETON SINGS
MISS SEETON DRAWS THE LINE
WITCH MISS SEETON
PICTURE MISS SEETON
ODDS ON MISS SEETON

*by Hamilton Crane*
HANDS UP, MISS SEETON
MISS SEETON CRACKS THE CASE
MISS SEETON PAINTS THE TOWN
MISS SEETON BY MOONLIGHT
MISS SEETON ROCKS THE CRADLE
MISS SEETON GOES TO BAT

*by Hampton Charles*
ADVANTAGE MISS SEETON
MISS SEETON AT THE HELM
MISS SEETON, BY APPOINTMENT

**SISTERS IN CRIME:** Criminally entertaining short stories from the top women of mystery and suspense. "Excellent!" —*Newsweek*

*edited by Marilyn Wallace*
SISTERS IN CRIME
SISTERS IN CRIME 2
SISTERS IN CRIME 3

SISTERS IN CRIME 4
SISTERS IN CRIME 5

**KATE SHUGAK MYSTERIES:** A former D.A. solves crime in the far Alaska north . . .

*by Dana Stabenow*
A COLD DAY FOR MURDER
A FATAL THAW

**DOG LOVER'S MYSTERIES STARRING HOLLY WINTER:** With her Alaskan malamute, Rowdy, Holly dogs the trails of dangerous criminals. "A gifted and original writer." —Carolyn G. Hart

*by Susan Conant*
A NEW LEASH ON DEATH
DEAD AND DOGGONE

A BITE OF DEATH
PAWS BEFORE DYING

# MISS SEETON
# GOES TO BAT

## HAMILTON CRANE

BERKLEY BOOKS, NEW YORK

MISS SEETON GOES TO BAT

A Berkley Book / published by arrangement with
the author and the estate of Heron Carvic

PRINTING HISTORY
Berkley edition / January 1993

ISBN: 0-425-13576-4

A BERKLEY BOOK®TM 757,375
Berkley Books are published by The Berkley Publishing Group,
200 Madison Avenue, New York, New York 10016.
The name "BERKLEY" and the "B" logo
are trademarks belonging to Berkley Publishing Corporation.

PRINTED IN THE UNITED STATES OF AMERICA

10  9  8  7  6  5  4  3  2  1

# chapter

## ~1~

OPINION IN PLUMMERGEN was divided.

Which division, in itself, was unremarkable. The population of this Kentish village has hovered around the five hundred mark since time immemorial: and during that time it has been a rare occasion when two hundred and fifty—or thereabouts—persons have not been at loggerheads with the other—approximately—two hundred and fifty. A few dauntless individualists through the ages have made a point of retreating to the safety of parentheses, but such neutrality has generally been frowned upon. It is seen as no more than one's plain parochial duty to take sides, for Plummergen does not so much indulge in as thrive upon argument, controversy, discord, and strife. What was good enough in 1189 at the accession of King Richard I is certainly good enough in the latter quarter of the twentieth century. Vengeance may traditionally be the Lord's, but perennial ideological divergence is, just as traditionally, Plummergen's.

Such division of opinion, therefore, was unremarkable. To the true Plummergen expert, however, certain refinements must surely present themselves as remarkable in the extreme: these refinements being the unexpected subdivisions of opinion into which the current convoluted dispute had diversified, such subdivisions being a complication to which Plummergen is not accustomed. And nobody was quite sure how it would all turn out . . .

It was Mrs. Flax who first polarised Plummergen in three different directions instead of the more usual two. With her basket over her arm, Plummergen's Wise Woman had made a majestic entrance to Mr. Stillman's post-office-cum-general-store, where a little crowd of shoppers was busy discussing the latest item of general interest, just as Mrs. Flax had expected—it being the middle of the morning, and village custom long established—would be the case.

Mrs. Flax listened for a few moments, her eyes beginning to gleam, while conversation surged to and fro about her. Gradually, this silent surveillance reduced the eager gossips to an uncomfortable muttering amongst themselves, as it dawned on them that Mother Flax was waiting to pronounce.

Which, with every face at last towards her, mutely asking her views, the Wise Woman duly did.

"At least," she pointed out, "she didn't do it *here*, did she?" And with these few words she split the village, Ancient Gaul-like, into three parts.

In Plummergen, when spoken with a particular emphasis, "she" can only refer to one person. Miss Emily Dorothea Seeton, who removed from London to Kent some seven years ago when her godmother died and bequeathed to her the picturesque cottage at one end of the village's main street, has, since her first arrival, been the subject of wildly differing theories and speculations. One school of thought considers her a positive asset to the place, the adventures into which she is plunged never failing to be resolved, with credit, by her own—innocent—actions. She is to be much admired, if not seen as an example to one and all.

The opposition counters this with claims that Miss Seeton has caused more trouble, and invoked more chaos—deliberately—than any one normal retired art teacher could reasonably be supposed to do: which the pro-Seeton lobby finds hard to deny without appearing ridiculous. Innocent or deliberate in her behaviour, Miss Seeton certainly makes her presence felt in unforgettable fashion . . .

But at least, on this occasion, she hadn't done so anywhere near Plummergen.

"Front page of the paper, so it was," said Mrs. Skinner, an avid reader—as is most of the village—of that popular publication, the *Daily Negative*. "Sensation in Scotland, it said. And didn't Miss Seeton go to stay with some lord in the Highlands only the other day?"

"And look whose name's on the top line," said young Mrs. Newport. "That Amelita Forby, as is always coming down here writing Plummergen Pieces, and about the Battling Brolly—stands to reason it's Miss Seeton again, doesn't it?"

Everyone had to agree that, though Amelita Forby had not specified Miss Seeton by name ("Yes, but she never does, does she? Sneaky, I calls it!"), the inference, to those familiar with the little spinster, was obvious. Miss Seeton had been At It again . . .

"At least," said Mrs. Flax, "she didn't do it here, did she? Peace and quiet, for once—and I'm sure," she added virtuously, "there's nobody likes a peaceful life more than I do."

Thoughts turned to some of the Wise Woman's less peaceful pastimes—ill-wishing; love-philtres; the potent charms used to banish the aftereffects of the love-philtres' efficacy—but nobody ventured to contradict her. Nobody, that is, except Mrs. Scillicough, sister to young Mrs. Newport.

Mrs. Scillicough and Mrs. Newport were Plummergen's contribution to the population explosion, as well as a classic example of sibling rivalry. Mrs. Newport had four children under the age of five, and an automatic washing machine; Mrs. Scillicough had triplets, and a twin-tub. Mrs. Newport's brood was as well behaved—after an ambiguous start, sternly suppressed—as could reasonably be expected of so youthful a quartet; Mrs. Scillicough's triplets were a village byword for utter frightfulness. For which reason, a desperate Mrs. Scillicough had approached Mrs. Flax with pleas for help; had been prescribed various herbal concoctions and incantations; had used these with ever-increasing urgency—and had found them sadly wanting.

For which reason Mrs. Scillicough stoutly refused to afford the Wise Woman the respect Mrs. Flax, and most of Plummergen's other inhabitants, believed to be her due.

Mrs. Scillicough tossed her head and scowled. "Peaceful life? There's none of you knows the meaning of the word! But what if it *is* peaceful here when Miss Seeton goes away? At least she brings a spot of life to this dump! Pictures in the paper, and reporters—"

"And the telly," broke in Emmy Putts from behind the grocery counter, where she dreamed perpetually of being Discovered by some passing producer and whisked off to stardom in Hollywood

movies—or, failing the films, on television. "Lots of telly people we allus gets here when Miss Seeton's up to her tricks, don't
we? Only this time, they've all gone off to Scotland! It's not—it's
not fair!"

"Now really, Emmeline . . . ," began Mrs. Stillman; but her
protest went ignored. Emmy's plaintive cry seemed to have
touched a nerve with a certain rebellious element among the
shoppers, who murmured, and grumbled; though they still cast
doubtful glances in the direction of Mrs. Flax.

"Sensation in Scotland indeed," said Mrs. Henderson, with a
sniff, and a glare for Mrs. Skinner. These two ladies had fallen
out over the flower-arranging rota in church, and one had only to
support a particular party line for the other to be heard denouncing
it. "What's she want to go gallivanting off with lords for? Aren't
we good enough for her?"

"After all the fuss she made about retiring down here, when Old
Mrs. Bannet left her that cottage," said young Mrs. Newport, who
lived in one of the council houses at the far end of the village.

"She's gone on holiday," retorted Mrs. Scillicough, who lived
in another. "And if a body can't have a holiday once in a while,
it's a poor lookout, that's what I say!"

"Holiday? When that reporter woman's gone with her, as bold
as brass?"

"No more than a put-up job, so it was . . ."

"Gets paid for a story, line by line . . ."

"There's bin stories enough around these parts for a while, I
reckon . . ."

"But Miss Seeton—" emphatically—"lives here!"

Which five crisp words encapsulated the difference of opinion.
The pro-Seeton lobby had long ago given up arguing their hero-
ine's merits, unless pushed to the limit by utter folly on the part
of her detractors: life, said Miss Seeton's friends, was too short.
Besides, they tried to avoid shopping when the anti-Seetonites
were liable to be out in force: it was far less exhausting;
with the result that the group which harboured the darkest
suspicions of Miss Seeton was generally able to voice such
suspicions among others of a similar persuasion with perfect
freedom: a freedom which they were happy to exercise—and
frequently did.

But all at once the happy freedom had proved false, the similarity mere illusion. Miss Seeton had been up to her tricks yet again: well, this came as no surprise. A week seldom passed without her doing something to set local—if not, courtesy of the press, national—tongues wagging. But that she had performed these latest tricks many miles from her native—(or at least adopted)—hearth was nothing less than an insult—or a matter for relief and celebration, depending upon one's point of view. Of that fifty per cent of Plummergen which regarded Miss Seeton as . . . well, as *odd*, half were only too thankful she had removed that oddness from their vicinity for a time; while the other half were annoyed that she had apparently seen fit to ignore their claim to a share—albeit vicarious—in her fame by indulging in her antics at the opposite end of the country.

The group headed by Mrs. Flax found itself unable to understand that fronted by Mrs. Scillicough. Everyone felt at cross-purposes: but not in the usual way, which they could have accepted, and even enjoyed. They were all, to a woman, decidedly unnerved by the feeling. It went far deeper than most of their habitual skirmishes: they found themselves in agreement on one level while, at the same time, in absolute disagreement on the other. They had been knocked decidedly off-balance . . .

Of course, they knew who was really to blame. The odd influence of Miss Seeton clearly continued to exert itself even during her absence many miles away: on this, at least, everyone could agree. But as to the other matter . . . would either side feel able to back down, or to modify its views? Unlikely, given the intensity of previous quarrels, whether or not caused by Miss Seeton. They needed some new direction for their thoughts, in order to restore their former unity of sentiment and purpose . . .

But, though everyone saw the danger at the same time and undertook some frantic cogitation, nobody could think of anything. An awkward silence descended on the post office. People found themselves unable to meet one another's eyes. Mrs. Flax surveyed the havoc she had wrought and fell to brooding on Miss Seeton's skill in long-distance enchantment, which she herself, for all her vaunted prowess as a wise woman, had never possessed. Like Emmy Putts, Mrs. Flax felt it was unfair; and was about to risk the faraway wrath of that foreign witch by saying so, when the bell over the door tinkled—and in walked salvation.

The long and the short of it, in fact. Tall, thin, and equine of feature, Miss Erica Nuttel accompanied her friend, the dumpy, dark-eyed Mrs. Norah "Bunny" Blaine, noted in the village for her bad temper and her subsequent sulks. These two ladies, whose little house, Lilikot, is situated almost directly opposite the post office, spend every spare moment at their plate-glass windows observing Plummergen life and passing public comment on it thereafter. The accuracy of such comment is a matter of small importance to the Nuts, as Miss Nuttel and Mrs. Blaine are collectively known. Plummergen has always regarded any bulletin from The Nut House with great interest and with much scepticism; but it is supposed there is always some grain of truth in these bulletins somewhere, if only it can be found.

And, if it can't, who cares? A good time is nonetheless had by all. Plummergen not only thrives on argument, controversy, discord, and strife: it revels in speculation, gossip, and wild surmise as well. And it now welcomed the Nuts with smiles of relief and expectant looks: it recognised the demeanour of people with News to impart.

Miss Nuttel surveyed the assembled shoppers with an air of lofty disinterest and took herself off to study the revolving book-stand while Bunny fumbled in her string bag for the inside-out envelope on which she had jotted her list. Neither Nut seemed aware of the pregnant hush which filled the post office; and Mrs. Blaine was ushered to the front of the queue with little cries that no, of course it didn't matter, they were in no hurry and she was to go right ahead. The Nuts invariably impart their most interesting news when pretending to be busy doing something else.

"Well," said Mrs. Blaine with demur, "if you're sure you don't mind . . ." A general chorus insisted that they didn't. "Too considerate of you all, when we're in such a hurry to catch up—Eric and I are a little behind this morning." And not a smirk was directed towards Mrs Blaine's ample rear: matters were too important for such levity. When would she come to the point? "Eric," called Mrs. Blaine—an indrawn collective breath. Was it to be now?—"Eric, I can't quite make out what I wrote. Can it really say *bicycle spokes*?"

The collective breath was exhaled with relief. It was to be now. Even for the Nuts, a reference to bicycles would be so bizarre that Plummergen knew it must in fact refer to whatever it was that Miss Nuttel and her friend wished to relate; and Plummergen waited eagerly for the rest of the equation.

"Better let me see," said Miss Nuttel, striding across from the books and taking the proffered envelope, over which she frowned for a few tense seconds. Then she nodded and looked up. "Not *bicycle spokes*, Bunny—*Brussels sprouts*. Understandable mistake, though."

"Yes, of course, too silly of me." Mrs. Blaine, beaming, retrieved her list and turned to Emmy Putts. "Two pounds of stone-ground flour, please, Emmy. I suppose it was because of seeing that girl. Too muddling—and a packet of oatmeal—when she rode that bicycle as bold as brass up to the door of the George—and a small bottle of olive oil. When one hardly expects any but the most exclusive—goodness, I had no idea the price had gone up so much. Better make that sunflower, instead. Such a remarkable-looking young woman, one has to admit. Perhaps," suggested Mrs Blaine, "she's an eccentric millionaire? Everyone knows how much Mr. Mountfitchet has been able to increase his charges since the Best Kept Village Competition, don't they, Eric? Eric?"

But Miss Nuttel's air of lofty disinterest, which had, after her deciphering of Bunny's scribble, been reinstated, was now changed to one of intense concentration on the view through Mr. Stillman's own plate-glass window. "Bunny!" cried Miss Nuttel, ignoring her friend's George and Dragon millionaire guest motif. "Across the road—look!"

Mrs. Blaine was promptly elbowed to one side by a concerted rush for a frontline view from the post office to the other side of The Street, as Plummergen's main thoroughfare is known: to Lilikot, otherwise known as The Nut House, at which the taller of the two Nuts appeared to be staring . . .

Or was she? As feet jostled for space, heads craned, and one or two more devious souls began to remove from the window the tallest items obstructing their line of vision, everyone saw that it was not what was happening to her house that worried Miss Nuttel. It was what was happening to the house next door which had caught her, and now their, undivided attention.

# chapter
## -2-

ASHFORD, FIFTEEN MILES northeast of Plummergen, is not the county town of Kent, but is nevertheless the headquarters for the local police force. PC Potter, who with his wife Mabel, his daughter Amelia, and Amelia's notorious tabby cat Tibs, resides in Plummergen's police house, is only one of many village bobbies who report to their town-based superior anything they feel Old Brimstone needs to know.

Superintendent Chris Brinton, based in Ashford, always suspected that he was regularly kept in the dark about certain aspects of rural life, but was never able to prove his suspicion; and was inclined to adopt the attitude that, on the whole, the ground force was a better judge of what was really important than the deskbound johnnie he was afraid he'd become. Ignorance, decided Superintendent Brinton, was definitely bliss in many cases, as far as he was concerned.

His one deviation from this comfortable working theory was in the case of Plummergen, home to Miss Emily Seeton. PC Potter had standing orders to disturb his superior—at home, if necessary—at any hour of the night or day should anything remotely untoward occur within a five-mile radius of the retired art teacher, or—in her absence—her house. It was—Superintendent Brinton advised his friend and colleague, Chief Superintendent Delphick of Scotland Yard—much safer that way. And Delphick, who had been responsible for Miss Seeton's first involvement with the constabulary—and had overseen her recruitment to the force as an Art Consultant—could in all honesty do nothing but agree with him.

But today's reports, over which the superintendent was poring, contained nothing from PC Potter; and Brinton hummed to himself as he reached the final sheet in the folder, and smiled. He reached into his pocket for one of the triple-strength peppermints to which he was hopelessly addicted, and smiled again. He even, as he popped the peppermint into his mouth, whistled a little tune.

"Hey, sir!" Detective Constable Foxon leaped from his chair and came rushing to thump his superior on the back. "Are you all right?"

Brinton, breathing heavily, glowered at Foxon through tear-filled eyes. "Some years ago," he wheezed, "for some reason which now escapes me, Foxon, I authorised your promotion to the plainclothes branch." He paused to cough and clear his throat. Blinking furiously, he went on: "Which, in case it has slipped your memory, Foxon, means that you are supposed to be—heaven help us all—a detective. And detectives, Foxon, are supposed to observe. And to follow clues. And to make intelligent deductions!"

He cleared his throat once more. "So what the hell do you mean by asking me if I'm all right? I've just swallowed a peppermint the wrong way—I nearly choked to death—do I *look* as if I'm all right?"

"Now you come to mention it, sir . . . ," Foxon began; then grinned. "Of course, far be it from me to suggest you might recommend me for the Police Medal, but—"

"Police Medal? When I've only this minute been telling you what a lousy detective you are?"

"But I did," Foxon pointed out, contriving to look both hurt and modest at the same time, "save your life, sir. You told me so yourself. Nearly choked to death, you said, with the inference that if I hadn't—"

Brinton hurled the packet of mints in the direction of his insubordinate sidekick, who ducked neatly with one hand outstretched, caught the mints, and returned them to the superintendent with a bow. "Yours, sir, I believe?"

Brinton muttered something, then cursed aloud as he surveyed the havoc he had caused among the papers on his desk. "I hate you, Foxon," he groaned, and raised despairing eyes to the ceiling. "Look what you've made me do!"

But his young tormentor was already on his hands and knees, collecting the scattered reports from the floor, to which they had been tumbled by the force of Brinton's outflung arm. As he shuffled the reports into some sort of order, Foxon whistled—successfully—with surprise.

"Three more burglaries last night and you're cheerful, sir? Isn't that a bit—well, unusual?"

Brinton grunted his thanks as the reports were handed back to him, and motioned Foxon to sit down. "We don't know all three of 'em happened last night, remember. It's the same old story. Only small items taken, no obvious signs of illegal entry, householder eventually notices something's wrong and starts checking—finds stuff missing and yells for help, no idea how long it's been gone. We're dealing with a regular pro team here, no mistake about that."

Foxon risked a faint smile. "Then at least we can rule out the Choppers, sir."

"For once, I'd agree with you. That gang of hoodlums might well be at the bottom of a fair amount of petty crime and local vandalism, but this sort of thing is miles out of the Choppers' league. Not that it's top-flight stuff, of course—these characters aren't exactly stealing to order, nothing fancy—but what they pinch is good quality. Easy to fence. Portable. Carefully in, and carefully out with a duffel bag over their perishing shoulders, crammed to the brim with goodies—that's the way the blighters work. And wouldn't I," growled the superintendent, "just love to catch 'em at it!"

"I think we all would, sir. May I, er, deduce that it was thinking of such a possibility that made you so cheerful? Something has occurred to you, sir. Inspiration has struck. Any minute now "

"Any minute now what'll be struck is you, Foxon. Didn't anyone ever warn you about taking the mickey out of your superiors? But, since you're so obviously trying to show me I was wrong to regret having turned you into a detective—apply yourself to these reports, laddie"—Brinton held the folder across the desk—"and then tell me what made me so cheerful. You have five minutes."

"Don't need 'em, sir." Foxon took the folder and handed it straight back to the startled superintendent. "I, er, couldn't help noticing, as I was putting it all together again—no report from

PC Potter, sir. Which, er, means there's nothing going on in Plummergen . . . at the moment," he added, just as Brinton seemed about to smile. The burgeoning smile vanished.

"She's in Scotland, laddie. Nowhere near this patch—nowhere near this country, thank the Lord! And I'll thank Him a second time, for giving us such nice, peaceful, harmless crooks—more or less—to chase after, for a change. I'm getting too old for the big-time stuff. Let's leave all that to the Yard!"

In the office of Detective Chief Superintendent Delphick, at New Scotland Yard, more reports were being studied. Detective Sergeant Bob Ranger, the Oracle's sidekick, stretched his massive frame and yawned.

"Coffee, sir? Might help to keep us awake."

Oracular eyebrows were raised. "No sergeant of mine is supposed to fall asleep on the job—but I have to admit," and he stretched in his turn, "this isn't the most gripping batch of files with which we've ever had to deal. Your suggestion of coffee is both timely, and apt. It is a source of much regret to me that you will be unable to fulfil it."

Bob grinned as he pushed back his chair and rose to his full height of six-foot-seven. "Well, would you settle for coffee-flavoured machine dishwater, sir? Or we could pop down to the canteen and have something a bit nearer the real stuff. Nobody's going to miss us for ten minutes or so . . ."

He cast a scathing glance at the heap of reports, midway between his in-tray and his out, on the desk before him. He couldn't remember the last time he and the Oracle were both so up-to-date with their paperwork. Very odd. Of course, the holiday season was in full swing—even crooks went away sometimes, and by late August those that hadn't were being nagged by their wives and pestered by their children—but it was odd, everything being so quiet. Unnerving, almost.

"Anne and I had a postcard from Miss Seeton this morning," Bob remarked, as he hunted in the filing cabinet for the cache of small change on which the coffee machine at the end of the corridor depended. He paused with his hand on the tin. What had made him think of Aunt Em out of the blue like that?

"Mine arrived yesterday," said Delphick, trying not to frown. "Didn't I mention it? Anyway, all she says is that she's having a good time."

"Same as ours, then. Of course, sir"—Bob rattled the tin glumly before removing the lid—"she wrote before Mel's story broke. I do hope she's still enjoying herself—oh." He tipped the contents of the tin into the palm of his hand. One five-pence piece winked forlornly up at him from the vast pink expanse. "Sorry, sir. Looks as if we'll have to slog down to the canteen anyway, unless . . ."

They both fumbled in their trouser pockets, Delphick's haul being an assortment of coppers, two fifty-pence pieces, and three of what, in pre-decimalisation days, had been sixpenny bits. "I'd intended popping out to the bank at lunchtime," he explained, with a sigh.

Bob's contribution was an even larger assortment of coppers, some florins—now known as ten-pence pieces—and two more fifty-pence coins. "So the only bob around here's me, sir," he said, with a chuckle. "The canteen, then? We can offload these horrors, at least."

"Legal tender, Bob. You shouldn't be so rude about them—though I agree they aren't my favourite coin of the realm. You'd think we'd be used to them after however many years it is, but they wear too many holes in my pockets for my wife's liking, and I consider them confoundedly heavy for the sum they're nominally worth."

Bob nodded. "How long ago is it—three, four years? And still nobody likes the things. So you have to hand it to those blighters Inspector Borden's lot are so busy chasing, sir—pretty smart of 'em to cash in on the way everyone hates them—sorry, sir"—as the chief superintendent groaned at the unwitting pun—"and go to all the bother of forging them. Mind you, if *I* had their equipment, I think I'd rather wait until someone invents a pound coin, wouldn't you? Make the game more worth the candle."

"Sergeant Ranger, you have a criminal mind. It comes as no surprise now that there was so little cash in the tin—yet on what, I have to ask, did you spend it? Was it squandered on riotous living—on wine, and song? Anyone with such a wife as Anne has no need of women, of course. Gambling, perhaps." Chuckling to himself, Delphick followed Bob as he marched down the corridor towards the lift. "A syndicate! I wish now that I'd locked the office door, since not even the hallowed floors of Scotland Yard seem safe from the taint of corruption. Or maybe you're paying blackmail over incriminating photographs?"

Bob jabbed a thumb on the call-button, sighed, and gazed in stony silence at the indicator light. Sometimes the Oracle let his sense of humour run away with him so fast, it made everyone within earshot dizzy—and thank goodness in this case there wasn't. Anyone within earshot. Who might misunderstand . . . And Bob scowled as he reproached himself for starting to sound—to think, he amended glumly—too much like Miss Seeton for his peace of mind. A couple of postcards, and she'd got the Oracle talking rubbish and him talking muddled. How on earth did she do it?

"Incriminating photographs," Delphick mused. "I trust the offender isn't dear old Cedric Benbow. My faith in human nature would be totally destroyed, should that prove to be the case. Might I enquire how much you have been asked to pay for the nega—Ah, good."

The lift, with a clunk, had arrived at their floor. Bob sighed again as the doors opened: with relief, that the lift was empty. If the Oracle was going to carry on like this all the way down to the canteen . . .

"You're right, of course." Delphick was completely serious now. "It's clever of them, whoever they are. Coins, of course, require less sophisticated equipment than notes, if you're going to forge them—and, once the equipment's up and rolling, always provided you're careful how you release the dud stock on an unsuspecting public, you're on an almost certain winner, I should say. And very few clues as to the identity of the coiners, or the whereabouts of their press . . . Although we could always suggest to Inspector Borden"—in a lighter tone, as they emerged from the lift on the canteen floor—"that he try searching in the Eyford area."

Bob looked sideways at his superior. "I've heard quite a few Fraud blokes talking about the case, of course—but I don't remember them mentioning a place by that name, sir."

"And why should they? It's my own idea entirely—or, rather, Sir Arthur Conan Doyle's: which Borden, since he has no clues worth speaking of, could do worse than follow. *The*

*Engineer's Thumb*—remember? The village of Eyford, near Reading, was where the unfortunate hydraulics expert met the self-styled Colonel Lysander Stark and his meat cleaver, as well as the beautiful English woman and the morose man with the chinchilla beard: the three persons who made up the gang of coiners with whom Sherlock Holmes would have crossed swords had they not set fire to the house and escaped with a selection of sinister, bulky boxes before his arrival."

"Oh," said Bob; there seemed little more to say. Delphick, however, wasn't going to leave it at that; and, as they joined the canteen queue, he went on:

"If my recollection of the story is correct, though the birds may have flown before Holmes arrived, the nickel and tin which they used in the coining process remained." Delving once more into his trouser pocket, he pulled out one of the fifty-pence pieces. "Easy enough, I should imagine, if you have an accurate die and a heavy press. No milled edge—just seven smooth sides, plus front and back, though I believe the technical terms are obverse and reverse."

"Heads and tails will do fine for me, sir," said Bob, as Delphick brushed away his offer to pay for the coffee. The chief superintendent chuckled again as they threaded a path through tables and chairs towards two empty seats.

"You really must try to control that gambling streak, Sergeant Ranger. What does Anne have to say about it? I'm sure she's as reluctant as I am to think of you living so dangerously. A quiet life has much to recommend it, don't forget." Then a quick sigh escaped him. "In moderation, of course. We must hope I'm not placing temptation in the way of Fate—but I suspect that many more days of this relative idleness, and you and I will be begging Inspector Borden to let us join him in his search for the coiners—who are, we must remember, almost certainly killers, as well. Old lags who claim to go straight, who have learned the art of die-casting, and who disappear from public view from time to time—and who are eventually discovered bound, gagged, tied in a sack and shot through the head—do not end up in such a fashion without, as Inspector Borden insists—rightly so, in my view—a degree of assistance from the criminal fraternity."

Bob, wondering whether to go back for a danish pastry—it seemed a long time until lunch—was glad of the diversion. He nodded. "I bet the poor bloke tried blackmail, sir, once he'd set up the presses and what-have-you for the gang, and they wouldn't wear it—well, nobody would, would they? Still, it's the first real slip they've made so far, being careless disposing of the body and someone finding it. On the whole, they're a clever bunch, I reckon. Very . . . restrained, sir, nothing over the top. Just enough snide to make it worth their while, but not so much that it's easy to follow their tracks. Somebody pretty smart's organised this particular scam, sir. Sir?"

Delphick was idly scratching with an abandoned fork at the Britannia side of another fifty-pence piece. "Extremely smart, I should say. How many people would think to check for snide? One always expects forgers to forge notes—high denomination ones, at that—not coins. And, provided the weight feels right, and everything looks in regular order . . . it's a serious precedent, Bob. Counterfeit currency—in sufficiently large quantities—could undermine the whole economy, given enough time. If the gang grows more greedy—if the equipment falls into the wrong hands . . .

"No wonder Inspector Borden's bothered. It's not just that they're ruthless enough to dispose of anyone no longer of any particular use to them, but the setup's potentially as dangerous as anything the Yard's had to deal with . . .

"So maybe we should be grateful for the peaceful life while it lasts."

# chapter

## -3-

IN PLUMMERGEN, MR. Stillman raised despairing eyes to the ceiling as his entire shopful of customers abandoned all pretence of buying anything and rushed to stare at what was happening on the other side of The Street. Even Emmy Putts, caught up in the excitement, darted from her post behind the grocery counter and forced her way to the door, there to stand gaping with everyone else as Mrs. Blaine, in her most horrified squeak, demanded:

"Oh, Eric! What on earth is That Man doing now?"

Plummergen is not generally noted for having a peripatetic population. Most of its inhabitants were born there—marry and raise families there—and intend (in their own good time) to be buried there. The village harbours deep suspicions of any incomers; it takes months, often years, to make up its mind about them. In Miss Seeton's case, as has already been noted, the passage of as many as seven years has not made it possible to reach any firm decision about her, though Miss Seeton, of course, is a special—not to say unique—case. Four or five years should be considered the usual period after which one may regard oneself as a Plummergenite of good—though not the highest—standing.

The highest standing belongs, naturally enough, to the natives, and to them alone. Miss Nuttel and Mrs. Blaine, for example, have lived a dozen years in the place, and are now thought of as Permanent Plummergen—but only of the Second Rank. The Nuts labour joyously under the illusion that they have achieved First Rank status; they suppose that, as such ranking was awarded to their erstwhile neighbours in Ararat Cottage—neighbours whose behaviour was, to say the least of it, peculiar—then it must surely be awarded them, whose behaviour is so very public-spirited.

The Nuts are mistaken. The Dawkins of Ararat Cottage may well have been members of the Holdfast Brethren, a religious sect with its headquarters in nearby Brettenden; but what does it matter that nobody else in Plummergen has ever belonged to the Brethren—whose customs, it must be said, are more than eccentric? The Dawkins, therefore, were also seen as eccentric—but acceptably so, they having been born in the village . . . though Ararat Cottage was best avoided after dark. Just in case.

With the death of Old Mother Dawkin, last of her line, the cottage became home to an assortment of migrant incomers who would lease it for a few months, make—generally—little impact on village affairs, and then move on. Nobody local would touch it. The estate agents regarded it with despair: the minimal rent they could charge, and the rapid turnover of tenants, barely covered their administration costs: Ararat Cottage, in short, was a white elephant. What they wanted was a Siamese nobleman to take it, once and for all, off their books.

What they got was a retired First Sea Lord. Rear Admiral Bernard "Buzzard" Leighton, whose first attempt at landfall had been with his widowed sister, was a reluctant best man when Bernice married a local Group Captain—like himself retired—and, muttering darkly about Brylcreem Boys, had decided he would like a change of scene. Ararat Cottage appealed to him before he'd even seen it: somewhere, he said, for an old sea-dog to rest his wandering ark at last; and, with typical Naval efficiency, he offered cash down for a quick sale at a reduced price, an offer which the estate agents were delighted—and relieved—to accept.

The admiral had now been installed in Ararat Cottage for five days: days during which his neighbours had worn themselves almost to shreds in running repeatedly from the front of Lilikot to the back. Nothing Admiral Leighton might do, the Nuts were determined, must escape their notice—and not much (they being experts at the game) did, though his most notable characteristic hardly needed their help to commend it to village curiosity. Ginger beards, however neatly trimmed, are rare birds in Plummergen. The suspicion with which the admiral's was viewed was tempered only slightly by the news that to make the cottage—he was heard to say—shipshape, he had brought in a team of builders from nearby Brettenden. The builders, being local, were duly pumped as to their employer's intentions. He wanted everything set to rights within the week, they said— had insisted on it—had proposed to invoke penalty clauses if it was not.

Miss Nuttel and Mrs. Blaine approved the idea of keeping tradesmen in their proper place, but felt it their duty to discover the reason for the admiral's haste, in case it had sinister undertones. Upon closer interrogation, the builders said they did not know. And the admiral always seemed too busy with carpentry, decoration, gardening, or general supervision of the work force to do more than nod from time to time at his next-door neighbours across the fence . . .

"Too suspicious, Eric," Mrs. Blaine pointed out, straining on tiptoe to see round the corner from Lilikot's bathroom window. Miss Nuttel, being so much taller, had elected to stand with one foot on the closed lavatory seat and the other on the laundry basket; a physical advantage which Mrs. Blaine thought too unfair. "Nobody can really be that busy when there's a whole truckload of builders working about the place—he's only pretending, I'm sure. Which means he must be up to no good, or else why is he hiding away and not talking to anyone? Except the builders, of course."

The builders arrived each morning at eight-thirty sharp and worked right through until half past five, with only the shortest of breaks, when absolutely necessary.

"Slave labour," said Miss Nuttel, who wasn't afraid of hard work, in moderation, but insisted on making sure Bunny appreciated her efforts with frequent cups of tea, cakes, and insistence that she had a little sit-down from time to time. "Not normal. Probably threatened to keelhaul them. Or the cat," she added.

Mrs. Blaine frowned. "Not a cat, Eric. Not a retired admiral. Surely he ought to have a parrot?"

"Of nine-tails, Bunny." Miss Nuttel shook her head for Mrs. Blaine's innocence. "The lash . . ."

"Oh!" Mrs. Blaine's blackcurrant eyes widened in terror, and her voice rose to a squeak. "Oh, Eric—you know how I abhor violence! And to think of it so very close—I won't sleep a wink, knowing he's just next door! Too dangerous! Unless—

well, maybe"—sometimes, the unthinkable did happen—"you're wrong, Eric. Oh, I do hope so . . ."

Firmly, Miss Nuttel shook her head. "Sorry, Bunny. Not a chance. Not normal to be so reliable—builders, I mean. Ever heard of such a thing before? Stands to reason he must have threatened them."

"Oh, Eric! Oh dear . . . But you're so right, of course. Nobody normal *ever* manages to make builders turn up on time like that every day, and as for getting the work finished when you expect it . . . he must have, well, *underworld connections*—too horrible to think of, in our peaceful little village! Of course he must be up to no good, else why would he bother? He's covering up for some dreadful crime—so dreadful, we can't begin to guess. Which means"—and Mrs. Blaine allowed her voice to sink to its most thrilling depths—"he can't really be an admiral after all, can he?"

Miss Nuttel was shaking her head again: she had started half-way through Mrs. Blaine's impassioned speech and looked rather giddy as she finally gave tongue. "Not *peaceful*, not anymore. Not since . . ."

Mrs. Blaine clasped plump hands together and uttered one of her most horrified squeaks. "Oh, Eric! You can't mean—an accomplice? Moving in while she's not here—pretending he knows nothing at all about her, when really . . . Oh, yes! You're right, of course. It explains everything."

Miss Nuttel now nodded her head with as much insistence as she had shaken it before. "An accomplice," she agreed, darkly. "What else? For That Woman . . ."

"Miss Seeton," breathed Mrs. Blaine, nodding in her turn.

And, having thus come to a conclusion with which both were happy to concur, the Nuts resumed their surveillance upon Ararat Cottage, and upon the self-styled Rear Admiral "Buzzard" Leighton (retired). The post office being conveniently situated almost directly opposite, even when the Nuts were doing the day's shopping they were able to maintain their watch . . .

"Oh, Eric! What on earth is That Man doing now?"

Mr. Stillman's other customers also wished to know. They recognised the Brettenden builders' lorry, which had already arrived once at the cottage that morning and decanted the greater part of its band of workers at the regular hour; it had then driven away with only two men in it. Seasoned observers took this as an indication that work on the cottage was coming to an end. These two were no doubt men whose services could be spared for some new project elsewhere.

But now the lorry was back; the two men were climbing out; their fellows were hurrying from Ararat Cottage, with the admiral close behind . . .

And, before the astonished eyes of Mrs. Blaine, Miss Nuttel, Mrs. Flax, and the rest, the entire band of half a dozen stalwarts began to manoeuvre down from the back of the lorry a very, very long wooden post, painted white. Which, having been duly manoeuvred, was borne out of sight around the side of the lorry; and failed to emerge again. Which could only mean . . .

"They're taking it into That Man's garden!" Without another word, Mrs. Blaine pushed through the throng to the post office door, wrenched it open, and hurried outside.

Everyone looked at everyone else; realised she must be right; and hurried after her. Mr. Stillman rolled his eyes at the ceiling and sighed. Mrs. Stillman glared at the assortment of items on the grocery counter and resolved that Emmy Putts would sell them, and Mrs. Blaine buy them, if she had to go out on the pavement and drag both parties back into the shop by force. "Emmeline!" she called, hurrying in turn to the door. "*Emmeline!*"

But Emmy Putts, in the middle of a cluster of erstwhile customers, was as deaf as they to her employer's call.


"The strangest thing," said Lady Colveden, as she passed his loaded plate to her son before settling to her own lunch. "When I drove past the post office, there they were outside—at least half the village, or so it seemed, staring across The Street at Lilikot. But the *really* strange thing was that Miss Nuttel and Mrs. Blaine were right there in the middle of the crowd, staring as hard as anyone! Well, I could hardly help noticing," she added, as Nigel's look of vague interest turned to a broad grin. "It looked so very . . . so very strange."

"You couldn't help noticing when you slowed the Hillman down to nought miles per hour, you mean." Nigel waved a cheerful fork in his mother's direction, ignoring her frown. "Did you manage to discover the nature of this, er, excessive strangeness before embarrassment caught up with you, and you were forced to drive on?"

"Why should I have been embarrassed?" His mother shook pepper on her vegetables with a careless hand, then sneezed twice. "Bother! When there was that enormous lorry blocking the road, and I wasn't in the Hillman, I was driving the station wagon. Naturally"—she turned wide, innocent eyes upon her undutiful son— "I had to slow right down. Your father would have been furious if I'd scratched the paint."

"Can't use me as an excuse, m'dear. Never been furious in my life." From behind the hallowed pages of the *Farmers Weekly*, held in quivering hands at the far end of the table, came the voice of Major-General Sir George Colveden, Bart, KCB, DSO, JP. "Bound to be a few scratches on a working vehicle—never expect anything else."

Lady Colveden shook her head at the *Farmers Weekly*, but, as its pages remained steadfastly open between herself and the well-loved, though exasperating, person of her husband, she turned back to her equally loved, and just as exasperating, son. "I shall ask you to remember what your father said, Nigel, when the next bill from Crabbe's Garage comes in. And if he even tries to grumble . . ."

"He wouldn't dare." Nigel raised his voice in the direction of the *Farmers Weekly*, from the direction of which a snort had emerged. "Besides, Dad has more important things to worry about—so do I, come to that. If it rains again before harvest's over . . ."

An apprehensive rustle came from the upheld pages at the end of the table, though Sir George still did not speak. On the face of his son and heir, normally so cheerful, a frown had imposed itself. "And if it's bad on the day of the big match—"

"There!" Lady Colveden clattered her knife in triumph on the edge of her plate. "I knew I meant to tell you something important, if you and your father hadn't muddled me with talking about the Nuts, and the lorry delivering that huge white stick thing to the admiral's house—"

"Stick?" Nigel looked up from his plate with interest. "Or stake? Perhaps he's planning to sharpen it and creep out at midnight and skewer Miss Nuttel or Mrs. Blaine through the heart with it. Isn't that supposed to keep witches well and truly in their place?"

"Vampires, I think," his mother began, as a muttering was heard from behind the *Farmers Weekly,* and its pages were lowered to disclose Sir George's ruddy face.

"Leighton planning to settle the hash of that vicious pair from Lilikot, is he? Good show. Lend him anything he likes." He nodded to Nigel. "Whetstone in the toolbox, last time I checked. Sickle, scythe—billhook, if he'd prefer."

"George, really! And Nigel, don't pay any attention to your father. Admiral Leighton couldn't carry it on his own, for one thing. It took six men to lift if off the back of the lorry, with the admiral telling them all what to do, and organising it beautifully, what's more."

"Trust the Navy. Senior Service. Organisation nearly as good as ours." Which compliment, from an Army man, was the highest Sir George could pay.

Nigel reached around the *Farmers Weekly* for his father's plate. "I suppose you weren't driving, er, slowly enough to see where they took it and what they did with it, after all the effort, were you?"

"Somebody came up behind me and hooted," Lady Colveden said, with a sigh, as she rose to collect the empty vegetable dishes. Then she brightened. "But really, it was as well I came home when I did, because otherwise I would have missed Molly's call, and she seems to think there's not much time to arrange something before it's too late. Naturally, I told her that you and Nigel, George"— another wide-eyed stare—"would be the ones who'd know most about that. And especially Nigel, of course," she added over her shoulder, loading crockery through the hatch into the kitchen.

Father looked at son; son looked at father. Shoulders were raised in identical shrugs. Sir George fingered his moustache thoughtfully. Miss Molly Treeves, sister to the Reverend Arthur Treeves, was—as everyone except the Reverend Arthur recognised—the true power behind the rectory throne; and was forever—or so it seemed to the baronet—approaching his wife with various *arrangements,* supposedly for the benefit of Plummergen, which always—he felt—ended up with poor Meg doing more than her fair share of the work. Duty to the village, of course: couldn't deny that. Put in more than you take out: sound motto. Hard work the price you paid for having a good life yourself: matter of giving thanks for one's own luck—count one's blessings. If the current plan had the vicar's approval . . . "Padre in on this as well?" he enquired at last, while Nigel added quickly:

"Whatever it is. Mother darling, do stop rattling and explain. Anyone would think you'd been talking to Miss Seeton—and she's not due back from Scotland for another few days, surely?"

"Well, of course she isn't. And that's why," said his mother, as if to a very backward child, "Molly says we must decide what needs doing, and how much we need to raise, so that we can tell her as soon as she comes home—well, not the minute she walks through the door, but you know what I mean—and then she can start painting, or whatever she decides to do. Though I imagine she'll paint—she seems to prefer that, doesn't she? And isn't it lucky," concluded Lady Colveden, "that the admiral has the builders in?"

# chapter

## ~4~

"ISN'T IT!" NIGEL followed his mother into the kitchen to help with the coffee, while his father, stifling a groan, gave up the unequal struggle and retired again behind the shelter of *Farmers Weekly*. "An amazing piece of luck," said Nigel, putting dishes with saucepans to soak in the sink. Lady Colveden frowned at the percolator and wondered whether it would be too much of an extravagance to drop hints to Sir George in plenty of time for her birthday. "One of the best bits of news I've heard for ages . . ."

His mother switched her frown from the slow burps of the percolator to her son's mischievous face. "Don't be sarcastic, Nigel. I can't think why, but you've been in a silly mood right through lunch. If you were younger, I'd ask your father to put you across his knee and spank you."

"Even if you did, he wouldn't." Nigel twiddled taps happily, watching detergent bubble. "Cruelty to children—besides, he'd be sarcastic too, if he emerged from his paper long enough. He wouldn't think it was playing the game to slipper me for what he wanted to do himself—because don't you understand, Mother darling, that neither of us has the faintest idea what you're talking about? Except—brilliant guesswork here—it has something to do with Miss Seeton." He shook his head. "When you start rattling in all directions like that, it usually has. And"—he raised his voice above her indignant protest—"as what began it this time was my mentioning the big match, I suppose there's some connection with cricket as well, though I hardly see Miss Seeton knocking Murreystone for six all over the field, even with her brolly on top form. And as for letting her loose on the scoring, or the teas—"

25

"It's the pavilion." His mother unplugged the percolator, loaded it on the waiting tray, and handed the tray to Nigel. He took it, staring at her.

"You want Miss Seeton to paint the cricket pavilion? Don't you think that's, er, rather beneath a qualified art teacher? Not that she'd see it like that at all, of course, especially if you and Miss Treeves asked her nicely, but—"

"I was talking about the admiral's builders," interposed Lady Colveden crossly. "As you knew perfectly well, Nigel." She held open the kitchen door. Nigel bore the coffee tray with due solemnity into the dining room. Having set it down on the table, he turned to his mother again.

"The admiral's builders, not the pavilion. You and Miss Treeves want Miss Seeton to paint their great big stick? But I thought you said earlier it was—oh, I see. That was the undercoat. Miss Seeton's going to give it the gloss. Though what that has to do with cricket . . . Does the admiral know, I wonder, what fate has in store for him?"

He skipped nimbly to his seat as his mother threatened him with a coffee spoon. "What fate ought to have in store for you, Nigel, is . . . is . . . George, do listen to the way your son's making fun of me. George!"

"Quite right," replied Sir George, ambiguously. The pages of his journal shook. Lady Colveden caught Nigel's unrepentant eye and poured coffee into cups with a sigh of resignation. Nigel passed one to his father, collected his own, and courteously passed his mother the sugar bowl.

"Cricket," he murmured, just loud enough to be heard. "You know, maybe I *can* visualise it, after all. Miss Seeton at the crease—she takes guard (middle and leg, I should think)—the sunlight from the handle of that gold brolly of hers dazzles the Murreystone bowler—he sends down a bumper—Miss Seeton turns out to have a hitherto unsuspected and distinctive late cut—she whacks the ball straight at—"

"Nigel!" Lady Colveden didn't know whether to giggle or scold. She took a deep breath. "Molly says her brother was looking for his old cricketing cap this morning, to keep the sun off while he was digging the garden, and he realised he must have left it in the pavilion after the last match. Not that he was playing, of course, but you remember how he does enjoy—yes, well," as Nigel started grinning again, and the pages of *Farmers Weekly* quivered. "So the vicar hunted up the key from Mr. Jessyp and went off by himself, because Mr. Jessyp was trying to work out the timetable for next year—you know how quickly the school holidays seem to be over now, almost before they've started. And with poor Miss Maynard's mother still no better . . ."

At another warning look from Nigel, and a pointed cough from her spouse, she had the grace to blush. "Anyway, the vicar was prowling round the pavilion all alone, and goodness knows how, but he managed to trip and almost knocked himself out, Molly says. She says that if something isn't done soon about the roof, it's sure to collapse when the bad weather comes. You know how we've had one or two really heavy downpours recently. The floor's a disgrace, especially in the kitchen." This, with feeling: Lady Colveden served on the Tea Committee. "The underlay, or whatever it is, seems to have soaked up the damp and buckled dreadfully, so that tiles are coming away all over the place."

"Floor and roof alike," agreed Nigel, while his father blew through his moustache and muttered that it was a bally shame things had been allowed to slip so far, but people seemed to have had other things on their minds recently . . .

"So Molly suggested," ventured Lady Colveden—by what process of thought, her husband and son could only begin to guess— "asking Miss Seeton to paint a picture of a Plummergen cricket match with the refurbished pavilion in the background, to be the star attraction at the auction"—she shot a quick look towards the *Farmers Weekly*—"where she thought you, George, might like to be the auctioneer. With a gavel, and Nigel to hold the lots up for people to see, and all the trimmings—a catalogue and so on . . ."

Sir George was observed to perk up a little at this suggestion, stroking his moustache with the tip of a thoughtful finger. Lady Colveden smiled, and frowned at Nigel, who had seemed about to speak.

"Of course, if you didn't fancy that idea, she thought perhaps drawing a plan, and having people put their names on individual tiles—or a raffle . . ." She smiled again as her husband's face fell. After more than twenty-five years of matrimony, Meg Colveden was an expert at making him do what he hadn't, at first, supposed he wanted to. "Though that's so *ordinary*, isn't it? Whereas an auction would be different, and much more *fun*. Everyone can join in together—a real community effort—and it is," she reminded her menfolk, "for the benefit of the whole village, after all."

Nigel, full of admiration, drained his cup, and held it out politely for a refill without saying a word, though his smile was as knowing as his mother's. At the end of the table, his father sat and huffed quietly to himself.

"And if they do a good job on the admiral's house, Molly says we should be able to trust the builders to do as well with the pavilion. She says we ought to ask them for an estimate— or do I mean a quotation?—while they're still here, instead of asking them to make a special trip out from Brettenden. Which is why"—and Lady Colveden poured fresh coffee with a defiant air—"I said it was lucky they were still in Plummergen, because it means we'll know that much sooner how much money we have to find."

"The pavilion certainly needs some work doing to it," said Nigel at last. "That storm the other day didn't help the state of the roof, or the floor." He raised his voice slightly. "And I must say I think Dad would make a nifty auctioneer—we'll dig out his old tails, and wax the tips of his moustache to look more the part; and I'll borrow a set of overalls from Jack Crabbe, if you like, to do the holding-up in real style. Pity there's no time to arrange it all before the big match, because it's a splendid idea—on the whole," honesty made him add. "You know, Mother, I can't help wondering if it's *altogether* wise . . ."

There was a pregnant pause. The brooding look on Sir George's face was identical to that on his son's. Lady Colveden glanced from one to the other, puzzled at first; then light dawned, and she was rather annoyed.

"Oh, really! All we're going to ask her to do is paint a picture of the cricket pavilion on a summer's day—almost like a chocolate box. For someone like Miss Seeton it would be the easiest thing in the world, and people are sure to want to buy it—so I do wish," she said firmly, "the two of you wouldn't sit there making me feel nervous. Whatever trouble could Miss Seeton possibly cause, painting a cricket pavilion?"

"Whatever trouble would anyone have expected Miss Seeton to cause by going to spend a couple of weeks in Scotland?" countered her son, with a rueful grin. "I bet they've had a high old time of it in Glenclachan while she's been there—and another bet says Mel Forby didn't write half the true story in the *Negative*. We'll have to pump her for the rest when she's down here next. Which will not," he predicted cheerfully, "be too long, if I'm any judge."

"Really, Nigel, as if . . ." But Meg Colveden's protest lacked conviction. She sighed; shook her head; then smiled. "If Mel comes, it'll be to write up all the burglaries, of course. And nobody could say Miss Seeton's anything to do with them, because they've been happening the whole time she's been away."

"They started before she went, though," Nigel reminded her. "Thrudd Banner had a couple of pieces about them in the *Blare* a week or so back, and I spotted a full-page article in the latest *Anyone's . . .*"

Then it was Nigel's turn to fall silent with embarrassment, though his blush was less noticeable than his mother's had been. He was, after all, a working farmer. Lady Colveden and Sir George turned wide, wondering eyes upon their son.

Poor Nigel blushed again. "Well, I just happened to be talking to . . . a friend who happened to have a copy in, er, her gear, and . . ."

"A friend?" His mother's eyes carefully avoided even an oblique meeting with his father's. "Somebody from the village, of course. That is . . . nearly everyone in Plummergen reads *Anyone's*, don't they?"

Nigel finished the last of his coffee at one gulp and rose to his feet, at which he found himself staring as he replied. "Well, they may do, but she isn't—from Plummergen, I mean, though she's staying at the George and Dragon. She, er, arrived by bicycle this morning—from Brettenden, I think—just as I was popping up to the garage to ask Jack Crabbe about my timing chain—I don't like the funny sort of jangling sound the MG's been making over the last day or so—and . . ."

"So it *was* the MG outside the bakery," said his mother. "I thought I recognised it, but with being so busy thinking about the admiral and that great stick thing . . . Anyway, at your age you hardly need your mother checking up on you all the time, do you? Nobody," and Meg Colveden managed to look innocent and indignant at the same time, "could possibly say I was one of those dreadful *prying* mothers, could they? I'm not what anyone would call *nosy,* am I?" There was a pause. "Is she a pretty girl?"

"Get it fixed?" was his father's more pertinent enquiry, as his son choked back an embarrassed laugh, blushing again. The major-general might well have his son's eye for a pretty girl, but he had also—he hoped—his priorities right. "Do no good to neglect it, y'know. May last awhile longer, but when it goes . . ."

"Oh, well," said Nigel, relieved to be talking about a less controversial topic. "You know how it is—by the time the engine had warmed up, it didn't sound so bad. And after I'd helped Annabelle take her things into the George . . ."

He swallowed the rest of the sentence and snatched the empty cup from his father's hand before Sir George had put it back on its saucer. "I'll, er, clear away, shall I?" And, as his parents looked at each other and smiled, young Mr. Colveden collected everything together, loaded it on the tray, and scuttled out into the kitchen without a word.

Only three passengers alighted from the train at Brettenden two mornings later: a middle-aged couple and a small, grey-haired woman wearing a tweed suit and a distinctive cockscomb hat, and burdened with two small suitcases, a capacious handbag, a raincoat over one arm, and an umbrella.

The carriage from which this laden little lady alighted had arrived, by sheer chance, at the foot of the stairs; and she stood puzzling now over the baggage which had been taken out by a fellow passenger and deposited for her convenience on the platform. She looked round for a porter: there was none to be seen. She recalled that it was time for the mid-morning break, and that Brettenden's stationmaster belonged to the Holdfast Brethren. Everyone knew about the Brethren. If the letter of Union law decreed that fifteen minutes must be taken for leisure and refreshment, then fast to the letter of that law would each Brother hold, both on his own account and for the benefit of those working under him. Which was, she reminded herself, only fair—one would not wish to be a nuisance, or to exploit anyone—but it did, one had to admit, have its inconvenient aspect.

She tucked the umbrella under one arm and bent to pick up her cases. As she straightened, her mackintosh slid down and tangled itself round the point of her umbrella. With a clatter, gamp and gaberdine fell to the platform, and their owner was heard to utter a little cry of "Drat!" as, making an instinctive grab for her precipitating property, she let fall both suitcases and narrowly missed her toes.

"Dear, dear. How very careless." She sighed, shook her head, and bent to retrieve her belongings.

"Allow me." The elderly lady had been so preoccupied that she had missed the approach from the train's farther end of the middle-aged couple. Now, above her little squeak of surprise, the husband reached round her to seize a case in either hand. "No, no—nothing to it, believe me. They balance beautifully, and they hardly weigh a thing. Will you manage all right at the other end, though? Where are you going?"

"You'd be welcome to share our taxi," said his wife, who had slowed her steps to match those of the small woman as she trotted anxiously up the concrete steps in the wake of her vanishing valises.

"That is really most kind, but I have arranged for a car to collect me—from the garage, you know. In Plummergen. That is, the car is from the garage—dear Jack Crabbe is always so reliable—but he is, of course, to collect me from Brettenden. And take me home. To Plummergen, which is where I live. Although I have recently been in Scotland, of course—not to live, but on holiday. Which is why I have so much luggage to carry—and it really is," she repeated, "most kind of you."

"Not at all." The answer came easily—and with truth, the middle-aged man being almost a foot taller, and several stone of muscle heavier, than the agitated and apologetic little lady in the tweed suit. "Nearly over the footbridge now, and then it's downhill all the way. Don't worry about it," as she began to apologise again. Her knight-errant's helpmeet, fearing that she would apologise herself into exhaustion, interrupted quickly, but firmly.

"Do excuse me, but—what an unusual umbrella! Black silk and—surely it can't be a gold handle?"

At once, the flow of breathless apology ceased. A proud smile brightened the brolly-owner's face. "Indeed, yes—a souvenir from a most courteous gentleman of a little adventure which we shared, some seven years ago now. Not *solid* gold, of course, for that would have been rather awkward to carry—the weight, you see. And I do not believe superintendents of police, even from Scotland Yard, were paid extravagant salaries—but gold, certainly. Any more than they are now, that is. Hollow, though, not plated—the cost, you see—and of course, staying with an earl, it seemed the least I could do. It is my very best, you see."

Neither the middle-aged man nor his wife could *see* very much of all this, but, after the fashion of long-married couples who can almost read each other's mind, they decided not to press for enlightenment. Life, they felt, was too short. And they had an appointment to keep: though they would dearly have loved to know how their new acquaintance had come, seven years ago, to be sharing little adventures with superintendents from Scotland Yard . . .

# chapter

# ~5~

"HERE WE ARE, then!" The trio had negotiated the downward flight of steps, had passed through the barrier and left their tickets in the labelled box, and were now standing in the station forecourt.

Husband turned to wife. "That taxi might do for us, but what about our friend here? I don't see anything that looks like a hire car, dear lady. Perhaps you'd better—"

He broke off, interrupted by a brisk tootling from the horn of a vehicle which had just rounded the corner from the main road into the forecourt. The driver, observing three faces turned in his direction and recognising one of them, tootled a second time, even more briskly.

"Sorry, Miss Seeton!" Tall Jack Crabbe came leaping from the car with a wave and a shamefaced grin. "Not like me to be late, I know, only young Nigel's not too happy about the timing on his MG, and I didn't rightly see as I ought to let him keep driving without I had a look under the bonnet first. This lot yours?"

He scooped up a case in either hand, nodded vaguely to the middle-aged couple as it became clear they were no more than chance met travellers with the same destination, and led the way to the car. "You hop in the front while I dump these in the boot— and there's something for you to take a look at, if you like, seeing as you were so kind as to show an interest in my puzzles." Jack Crabbe, though he worked regular hours as a mechanic in the family garage, was famed in Plummergen as the village's resident cruciverbalist, the crosswords he composed being highlights of the learned periodicals to which he regularly contributed. His identity was concealed from the rest of the country under a pseudonym, but it was widely known throughout his native heath that "Coronet" was in truth Jack Crabbe: who had, as he would explain to the curious, a very kind heart, really.

Miss Seeton, who from time to time essayed the crossword in *The Times*—but with varying success—had always been much impressed by Jack's skill. When he drove the twice-weekly shoppers' bus from Plummergen to Brettenden, he would spend the hours between arrival and departure with a thesaurus, a dictionary, and a sheaf of blank forms; it was a bad day when he couldn't complete at least half of a puzzle, and he generally managed more. Plummergen was proud of Jack; it mostly didn't understand a word of what he did, but nevertheless was always happy to lean over his shoulder and make helpful comments, to which he would listen with polite and noncommittal interest.

Miss Seeton had recently supplied him with a clue which had greatly pleased him, and he had promised her a copy of the magazine which contained it, when it was published.

"Which there it is," he said, as he climbed back into the driver's seat and started the engine. Miss Seeton made appreciative noises as she opened the journal at the page with the slip of paper poking out. She smiled.

*"Bird's cough sounds rough despite inhalation of hydrogen,"* she read. "Six letters. Dear me. And all because we visited the Wounded Wings sanctuary . . ."

"You keep that, Miss Seeton—I got one extra, just for you. Brought me luck, so you did. They're going to pay me five pounds more, starting with this." Jack brushed aside her exclamations of pleasure with further thanks of his own, then changed the subject by asking if she'd had a good time in Scotland, adding that he hoped she felt back on top form after her holiday because of this cricket picture he'd heard people talking about.

"Cricket?" Miss Seeton, with her mind half on her holiday, half still on the crossword, looked blank. "Picture?" Then, with a sudden smile: "Of course—Charters and Caldicott—Basil Radford and Naunton Wayne. *The Lady Vanishes.*" Miss Seeton was a keen cinemagoer when circumstances permitted. "Forever worrying about the cricket score . . . Not that I understand the scoring, or indeed much at all about cricket, though of course such an understanding was not, as I recall, essential to the plot. It is many years since I last saw the film, of course. How pleasant that it is to be reissued. I shall make a point of going."

Gently, Jack explained that as far as he knew there were no plans for a revival of the Hitchcock classic, and he was sorry to have misled her. As for understanding cricket, if kiddies played it in school then it couldn't be too difficult, could it? Miss Seeton supposed he was right. It was, she remarked, one's national game, and therefore one could not help but feel some sense of regret that one's understanding was so very, well, limited . . .

Jack, who kept wicket for Plummergen, was justly proud of his ability to whip off a bail with the best, and decided that he was as good a man as any to explain the basics of the national game to one who—though she did not yet know it—was to immortalise on canvas the climax of Plummergen's encounter with Murreystone. He cleared his throat. A frown appeared between his brows. He cleared his throat again.

"It's simple enough, Miss Seeton—the basics, that is. There's eleven of them, and eleven of us. And *our* eleven is hell-bent—begging your pardon—on beating theirs. See?"

Cautiously, Miss Seeton admitted that, so far, she saw.

"Well, er, that's it, really." Jack frowned again, and with relief saw that they were coming into Plummergen. Perhaps, he reflected, he was *not* as good a man as he thought he was. It was easy enough to *do* it—but nowhere near as easy to tell someone else what you did. He drove on slowly down The Street, wondering whether there was anything else helpful he could find to say.

But The Street—Plummergen's main thoroughfare—is not more than half a mile long. Running in a gentle curve from north to south, it narrows at its southern end to a near-lane between high walls, which lane runs over the Royal Military Canal and, turning sharp right, on to Rye, some six miles to the southwest. Before it crosses the canal, The Street makes another sharp right turn towards Rye, becoming known as Marsh Road. The cottage owned by Miss Seeton is situated on this odd little peninsula of Rye-bound roadways, her back garden having as its southern boundary the canal, and as its eastern, one of the high brick walls.

Sweetbriars is a pleasant spot, of which Miss Seeton is particularly fond; but it is hardly a great distance from a driver's first glimpse of the village nameplate at Plummergen's northern boundary. Which gave Jack Crabbe very little time to frame some telling and memorable phrase by which his passenger might feel slightly more conversant with the laws of cricket than she had felt before . . .

The car slowed outside the George and Dragon, and Jack prepared to swing it in a semicircle to stand across The Street outside Miss Seeton's cottage. His expert eye judged the amount of swing necessary: "swing" reminded him of bowling a cricket ball; and sudden inspiration struck.

"It's like this, Miss Seeton. When we're batting, we want to hit as many runs as we can off their bowling. But when *they're* batting, we want to stop them by our fielding. And, er, the same for them, the other way round. See?"

Feeling rather pleased with this, he brought the car to a halt, climbed out to open the passenger door, collected Miss Seeton's bags and raincoat from the boot, and escorted her up her front path. Then, having seen her safely home and accepted his fee, he swung the steering wheel in another skillful curve, and headed northwards for home.

Inside her cottage, Miss Seeton closed her eyes and gently inhaled all the familiar, welcoming scents. Dear Martha must have come in earlier and left a little snack, though today was not one of her regular days. A fruitcake too, if she was not mistaken! Miss Seeton breathed in once more, savouring the hint of spice, of polish and fresh flowers and . . . well, of home. She had enjoyed her holiday, of course—the scenery of the Scottish Highlands was spectacular, and there were several sketches in her portfolio of which she was rather proud—but there was, indeed, no place like home. Especially if one was, perhaps, rather more tired from one's journey than one had expected to be, when the sleeping compartment had been so very comfortable . . . And Miss Seeton found herself stifling a yawn.

"Dear me." She glanced at her watch and clicked her tongue. She could hardly go to bed so soon after having left it—or rather, having left her bunk, she supposed she should say. She sighed; the sigh turned into another yawn. She clicked her tongue again.

"A cup of tea," she told herself firmly. "And perhaps the unpacking—and the washing—" she sighed again—"could wait until afterwards . . ."

In the kitchen, she found a tray ready laid, the kettle full, and a note from Martha Bloomer saying she'd put all Miss Seeton's letters in the sitting room, and she wasn't to go worrying herself over reading them until she'd had a nice sit-down over a good hot cuppa, and a slice of cake as well, always minding to leave room for her lunch, which she'd find in the fridge, being cold meat and a salad, already washed, and some apples and a banana or two, and eggs, of course . . .

Miss Seeton's eggs come from the chickens which inhabit the henhouse at the bottom of her back garden. The garden, and the hens, are cared for by Stan Bloomer, Martha's farmhand husband, without charge; he selling any surplus eggs, fruit, flowers, or vegetables for profit, enhancing his reputation around the village as a strong, silent, and invaluable worker. Martha comes in twice a week to clean for Miss Seeton, who is cousin, goddaughter, and heir to Old Mrs. Bannet, Martha's previous employer. Mrs. Bloomer happily "obliges" other households about the village; but resembles Mrs. Micawber in her insistence that she will never desert—no matter what inducements are offered by those attempting to poach her services—her "Miss Emily," to whom she, like Stan, is devoted. As Miss Seeton, in turn, is devoted to them . . .

"Dear Martha." Miss Seeton's eyes were bright as she read her henchwoman's note. "I do hope she will like the little gift I have brought from Scotland . . ."

The kettle's whistle broke into her reverie, and she set about following Martha's kind advice to make herself a good hot cuppa. An English gentlewoman, no matter how weary, can brew a cup of tea almost by instinct. Take the pot to the kettle—rinse with boiling water to warm it—pour the rinsings away—spoon in just enough loose tea from the caddy—some say one spoon for each person and one for the pot, but Miss Seeton prefers hers less strong—pour on boiling water—put on the lid—pop on the cosy—and wait.

"Four minutes," murmured Miss Seeton, glancing up at the clock before hunting out milk from the fridge and cake from the tin. She poured milk, sliced cake, tidied away as the clock ticked on; the time was up, and she took a teaspoon to the pot, stirred briskly, allowed the leaves to settle, and poured. And smiled. And carried the tray into the sitting room . . .

The comfortable chink of china was interrupted by a yodelling wail from just beneath the window, and Miss Seeton started, sending a splash of tea into her saucer. The wails turned into growls, and there came a hasty, spitting sound, followed by a series of vegetable crashes, and a bump.

"Oh, dear," said Miss Seeton, knowing what these noises signified. She had moved to the window, and now looked out to see a black-and-white furry streak disappearing down her front path, hotly pursued by a victorious tabby thunderbolt. "Tibs!" Miss Seeton banged on the window, rattling the glass. "Tibs!"

But little Amelia Potter's infamous pet, though normally holding Miss Seeton in some respect, was deaf to all remonstrance as she chased the interloping moggy through the gate and out of sight behind Miss Seeton's wrought-iron fence, leaving Stan Bloomer's herbaceous borders looking less tidy than they'd been two minutes earlier. "Oh, dear," said Miss Seeton, hearing distant sounds of combat; but she knew there was nothing to be done. Tibs, with the light of battle in her eye, can move extremely fast, and will cheerfully chase any foreign feline from one end of The Street to the other—indeed, had probably done so on this occasion, since her home in Plummergen's police house is on the northern edge of the village, while Sweetbriars lies towards the southern.

Miss Seeton sighed and returned to her neglected tea. She ate cake and poured herself a second cup; she yawned. It had been a busy time: everyone had been so kind, but home was, after all, the best place to be, though her memories of Scotland were indeed happy. She would look back through her sketchbook to refresh them, while she drank her second cup; Jack Crabbe's magazine was a treat which would need rather more concentration than she felt able, at present, to apply.

Miss Seeton's sketchbook was on the top layer of her suitcase, and easily found. Automatically, she took pencils and her eraser back with her into the sitting room; and, as she leafed through the pages, found herself drifting into a happy daydream of sights she had seen, people she had met.

After the final drawing, she allowed the book to rest open on her lap, while she pondered Miss Philomena Beigg, naturalist and author, whose signed copy of *Bird Life of the Glens* had been packed next to the sketchbook in Miss Seeton's suitcase. She must remember to tell Mrs. Ongar, who did such splendid work at the Wounded Wings Bird Sanctuary, all about her new friend from Scotland . . .

"Good gracious." Miss Seeton came to herself, blinked, and looked down at the page before her, which was no longer blank. At some point in her reverie she must have picked up her pencil and started to draw. No doubt she had started—though one had no conscious recollection of this—with the intention of committing to paper another memory of her Highland holiday: surely those were rocks she could see in the distance? Cluttered and tumbled as they were, it was difficult to be sure, especially as the foreground was filled with images of birds. Birds which were all grey, large, long-necked, their huge wings tipped with black, their tails short, their beaks sharp—birds distinguished from other avian sketches Miss Seeton had from time to time drawn by the injuries closer inspection showed had been suffered by every one.

"Oh, dear!" Miss Seeton stared at trailing wings, damaged bills, torn feathers, broken legs. "Oh, dear . . . But, of course, as I was only just now thinking of Wounded Wings . . . And that splendid book *The Flight of the Heron,* which I recall reading at school. D.K. Broster—such a vivid Scottish setting . . . or are these, perhaps, cranes, rather than herons? They are sometimes so easily confused—and it is, of course, a common error in some parts of the country to refer to *Ardea cinerea* as a crane when it is, in fact, the Grey Heron—yet an understandable error, when one examines these sketches—if even I cannot be sure which it is . . ."

Miss Seeton frowned, shook her head, and began to murmur "Heron? Crane? Heron? Crane?" as if these words were some rare mantra recently discovered during her reading of that invaluable book *Yoga and Younger Every Day.* Her study of its precepts had done wonders for her knees, and indeed for the rest of her. Miss Seeton, for her age, was in remarkably good shape, both physically and mentally; she had no real need of mantras to help her relax; and she came drowsily to the decision that the birds were cranes—

and that it didn't matter much in any case. She was far more interested in the strange circular shapes which had now appeared in the air above the injured birds—hailstones, perhaps? There had been one or two spectacular storms around the glen, certainly, yet no hail, that she recalled. And, strangely, one had drawn no lightning, which had been so vivid a part of those storms . . .

One had to hope the weather would be better on Saturday, when Plummergen were to meet Murreystone. Dear Jack Crabbe. What a very clever young man he was, and how kind to let her keep the magazine . . . She feared she had not altogether understood his description of cricket, though naturally, being English, one knew a little . . .

Dreamily, Miss Seeton began to sketch what she could remember of the game of cricket, as played by the Plummergen team. One might not understand the laws, but one supported one's home side to the best of one's ability—and there was little hardship in sitting among friends in deck chairs, with wide-brimmed hats against the sun, watching white-garbed figures moving on emerald grass . . .

Daniel Eggleden, village blacksmith and mighty bowler—dear Nigel Colveden, who batted, so his parents explained, so skillfully—Jack Crabbe, the wicket-keeper . . .

Warming to her task of capturing on paper her many dear friends engaged in one of their favourite pastimes—no, she must not use this word, even in her thoughts. Miss Seeton smiled as she heard again the distant voice of Nigel thrilling with horror, informing her that cricket was nothing less than a religion—dear Nigel, such a lively, charming, good-humoured young man . . .

Such a dear friend—as, after so many years, were they all. Miss Seeton roughed in the final outline, added a hint of shadow beneath the umpire's feet, and held her sketch out at arm's length to see whether she had, indeed, captured on paper even part of the mystique that was cricket . . .

And at first smiled, pleased with the translation of her happy vision from her mind's eye to reality.

And then looked more closely, and blinked.

"Good gracious me," said Miss Seeton.

# chapter

# ~6~

"GOOD GRACIOUS ME." She blinked again. The picture did not change. There was Plummergen's playing field, on which in winter football matches were fought out with rival teams, but which in summer was dedicated to England's national game— no, religion. Miss Seeton, thinking of Nigel, smiled; but the smile was soon replaced by a puzzled stare, as she continued to study her picture. The pavilion, in which Lady Colveden and her friends served such delicious teas, looked—as it had done on the occasion of Miss Seeton's last visit—somewhat the worse for wear: which was understandable, as the summer had been hot and dry for some weeks before several heavy storms had broken the drought. Wooden buildings, unless of oak, are painted against the ravages of the English climate—and paint, during hot, dry spells, peels.

There was the pavilion—in the background, but still recogniseable. In the foreground, the back view of a watching umpire, his shadow flickering on the grass. The players he was watching stood together, close to the familiar three-stumped shape of the wicket, as if about to discuss some change of tactics; with their heads—their faces—turned so that the umpire, and anyone looking at the sketch, could clearly see them. There they were: Daniel Eggleden, Nigel Colveden, Jack Crabbe, and the rest of the team: all of them old friends, all of them—having been born east of the Medway—Men of Kent, as opposed to those who, born west of the river, must be called Kentishmen. But English through and through, of that there could be no doubt . . .

So why, wondered Miss Seeton, were their facial features so very . . . oriental? The slanted, dark eyes; the flattened noses; the

41

hint of swarthiness about the skin . . . She knew, of course, who they were—who they were supposed to be—but somehow, well, they weren't. And why did some of the players sport, instead of the traditional cricketing caps, peaked and soft-crowned—or even the newly popular soft towelling hats, about which Nigel, the traditionalist, had been so rude—wide-brimmed coolie straws? When the game they were all playing—when the setting in which they were all playing it—when *everything* was so very English . . .

"A touch of the sun," said Miss Seeton firmly and shook her head, and felt a yawn coming on. "I really think . . ."

She folded her sketchpad, set it to one side with her small selection of drawing tools, picked up Jack Crabbe's magazine, and decided that a little lie-down upstairs would not, in the circumstances, be very self-indulgent, after all—not when one had travelled so far, and when—

Miss Seeton froze in mid-movement. What was that noise?

As she stood stock-still, she heard it again: a light, scrabbling, pattering sound from the far corner of the room. A further pattering, and a squeak.

"Oh, dear." Miss Seeton clicked her tongue. Some poor animal—a mouse, a shrew, a vole—had found its way into her house from the garden, and seemed unable to find its way out. How dreadful—she had been away for almost a fortnight. For how long must the poor creature have been starving here while she—

"Martha," said Miss Seeton, with a sigh of relief. Dear Martha would have chivvied that mouse outside the moment she heard its tiny claws on the floorboards—Miss Seeton shut her mind to the horrid possibilities of the spring-loaded mousetrap—and she had visited Sweetbriars every other day, the last time having been only that morning. Which meant that the mouse—or whatever it was—must still be in good health. She would not, when she went to look for it, find a weak, gasping near-corpse with fading eyes . . .

The pattering came again. Miss Seeton frowned. One had no wish to harm the poor creature, but it could hardly be permitted to remain indoors: Martha usually chased them with her broom when she spotted them, which wasn't very often, but was known to happen. Living in the country, one had to expect such incursions. Miss Seeton frowned again. By the time she had hurried out to fetch dear Martha's broom from the hall cupboard, the mouse would have vanished—one knew how quickly they could move.

"Oh, dear!" Thoughts of speedy movement reminded Miss Seeton that Tibs was on the prowl at her end of Plummergen. Tibs caught more mice, rats, birds, and even rabbits than any other cat in the village. The mouse, or whatever it was, must be released into Miss Seeton's back garden, behind the safety of the high brick wall—and she must be sure not to tell Stan, who would grumble about his vegetables . . .

But first, to catch it. Miss Seeton's ear was keen, and she knew that the creature had come to a halt in its patterings over in the far corner of the room. There were no convenient holes in the floorboards down which it could escape: it was trapped— she flinched—it was cornered. She would catch it, and carry it outside . . .

She took two wary steps towards the now-stilled pattering, and peered into the distance. The eye of an artist is not deceived by shadows, by light and dark and outline: she peered, she concentrated, and she saw A small, grey-brown, long tailed, bright-eyed, panting creature had seen her move, and was quivering as close against the safety of the skirting-board as it could.

One could not, of course, go on peering indefinitely: it was hardly, well, practical. Miss Seeton thought wildly of dusters, with which she was wont to catch spiders before putting them out of the window—could she snatch one of her antimacassars from the back of an armchair and drop it over the mouse as if it were a spider? But spiders, of course, did not bite. Except tarantulas, and red widows, and others of foreign origin. What manner of poisonous spider, Miss Seeton found herself wondering, inhabited the Orient?

"What nonsense!" She shook her head, and the mouse was observed to jump. It emitted a terrified squeak. Miss Seeton frowned, and looked about her once more.

She smiled. Not taking her eyes from the mouse in case it should make a dash for it, she reached sideways, tipped the dregs of her tea into the slop-bowl, gathered up her saucer, and, cup in one hand, saucer in the other—a pair of porcelain pincers—she advanced slowly, steadily, upon the corner of the room where the mouse lurked . . .

And, swooping, scooped it triumphantly into its unorthodox crockery cage, where it scuttled and squeaked in great alarm while she bore it breathlessly out of the sitting room to the kitchen, set it on the draining board while she opened the back door, and, walking carefully to the middle of the lawn, released it.

Miss Seeton was rather proud of herself as she returned to the sitting room. The mouse, after a moment's terrified paralysis, had darted to the edge of the lawn and disappeared into the shrubbery with—she could almost have sworn—a farewell flirt of its tail as it vanished. Evidently it had suffered no lasting harm from its little adventure; now she must discover whether she, or rather her dear cottage, had suffered any harm from the mouse. Teeth—and scratching claws—and, of course, droppings . . .

After a careful search around the entire ground floor of Sweetbriars, Miss Seeton could be confident that her small visitor had caused no damage. The search, however, had left her rather tired. And thirsty. "Just one more cup of tea," she promised herself; then she would start work. Answering letters, paying bills, putting her washing in the machine—no, she'd better do that first, so that it could be soaping and spinning and rinsing while she drank her tea and read through the pile of correspondence. Although . . . when dear Jack Crabbe had been so kind—one's own personal copy of his magazine—and he was sure to ask what she had thought—and there was always the risk, when one was drinking, that a sudden clumsy movement might spill tea over papers one would prefer to remain tidy . . .

Miss Seeton was just carrying her tray into the sitting room for the second time when, at the end of the hall, the telephone rang. She trotted towards it, set the tray down on the table beside the umbrella rack, and picked up the receiver with a smile.

"Plummergen 35 . . . Why, Lady Colveden, what a pleasant surprise!"

Meg Colveden was careful to begin by asking whether Miss Seeton had enjoyed her holiday, and—having heard how much she had—hoping that the journey home had not overtired her. Miss Seeton, with a guilty glance at her second cup of tea, hurried to assure her friend that it had not.

"That's splendid," said Lady Colveden, with perhaps more enthusiasm in her voice than might normally have been expected.

"So you're fully refreshed and ready to go! Though you'll be busy this afternoon sorting things out, I suppose. But will tea tomorrow be all right for you? We'd all be so pleased to see you. We rather hope"—her voice sank to a conspiratorial murmur— "to persuade Nigel's latest conquest to join us, too—at least, *he* may not have conquered her, but *she* certainly seems to have had an overwhelming effect on him." She stifled a giggle. "George and I felt almost sorry for the poor boy at luncheon, when he was trying so hard not to look embarrassed—you know how he is . . ."

Miss Seeton knew: how could she not? Everyone in Plummergen knew that young Nigel—as he would no doubt remain for years to come—had inherited, along with his father's eye for the ladies, his mother's generous heart. The baronet's heir fell in and out of love nearly as often as Miss Seeton tumbled in and out of adventure—nearly, though not quite. Miss Seeton, of course, did not acknowledge the adventures, even in thought, but she had to acknowledge the susceptibility of her young friend to an attractive face and graceful figure. And one had to confess to a little twinge of curiosity at the chance of meeting the latest object of Nigel's fancy . . .

"Then that's agreed, Miss Seeton. We'll see you at tea tomorrow—and perhaps," added Meg Colveden, "you might like to bring your sketchbook to show us? I'm sure you've drawn some marvellous views of the Highlands, and we'd all be so interested to see them . . ."

Which artless invitation, unconscious of the cricketing-sketch scheme lurking in her hostess's mind, Miss Seeton was—after some moment's polite demur—happy to accept.

She settled herself back in her favourite chair in the sitting room and began to read the magazine which dear Jack Crabbe had so kindly given her. The clock on the overmantel merrily ticked, the washing machine busily whirred in the background. Miss Seeton sipped her tea, and leafed through learned pages, and felt so very glad to be at home again. How peaceful it all was . . .

Peace might well reign in Sweetbriars, but in Lilikot there was much frenzied whispering and frantic peering from upper windows as the Nuts tried to make out what Admiral Leighton planned to do with his long, white wooden post. They had, with the rest of the shopping gossips, watched the six workmen carry the post round the lorry and into the garden of Ararat Cottage; and Mrs. Blaine had been induced—by a display of willpower Mrs. Stillman hadn't realised she possessed—to come back and complete her purchases, though it had not been Emmy Putts, resolutely deaf among the gossips, but her employer who eventually served Bunny with the oatmeal, sunflower oil, brussels sprouts, and other items she was not to be permitted to forget.

Having paid for her groceries and stuffed them grumpily in her bag, Mrs. Blaine went back outside to collect Eric, who hurried home with her and then meanly—so thought Bunny—rushed to lay claim to one of the best snooping spots in Lilikot, while *she*— too unfair—had to unpack the shopping and put it away. The kitchen, at the back of the house, was downstairs: the best view of the admiral's mysterious wooden post was to be had from the landing, upstairs. Mrs. Blaine's little black eyes snapped as she banged tins on the counter, and slammed drawers, and made a great clatter among the cupboards.

It was with an angry face that Mrs. Blaine at last joined Miss Nuttel by the open window; but Eric was too enthralled by what was going on below to take any notice of Bunny's moods. On sensing her friend's arrival, she grunted a quick greeting and then moved a token inch to one side, not relaxing her concentration for a moment from the sight and sound of Admiral Leighton in his front garden, urging on his crew to the completion of their task. And Mrs. Blaine, still determined to let Miss Nuttel know just how cross she felt about it all, soon found her own attention caught by what was happening.

"Why, I never noticed them digging that hole! Did you, Eric?" Mrs. Blaine felt aggrieved all over again. Somehow, she had missed the chance to speculate that the admiral, his underworld connections now a certainty in her mind, planned to bury the corpse of some criminal colleague in an unmarked grave in his own front garden. Her only consolation would be if Eric, too, had missed it.

Miss Nuttel shrugged; she'd had time to overcome her own sense of grievance, time to prepare herself to sound casual and knowing. "Could have been a rosebush," she said. "Or a tree . . ."

Eric's share of the Lilikot lifestyle involved much outdoor work which Mrs. Blaine found lacking in interest, as well as too physically wearisome.

"Flagpole, though," said Miss Nuttel. For, by the time Bunny appeared at her side, it had become clear to Eric that the long, painted post brought by the builders and now being erected in the front garden of Ararat Cottage could be nothing else. And, peeved though she might be, Mrs. Blaine knew that the muttered identification her friend saw fit to offer could hardly be denied. Even she could recognise the metal rings, the arrangement of strings and ropes and—

"Halyards," said Miss Nuttel, in assured accents, as the admiral, his flagpole now finished, began experimenting with hoists and pulleys, checking that everything moved smoothly. The concrete already looked less runny than it had before; ballast and gravel and wedges had played their part; and the admiral appeared pleased by the successful conclusion of his arrangements, turning to the workmen with a cheerful invitation to come into the house and splice the mainbrace while he wrote out the final cheque.

"Well!" Mrs. Blaine, being so much shorter, lost sight of the little procession before Miss Nuttel did. She turned to stare again at the flagpole where it stood proudly in its solid base, bare of flag or pennant or standard. "Too sinister, Eric, I must say! Everything done in such a hurry—digging that hole so quickly— so much concrete, and drying so very fast—I'd be interested to know"—darkly—"whether there's anything else at the bottom of that hole besides earth and cement. Or"—even more darkly— "any*one*. You," with a monumental sniff, "had by far the best view. Didn't you notice anything? You must have done!"

Miss Nuttel grunted. She had indeed had a grandstand view of almost the entire proceeding; and, much though she would have enjoyed the idea of a mysterious bundle at the bottom of the hole, had seen nothing of the sort and took much delight in informing Mrs. Blaine of this fact. If Bunny was going to be disagreeable, Eric in her turn was just as capable of disagreement. Besides, she had other matters on her mind: other questions to be asked, other speculations to be made . . .

"Suspicious," said Miss Nuttel, with a backward jerk of her head in the distant direction of Sweetbriars, at the far end of The

Street. "Came back today, didn't she? Crabbe's sent a car—and now this." Through the open landing window she indicated the flagpole in the admiral's garden, in full view of every passerby.

"*Signalling*," said Erica Nuttel, and slammed the window shut.

# chapter
## -7-

WHILE THE NUTS were so preoccupied with the problem of the admiral's flagpole, the matter of the mysterious cyclist, whose appearance that morning at the George and Dragon had prompted Mrs Blaine's remarks about brussels sprouts and eccentric millionaires, faded utterly from their minds. On an ordinary day, however, they would happily have thrashed the topic to microscopic pieces amongst themselves and the rest of the customers in Mr Stillman's post office, because she was really a remarkably attractive girl . . .

She was really a remarkably attractive girl. Nigel Colveden, driving from Rytham Hall with half his attention on the MG's engine and the other half on the road, had first spotted her as she slowed to a halt outside the hotel, then dismounted to push her laden bicycle across the paved front yard and rest it against the porch step. Nigel was no snob. Landlord Charley Mountfitchet's guests could arrive on foot if they liked, or by bus; but the normal style of arrival was by car, whether the visitor's own vehicle or one of the local taxis. Newcomers to the district might wheeze and lurch their way from Brettenden railway station in aged Mr Baxter's asthmatic hire car, old hands preferred the more reliable service offered by Crabbe's Garage. But Nigel couldn't think of anyone who'd ever arrived by bike before, and he looked at the cyclist with some interest . . .

And then looked again, with a great deal of interest, for she was really a remarkably attractive girl. Long, wavy blonde hair which gleamed richly in the sun; a shapely form, and—she was wearing shorts—sensational legs. Nigel gulped, and breathed in hard as he

49

brought the car to a juddering halt on the corner where Marsh Road joined The Street; and continued to stare at the vision on the front step of the George and Dragon opposite.

The vision turned as she heard the note of the MG's engine change. Even from the other side of The Street, Nigel could see that her eyes were a deep cornflower blue; her skin flawless and lightly tanned; her lips a full, generous, soft pink; and her teeth, as she parted those lips in a smile, a row of perfect pearls. "Gosh," breathed Nigel as the vision smiled again, unoffended by his obvious interest. And no wonder: she must be accustomed to admiration from everyone everywhere she went . . .

"Oh, gosh," said Nigel again, as the vision ventured a little wave in his direction and smiled all the more. What further hint could a red-blooded male ask? Nigel swung the MG round sharply to the left, pulled in to the kerb outside Winesart's bakery, switched off the engine, and darted diagonally across The Street to enquire, still breathless:

"I say—do you need any help parking your bike?"

It was the best he could manage at such short notice, and he felt rather foolish as he said it. She didn't laugh at him, though; she simply smiled again and shook her head.

"Thanks. You're very kind, but I can manage." Her voice was lilting and low, with a touch of huskiness that sent delightful shivers down Nigel's spine. "We're used to coping by ourselves, Edgar and I—still, thank you for offering. I appreciate your kindness."

The look in those blue eyes spoke volumes for the sincerity of her appreciation, and Nigel wondered whether it would be pushing his luck to risk the wrath of the as-yet-unseen Edgar by continuing the conversation. After a quick look up The Street, which showed no signs of movement, cyclic or otherwise, he ventured:

"Are you, er, planning to stay at the George?" Another foolish question—what else would she be doing on the doorstep, if not wanting to go in? Though she could, of course, be looking for work, rather than having a holiday. Those baggage carriers strapped to the rear frame of her bike, the fruit-juice containers at the front, suggested a seasoned traveller. She might be an Australian or a New Zealander, backpacking round the Old Country, surviving on casual employment; though she'd sounded as English as his own family.

"It seems to be a nice hotel." The girl smiled again. "Would you say it was sufficiently respectable for a lone, lorn female?"

Nigel blinked. He glanced up The Street again. "You're by yourself?" His heart gave a little thump. "Aren't you—aren't you waiting for your, er, Edgar?" They'd had a quarrel—he'd tried to bully this sweet creature—she'd fled in panic—he himself might be her only hope when the angry Edgar caught up with her . . . And Nigel squared his shoulders, made muscular by years of working on the farm, and did his best to look like Sir Galahad waiting to slay the dragon—or, he added to himself with a smile, Saint George.

The girl smiled back, her trill of laughter as musical as birdsong. "Oh, I've no need to wait for Edgar—he's as punctual as I am! And he never goes anywhere without me, just as I hardly ever go anywhere without him." She patted the handlebars of her bicycle. "Let me introduce you to Edgar—and, before you ask, it's because *my* name is Annabelle Leigh, although . . ." She spelled it for him, and smiled again, ruefully. "My parents shared an enthusiasm for Poe—I'm only thankful it wasn't for Tennyson. Imagine being called Maud, in this day and age!"

Nigel, trying to imagine it, shook his head as he introduced himself. Annabelle suited this glorious girl as no other name possibly could: why she should even dream of being called Maud he couldn't think. But Annabelle Leigh had a delicate, romantic, poetic sound . . . "Annabelle," he said and returned her smile. "I do hope you're going to stay in Plummergen a good, long time."

"I might. It seems an attractive place." Had he heard a slight pause before that final word? Her beautiful eyes sparkled at him, and Nigel allowed himself to hope that he had. "Very . . . flat," she said, patting the handlebars once more. "My last working holiday was in Norfolk."

"Prairie farming," came the automatic response before he checked himself. "Er, yes. You know, I'd always assumed Australians had an accent you could cut with a knife, but your voice is, well . . ." And, struggling for a compliment of sufficient force, he mumbled into a confused silence as the wide cornflower gaze showed nothing but pure amazement.

"What on earth made you think I was Australian? I'm as English as the next man—or woman! Oh, of course," and she nodded towards the loaded baggage carriers. "The working holiday bit. Well, I just thought one day, if the Aussies and Kiwis can do it, why not me? I don't mind hard work, though it's better to find something you're good at, and which you enjoy—especially if the money's not brilliant—which I have. I'll bet," she told him with pride, "I'm the first journeyman artist you've ever met, aren't I?"

Nigel blinked again. "I, er, suppose so," he said, with caution. *Artist,* of course, he recognised—a vision of his old friend Miss Seeton floated briefly across his inward eye—but as to *journeyman* . . . "You, er, must travel a lot," and he studied the sturdy bicycle tyres with their deep treads, and tried not to let his glance drift to Annabelle's legs, in their practical—but so flattering—shorts. Anything less masculine than their slim, tanned, smooth shapeliness it was hard to envisage.

Annabelle smiled. "I travel, yes—I need to breathe different air all the time, I need to be free, though that's not why I call myself a journeyman artist. It comes from the French," she explained kindly. "*Journée*—the length of one day: the period for which a journeyman is paid for his, or her, work. Just as I'm hired on a daily basis, so I'm paid the same way. I'm free to come and go as I please, you see—anywhere"—as she patted the handlebars again—"provided there aren't too many hills."

"Say it again," begged Nigel. "You were absolutely perfect—I mean, that's how it sounded. The French, I mean. So . . . so attractive." And he wondered briefly whether it had been thoughts of Miss Seeton that made him so confused, or the devastating closeness of Miss Annabelle Leigh. The latter, he decided, as once more her lips parted, first in a smile, then in slow motion as she obligingly murmured "*Journée,*" adding:

"The attraction of opposites, perhaps? You don't speak French, obviously. But do you know what the opposite of day is, Nigel? Night—*la nuit,* in French. The moon is *la lune*—the stars are *les étoiles.* Love is *l'amour* . . ."

"Gosh," said Nigel, as she came to a halt. "I mean—it sounds so . . . so French, when you say it."

"So it should—I read French at university before I decided to treat myself to a sabbatical. I don't want to settle down and join the rat race until I've spent a couple of years just travelling about and seeing the world—seeing England, anyway, for a start. I haven't been on the road long. Next year, once I've got the hang of things, I might take off round Europe—or go to Africa—or America . . ." She smiled at the admiring, almost envious look he gave her. "Making up," she explained, "for the years I spent in the convent, you know. My mother packed me off there after my father died."

"I'm sorry." Sir Galahad, Nigel felt, would have said something rather more memorable; but Annabelle Leigh didn't seem to mind. Indeed, she laughed.

"I'm not! Sorry about going to the convent, that is. It wasn't as bad as it might have been, though I hope you don't believe the popular mythology about convent girls being so very much wilder than the rest. It isn't true in the least." But her eyes twinkled as she said this, in a way which puzzled poor Nigel until he realised she must be joking. He twinkled back at her.

"Perish the thought, Miss Leigh—and would I be so formal if I supposed you'd allow me to take liberties? Er, how would it be if I took your bicycle instead, while you see if Charley Mountfitchet has a room? I mean, I could take care of it for you, outside. Not that there's what you'd call a crime wave in Plummergen, but . . ."

He broke off as he remembered Miss Seeton again, clearing his throat with unnecessary vigour. Annabelle looked decidedly startled. "I mean," said Nigel, "it might just fall over, or something—or be rained on . . ."

Annabelle looked upwards to a sky as cloudless and blue as her eyes, and another smile curved her lips. "You're very kind," she said gravely. "Thank you. And perhaps, if Mr—Mountfitchet, did you say?—has a room for me, he might also have a map. I'd like to know exactly where I am before I begin exploring and trying to earn some money."

Nigel looked a silent question, and she pointed to those bulky bags in their carriers. "My artist's equipment," she explained. "Sketchbook, pencils, paints, palette—folding easel, eraser, shooting stick—the works, in short. Three changes of underwear," she added mischievously, watching his sudden blush, "and a spare pair of jeans," taking pity on him. "I travel light, and I work hard."

Since she obviously wasn't going to think it impertinence on his part, Nigel ventured to enquire further as to the nature of her journeyman's work. Annabelle spread her arms in an expansive gesture.

"I paint—I immortalise. Look at this lovely old pub—it's simply crying out to be captured on canvas! I'll ask Mr Mountfitchet if he'd consider reducing my bill in return for a signed Annabelle Leigh picture of this place—and if he says yes, then I've earned part of my keep before I've left the village. If he says no, then I hop on Edgar here and cycle off to find other likely buildings—I check if the owner's at home first, of course, no sense in wasting my time on an empty house—and I ask if they'd mind my sitting outside in the road for a while. I tell them why I want to, naturally, but I never"—her eyes twinkled again—"mention money, at this stage. Time enough for that when they've seen the finished article. It usually sells itself, and, if it doesn't . . ."

She concluded with an expressive shrug which was entirely French, and her lips formed a careless *moue* which Nigel found altogether enchanting. With a quick flash of sympathy, he felt he understood exactly what she meant; and for a few wild moments he envied Annabelle Leigh her freedom, her independence, her gay spirit, her glamorous, gypsy lifestyle—which captivated him to such an extent that he found himself wondering whether he really wanted to stay in Plummergen for the rest of his born days. Living and working on the family farm, inheriting—eventually—and inhabiting the family home . . .

"Rytham Hall," he said, with a gulp, dragging his eyes from Annabelle's and becoming, with an effort, Nigel Colveden again. "Where I live—just up the road there. I think it's rather old, and—I mean, I know it is, so you might be interested . . . a couple of the rooms are William Morris, and they're supposed to be some of the best in the country—but they're inside, of course, so I suppose you wouldn't paint them, would you? Rooms, I mean—interiors. But if you'd like to come along and paint the exterior—or sketch it, or draw . . ."

Annabelle hesitated. "You know nothing about me," she began; but Nigel broke in to say that he knew everything he wanted to know. For the present.

"Nothing about my talent," she enlarged, ignoring this hint and speaking in a serious voice. "For all you know, I could be a hopeless artist—don't you even want to check me out before making such a rash offer?" She gestured towards the laden bicycle panniers. "While I'm, er, checking in," she said, smiling at the shared joke. "That's if you don't mind keeping Edgar company while I see if your Mr Mountfitchet has room for me. After all, there's no point in asking me to paint Rytham Hall if I'll be miles away from here by this evening. If you wouldn't mind waiting while I ask . . ."

It hardly took those cornflower eyes to persuade Nigel that he didn't mind in the least; and Annabelle thanked him prettily, blew him a hasty kiss, and opened the front door of the George and Dragon, leaving her own St. George on the step outside, wondering if he dared couple an invitation to tea with a request for a signed likeness of his home.

"Oh, gosh," said Nigel, patting Edgar's handlebars, not caring if his panniers contained the work of a Royal Academician. "Annabelle. Annabelle Leigh . . ."

# chapter
# -8-

MRS. BLAINE, NORMALLY so insistent that Eric should digest her meals properly before doing anything about the house or garden, had almost thrown the plates on the table at lunchtime, and herself had set to with knife and fork before her friend had time to pull up her chair. She glowered at Miss Nuttel, daring her to comment on the meal, which was far less elaborate than usual: but Miss Nuttel understood, and ate in a hurried silence. If a watch was to be maintained on the admiral, as little time as possible should be wasted in eating.

"Weed the borders in the front this afternoon, I think." Miss Nuttel swallowed a final, hastily chewed mouthful and washed it down with a glass of water drawn from Lilikot's private pump. "Mow the lawn too, perhaps. Compost."

Mrs. Blaine did not point out that the lawn had been mown only three days earlier. She nodded sagely. "August, too hot—everything grows so much faster, doesn't it? And with all the rain, as well—I thought, you know, that I really ought to clean the windows. They've been too splattered by the dust . . ."

Five minutes later, both Nuts were busy at their respective stations, Miss Nuttel carefully weeding, Mrs. Blaine wielding a languid shammy leather across the vast expanse of plate glass along Lilikot's front wall. A casual onlooker must have marvelled at how they managed to keep the good work going all afternoon. Anyone else would have been finished within the hour. But the Nuts were not anyone else: they had spent years nosey-parkering, which they considered the perfect pastime; and they could pass that time as slowly, or as fast, as circumstances might demand. Three hours after they had first begun, Miss Nuttel was still clearing weeds from her herbaceous borders, and Mrs. Blaine was still dipping her leather washcloth into soapy water that was by now stone cold, and from which the froth had long since faded away.

The admiral, alone in Ararat Cottage following the workmen's departure, was at one time heard through the open windows, hammering nails. Mrs. Blaine, with a squeak, dropped her shammy and darted across to Miss Nuttel, bleating that he must be building a coffin for another underworld corpse, and what did Eric think they ought to do about it. Miss Nuttel, whose ear was more expert and whose indigestion was more intense, retorted that he was probably putting up bookshelves, and Bunny had just trampled on her prize *Limnanthes Douglasii*. Mrs. Blaine, with a toss of her head, muttered something and stamped off back to her bucket and washcloth.

Miss Nuttel's pangs of indigestion died down enough for her to contemplate the thought of a cup of herbal tea, if Bunny could be coaxed into making it—but how to approach her, in this mood? For her part, Mrs. Blaine began to feel hot and thirsty—the very sound of sloshing water made the problem more acute—and wondered whether Eric was still in such a mood, since someone ought to stay on patrol while the other put the kettle on. They each looked up from her task, caught the other's eye, pulled rueful faces, and stopped what she was doing; but, as neither was prepared to admit she was in the wrong, they went indoors together . . .

And together rushed out of the kitchen before the kettle had finished boiling. Through their open back door, they heard the sound of Admiral Leighton's own door closing—his footsteps round the side of Ararat Cottage, marching down the path towards his front gate . . .

There was a squeak from Mrs. Blaine and a grunt from Miss Nuttel as their two selves collided in a doorway designed to allow the comfortable passage of only one. Neither was at first prepared to yield—they struggled, and squeezed, and snapped at each other, Miss Nuttel's bony elbows prevailing at last over Mrs. Blaine's more easily bruised padding, and Eric raced along the hall with Bunny in close pursuit, heading for the all-seeing safety of the net curtains, and the windows that overlooked The Street.

Side by side the Nuts peered out through the plate-glass spy-hole. "Post office," said Miss Nuttel, as the admiral's sturdy form strode in the direction of that establishment.

Mrs. Blaine rubbed a thoughtful bruise, and pouted when Eric took no notice. "He might be going to Crabbe's Garage, you know. To ask about the bus service, as he hasn't got a car, after all, has—oh."

"Post office," repeated Miss Nuttel, in tones of deepest satisfaction. "Buy everything this morning?" she added; and Mrs. Blaine understood at once. Forgiving her friend for her elbows and her disagreeable behaviour, she said quickly that she was sure there were a few things she'd forgotten, which wasn't surprising in the circumstances, was it, and if they were only to go back again she felt sure she would remember what they were. "But we really ought to go as soon as we can, before I have even longer to forget," she insisted; and Miss Nuttel nodded.

But before they had finished locking doors, closing windows, and hunting out shopping bags—all of which took far longer than usual, as both Nuts would keep rushing back to check on what was happening over the road—the door of the post office opened a second time, and the admiral appeared, smiling broadly behind his neat ginger beard. The Nuts saw that he had been buying things, for he now had with him two brown-paper packages he hadn't had before. Tucked under one arm was a heavy, string-tied, bulky bundle; in his free hand he held what was evidently a much lighter affair, which he swung jauntily to and fro as he stepped over the pavement, paused on the kerb, checked for traffic, and duly crossed The Street, back to his cottage.

Four interested eyes watched him approach the gate—he had left it open when he went out: now the Nuts knew why—and pushed it shut behind him with a careful foot as he held his packages fast. He marched up the path, round the side of the cottage and, presumably, in at his back door: which he then, with a thump, closed.

Miss Nuttel looked at Mrs. Blaine. Mrs. Blaine looked at Miss Nuttel. She seized her shopping bag and hurried to the front door without waiting to see whether her friend was behind her: she knew, without checking, she would be.

They were in such a rush to reach the post office that they narrowly missed being run over by Sir George, driving with his usual efficiency from Rytham Hall to Brettenden, in search of some necessary item of farm equipment Nigel, busy repairing the tractor, had said he needed. Lady Colveden's offer to save everyone time by going herself had been vetoed by her menfolk with ribald remarks concerning her shopping habits, and slanderous suggestions—from Nigel—to do with extravagance, especially in the matter of hats. So it came about that Sir George nearly ran the Nuts down: and they, with one more grudge against the manor to add to their tally—Lady Colveden's regular employment of that domestic gem Martha Bloomer was another—were faced with the delightful prospect of two different titbits for discussion: the buying habits of the admiral and the driving habits of the general. Their eyes gleamed, their steps quickened, and they entered the post office in a fever of excitement.

Their excitement was the greater as they were frustrated in their attempts to discover anything of what the admiral had bought. Emmy Putts, who had served him, had been the target of some bluff Naval gallantry, and now saw herself as his champion, and therefore mute. Moreover, Mrs. Stillman, who regarded Emmy as a Responsibility—what would she say to the girl's mother if Anything Happened?—kept a watchful eye both on her youthful employee, and on her tongue. For once, the post office was empty of other customers . . .

Baffled, Mrs. Blaine rejected three different brands of tinned tomatoes as having Political Undertones and stalked out without buying anything. After a few seconds' thought, Miss Nuttel followed her.

"Well!" Mrs. Blaine flounced up the garden path and with hands that quivered put her key in the front door. "Well, really, Eric, I never thought . . . too insulting! When all I did was require a civil answer to a civil question. If the post office prices weren't lower than the rest . . ."

But, since they were, this vague threat was as idle as both Bunny and Eric knew it to be; and Mrs. Blaine stamped in silence into the house, wishing she could slam the door to vent her feelings, but conscious that close behind her came Miss Nuttel. Who, to Mrs.

Blaine's surprise, shut the door with a thud, rather than a bang; and then—the only word for it—smirked.

"What is it, Eric? Not your indigestion again?"

"*Spirits,*" hissed Miss Nuttel, with a nod and a scowl in the direction of Ararat Cottage. After goggling at her for a space of three seconds, Mrs. Blaine yelped.

"Spirits? Sinister powers! Oh, Eric, how dreadful! We all know Old Mrs. Dawkin was simply *too strange*—and they say That Man asked *particularly* to buy her house. He said it would suit him *perfectly*! If he's in league with That Woman, then he must be a . . . a *warlock,*" in hushed accents. "A . . . a male witch—living right next door! Oh, Eric, what shall we—what *can* we do?"

The blackcurrant eyes widened, first with alarm, then with surprise that Eric was taking no notice. Indeed, rather than responding to her friend's understandable panic, Miss Nuttel was—was *smirking,* in that same infuriating way . . . And the blackcurrants narrowed to slits, sparking fire. "Eric, what on earth is the matter?" demanded Mrs. Blaine, as Miss Nuttel stared loftily down her equine nose, exuding an aura of self-satisfaction. "Eric, for heaven's sake! Don't keep me in suspense—what did you really mean?"

The smirk grew wider. "Looked at the shelves," replied Miss Nuttel, with a portentous nod. "While you were talking to Emmy—"

"Talking!" interposed Mrs. Blaine bitterly.

Miss Nuttel ignored Bunny's grumbles, as she so often had to do. "Checked what was missing—half the bottles gone. Spirits," she said again, with another nod. "Whisky, brandy, gin, rum. Mixers, too—tonic, soda water, bitter lemon. Stands to reason *he* bought them—all there earlier, weren't they?"

"And nobody else in Plummergen has ever shown signs of being an alcoholic—oh, Eric, how clever of you to notice! The mixers must have been a *blind,* to make us all think he was really going to use them—but everyone knows," said Mrs. Blaine, "what hard drinkers these Navy types can be. Look at the way they used to be served with a tot of rum every morning—positively encouraging the habit! He'll pour them down the sink, of course, and take the rest *neat.* No doubt he'll be singing sea-shanties in the middle of the night, and keeping us awake—too shocking, in our dear, peaceful Plummergen! We must be ready to telephone PC Potter the very instant he starts up. We don't," she said, in meaningful tones, "want any . . . incidents, do we?"

"Certainly not. Keep a careful eye on him, in case." And, suiting the action to the word, Miss Nuttel grabbed her outdoor shoes and gardening gloves from where she had flung them down earlier, and made once more for that ideal vantage point in her herbaceous borders.

It was while Mrs. Blaine, who was really too tired to wash any more windows, was reluctantly peeling potatoes at the sink that the next stage of the drama unfolded—literally. Miss Nuttel, without warning, rushed into the house and grabbed her friend by the arm, dragging her to the kitchen door. "Bunny, look!"

Mrs. Blaine followed the direction of the pointing fork, and looked. At the foot of his new flagpole stood Admiral Buzzard Leighton, with a roll of green-and-white cloth in his hands: a roll with a toggle at one corner and a loop at the other. These he attached to the flagpole halyards, and, by a practised hauling motion, he raised the roll of cloth— a flag, the Nuts guessed—to the top of the pole. As it hung there, swaying, he jerked once on the halyards, and the flag unfolded, to flap merrily in the evening breeze. The admiral stood staring up at the flag—a pennant, proudly flaunting its emerald-and-ivory length above his head—and gave a quick nod, as if pleased with his efforts. He walked to the garden gate, opened it, and looked up and down The Street; then he turned on his heel, leaving the gate open, and went back into Ararat Cottage by the front door—which, like the gate, he left open.

"Well!" said Mrs. Blaine.

"Exactly," said Miss Nuttel.

There was a pause. They gazed at each other, then out at the long green-and-white flag.

"Signals," said Miss Nuttel.

"Well, of course, Eric, it's too obvious he's signalling—and to That Woman, as we suspected all along. And he left the gate open for her to come sneaking in . . ."

There was, to the careful observer, a flaw in this argument, but Miss Nuttel rose above it. "Easier after dark for her," she said.

"Letting her know about it in good time, that's all—but best keep an eye open now. Just in case."

And, Mrs. Blaine concurring, they set up watch once more in the front windows of Lilikot: watching for any visitors to Admiral Leighton in Ararat Cottage—watching for Miss Emily Dorothea Seeton.

Since the Nuts were so sure they must soon see Miss Seeton, they gave no thought to any idea that others might respond to the admiral's signal. Great, therefore, was their astonishment when the first response to that green-and-white flag came from some-body else—somebody who, until then, had been generally thought a model of Plummergen probity.

She came briskly down The Street from the direction of Dr. Knight's nursing home, on her way to post the bundle of letters the Nuts could see clearly in her hand. Her eyes turned with quick interest to Ararat Cottage; and she halted in her tracks—stared up at the flagpole—was observed to smile. She thrust her letters into the box, dusted down her hands, smiled again; glanced at the gun-metal watch always pinned to her uniformed breast, then headed smartly across The Street to the open gate of Admiral Leighton's garden—passed through it—walked up the path, tapped on the front door—and, evidently hearing an invitation, entered. And vanished from view.

Miss Nuttel looked at Mrs. Blaine. Mrs. Blaine looked at Miss Nuttel. Together, they gave vent to their surprise and shock, in four explosive syllables:

"*Major Howett!*"

It was indeed that redoubtable personage, the backbone and boss of Dr. Knight's establishment, Major Matilda Howett. Retired from an Army career, the major had taken over as Dr. Knight's nominal second-in-command when matrimony, in the outsize form of Detective Sergeant Bob Ranger, removed his daughter Anne to a part of Kent from which commuting would have been impractical. Anne now worked as a doctor's reception-ist and nurse in distant Bromley; Dr. Knight and his wife, who had, while she still lived with them, innocently supposed them-selves to be in charge, had since discovered their mistake. The major Stood No Nonsense, and Got Things Done, and terrified malingerers into instant cures; though beneath her brisk exterior she was kindness itself to the genuinely ill. The Knights counted their blessings, and village wags christened Major Matilda the Howitzer.

"Oh," moaned Mrs. Blaine, "I never would have though it— never! When she's supposed to be such a friend to the vicar's sister—too hypocritical! What *can* a woman like Major Howett be doing in the admiral's house?"

"Better not ask," said Miss Nuttel, in tones to send shudders down poor Bunny's spine. "*Drink . . .*"

"White slavery!" breathed Mrs. Blaine, with as much glee as Emmy Putts—who found life in Plummergen very dull— was wont to speak of such things before being routinely suppressed by Mrs. Stillman. "Oh, it's too shocking! He'll dope her, of course—a Mickey Finn, isn't it?—and then That Woman will carry her off to Sweetbriars, where nobody will be able to find her—that high brick wall, remember?"

Miss Nuttel, nodding, remembered; choosing to forget, as did Mrs. Blaine, that Miss Seeton—who stood five-foot-nothing in her stockinged feet—was at best estimate half the size of the formidable major, and moreover didn't drive a car. Since it had already been remarked that the admiral also possessed no motor vehicle, it would seem that the mechanics of this particular abduction were inefficient, to say the very least.

"Nobody will be able to hear her calling for help," Mrs. Blaine said gloatingly, her eyes gleaming. "And oh, Eric, how can *we* be safe in our beds? What's to stop him creeping in here in the middle of the night . . . Eric? Oh, Eric! Oh, no!"

For, even as Bunny's lament had been building up to its thrilling climax, Miss Nuttel's attention had drifted from her friend, caught by what was happening outside.

Where a moving vehicle had slowed on its southbound way down The Street, and stopped almost exactly opposite, so that the driver could look in the direction of Lilikot—in the direction of Ararat Cottage next door—in the direction of the admiral's signal . . .

Which, having been duly observed, prompted the driver to switch off his engine, lock the car doors, and cross to Ararat

Cottage. Where, after a quick tap on the open door, he went inside . . .

Leaving the Nuts to gape at each other in horror.

"Oh, Eric, surely not! And he's a married man!"

# chapter

# ~9~

"I'M A MARRIED man now, sir, if you remember." Detective Sergeant Bob Ranger sounded slightly aggrieved. "I've got responsibilities."

In their office at New Scotland Yard, Delphick shook his head at his red-faced subordinate. "No, no. Don't you mean it's Anne who has the responsibilities? She's stopped worrying so much about all her patients in favour of trying to take care of her husband. And she's the one who's decided it's time you had a holiday, not you. Am I right?"

Bob blushed again, and grinned. "Well, sir . . ."

"I'm right. I thought so. And I'm not surprised. Your Anne isn't the only one who's noticed you've been working at full stretch recently, Sergeant Ranger. And, as things seem to have slowed down a little in our particular department—and we've even made noticeable inroads into the paperwork—in short, why not take a few days off?" Delphick quirked an eyebrow at the enormous young man on the other side of his desk. "Am I really such an ogre that you must stiffen your sinews and summon up your blood before daring to ask me for leave of absence? Surely not. Especially when, as I remember, you haven't used half your year's entitlement yet."

Bob shuffled his feet and cast uncomfortable glances in the direction of Delphick's in-tray. "Well, sir, I did sort of wonder . . ."

"Whether you could be spared? Nobody, Detective Sergeant Ranger, is indispensable—though there are times when some are less indispensable than others. And, since we have already

established that this might just be one of those times . . . Make
a break for it, Bob, before something happens to prevent it." He
stretched luxuriously. "Rest and recuperation—you can't beat
them. And who knows? As I appear to be in a sufficiently good
mood, you might wangle a long weekend out of me. Have you
thought where you might go?"

"Nowhere special, sir. Anne would like to spend a little time
with her parents, so—"

Delphick sat up with a jerk. "In Plummergen? Cancel my last
remarks immediately. A rest is the very last thing one expects to
enjoy, with Miss Seeton in full cry. She is, if you recall, back from
her Scottish holiday now, no doubt with her brolly primed and
her sketchbook on red alert." He shook his head. "Wouldn't you
prefer to be seconded to Inspector Borden to help him investigate
the coiner killing? A nice, safe murder that's nothing to do with
Miss Seeton . . ."

"No, sir, thanks all the same. You said yourself, the other
day, it *is* Fraud's case, not ours—besides, the poor bloke
they found dead may well have been a retired die maker,
but they still haven't definitely proved he was anything to
do with the coiners— or with us—or," some imp of mischief
made him add, "Miss Seeton, sir. So, if there's no logical
reason why I can't have a weekend in Plummergen . . ."

Delphick regarded him thoughtfully. "Use your imagination,
Sergeant Ranger. What else did I point out the other day? That
everything was unnaturally quiet in our specific operational
area—the lull, I now strongly suspect, before the coming storm.
There is, no doubt, an entire series of deaths in suspicious circumstances about to be discovered, all of which will successfully be
proved to lead back to the coiners—scrap metal merchants, plant
and machinery suppliers, drivers of delivery vans, hydraulics
engineers—with the inevitable and overwhelming result that
Fraud will be forced to ask for assistance." Delphick achieved
a frown of monumental bewilderment. "I doubt, however, if they
will ask it from us. I have noticed, in recent years, a marked
reluctance on the part of our colleagues to request the help of this
particular office." He shook his head. "I cannot for the life of me
imagine the reason . . ."

Bob, who could, grinned, and said nothing. The chief superintendent chuckled suddenly.

"You have your long weekend, Bob, and perhaps I'll treat myself to a day at the Oval beforehand. If the weather stays fine for the Test Match . . ."

"Tell you what, sir. If it's cricket you want, why not pop down to Plummergen on the Saturday? It's the annual Murreystone match—Anne's mother's helping with the teas—and, well, it might be interesting. Potter passed the word unofficially that they're still brooding about the Best Kept Village Competition, and a bit of, well, of muscle—" Bob tried to sound modest, with little success—"might come in handy, Potter says. Young Foxon from Ashford's likely to drop in too—he's a handy sort of bloke in a scrap, if you remember. But if Murreystone see enough coppers about the place, it might put them off—and they know us, sir, don't they? I mean, there'd be no need to let 'em know we weren't exactly on duty, would there?"

Delphick chuckled again. "Deviousness is not a trait I would previously have associated with you, Bob. So much for your urgent need for a holiday! You haven't just adopted Miss Seeton as an honorary aunt, you've adopted her village as your second home. And now you're trying to rope me in as moral, if not physical, support . . ."

"It was Anne's home first, sir," Bob began; then grinned once more, and shrugged. "Oh, well. After all this time, I suppose I do sort of think of it like that—Plummergen, I mean, as a second home. I get on all right with Anne's parents, and we've made friends with quite a few of the locals over the years. Most people are pretty friendly, once you get to know them—it's a decent sort of place on the whole, sir. The sort of place it'd be a pity to have bashed up by the local rivals just because of a cricket match. When it's normally such a—such a peaceful sort of place, sir . . ."

To which outrageous remark Delphick could find no suitable, or coherent, reply.

Miss Emily Dorothea Seeton has no idea that she is regarded by so many people with such circumspection. Never mind that she so frequently becomes, in Delphick's word, *embroiled* in adventures which are not of her choosing: never mind that the aftermath of such adventures is almost invariably chaos. Few save her sternest critics have accused Miss Seeton of being directly responsible for the chaos, for direct responsibility suggests choice, and free will, whereas it is generally recognised that Miss Seeton would consider it quite unsuitable for a gentlewoman such as herself to choose any path which is in the least out of the ordinary—and *out of the ordinary* describes her adventures to perfection. Since, however, she remains firmly convinced that she never undergoes adventures, whether ordinary or not, it is left for her friends and associates to bear the brunt of all the nervous strain which accompanies these adventures, and of the clearing-up which often, of sheer necessity, ensues. Miss Seeton never notices their efforts— or, if something especially out of the ordinary should manage to force itself to her attention, she is always sure that only by accident has she become involved in matters far too exotic for the retired art teacher she feels herself to be: and which, indeed, on one level she is. Her friends and associates, however, know otherwise . . .

But even for Miss Seeton, an invitation to afternoon tea at Rytham Hall was unlikely to result in anything other than an enjoyable time being had by both guests and hosts—some of them, anyway. Lady Colveden was always happy to see Miss Seeton, and looked forward to meeting Nigel's newest romantic interest; Nigel had changed his shirt in Annabelle's honour, and was staving off pangs of hunger by demolishing the emergency supply of scones in the kitchen—but Sir George, who had eaten no breakfast and little lunch, was sitting by himself drinking black coffee, and saying that the thought of clotted cream made him feel ill.

"Better not let Mother hear you say so," warned Nigel, who'd come to tempt his suffering father out of seclusion. "She thinks it serves you jolly well right—she was almost frantic yesterday when you didn't come home for so long. I was starting to wonder myself, I might add, though I managed to stop her ringing the hospitals to see if there'd been an accident—I said that everyone between here and Brettenden knows you and the station wagon, and somebody would've been sure to tell us. But the idea of an orgy—" Nigel grinned wickedly—"never occurred to either of us, of course."

Sir George groaned. "Strong drinks, in the Navy. Some time since I was on a troop ship. One forgets." He closed his eyes, and winced. Nigel snorted.

"That's hardly an excuse for scaring poor Mother into a blue fit and then waltzing in four hours later saying that the Howitzer wasn't such a bad sort after all. Is that any kind of example to be setting your only son? I'm young, and impressionable," Nigel informed his father in his most solemn tones. "It could do me no end of psychological harm to be the product of a broken marriage."

His father glared at him, but said nothing. Nigel tried again, producing from behind his back the blue-glass-lined, silver jam dish which Lady Colveden, before her son began to make such inroads into its contents, had filled with strawberry preserve. "You'll feel better," said Nigel, "once you've taken some sugar into your system. A scone or two, with a good dollop of jam on each—three lumps in your cup, and you'll be a new man. I'd hate Annabelle to think," he added carefully, "that my father was such a poor, broken-down specimen . . ."

Sir George managed a grin. "Poor breeding stock, eh?" Nigel looked startled, and blushed. His father essayed a chuckle, which didn't hurt as much as he'd feared. "Jumping the gun a bit, aren't you? Better see this filly of yours, though, or your mother'll never let me hear the end of it." With another groan, less urgent than the first, he raised himself slowly from his chair, took several deep breaths, and tried moving. He was pleased to find that he did not fall over. He made his cautious way across to the window and looked out down the drive.

"Here she comes, dressed to kill," he announced; and Nigel, with an exclamation, abandoned the jam dish on a side table, blushed again, and bolted from the room.

Ten minutes later Sir George, his spirits much improved by having played this little joke on his son, was talking to Miss Seeton in the sitting room while, in the kitchen, Lady Colveden made tea and, in the hall, Nigel lurked.

It had not been Annabelle Leigh whose coming Sir George had announced with such enthusiasm, but Miss Emily Seeton. Who, with her unique gold umbrella over her arm, her favourite string of beads—yellow glass, inherited from Cousin Flora—about her neck, and a neat straw hat upon her head, had walked the half mile from Sweetbriars under a lazy August sun; and when pressed had admitted that yes, she might perhaps be a little thirsty.

"We won't wait for Nigel's friend," Meg Colveden said as she headed kettlewards. "George, you stay and tell Miss Seeton about the admiral's party—I don't want her talking about her holiday until I'm back to hear it. I'm sure it was marvellous—Scotland is so beautiful—but for now . . ."

Lady Colveden smiled kindly upon her guest, nodded to her husband, and left them alone to prepare the tea. Miss Seeton, conscious of the good guest's duty, enquired:

"You have been to a party, Sir George? And at Ararat Cottage, of course. Dear Martha has told me—it was one of her mornings today, you know—about his coming to live in the village—Admiral Leighton, I mean. Such a pleasure for two such senior officers—oh, dear. I do beg your pardon. In rank, as opposed to in years, because I trust you understand that I would never . . ." Poor Miss Seeton turned pink. "Senior, that is." She took a deep breath. "Officers and, well, gentlemen . . ."

"Quite right, quite right." Sir George spoke quickly to spare her blushes, and—to reassure her that he'd perceived no insult in her remarks—nodded once or twice, until he remembered, wincing again. At Miss Seeton's subsequent look of dismay— had her apology been insufficient? had one still sounded impertinent—he made haste to justify his remarkable facial contortions.

"Gin pennant," said Sir George slowly, as if those two words explained everything: as, in a sense, they did.

But not to Miss Seeton, whose knowledge of matters military and naval was not so much limited as nonexistent. She regarded Sir George doubtfully. Had she heard him aright? *Djinn,* she knew from having read *The Arabian Nights* as a child, was the plural of *genie.* "In a bottle?" she murmured doubtfully, thinking of the hapless Scheherazade, and her thousand and one tales told night after night to ward off the penalty of death decreed by her husband, the temperamental sultan Schahriah. "Hardly," she murmured, "a model husband . . ."

Sir George looked startled. Accustomed as he was to the idiosyncrasies of Miss Seeton's thought patterns, it nevertheless surprised him that she, normally so considerate of other people's feelings—so reluctant to pass personal remarks—now should apparently think it her duty to censure him for having succumbed to the hospitable wiles of Rear Admiral Leighton. Most unusual—quite out of character for the little woman. Must have misheard, surely?

He became convinced that *someone* had misheard when Miss Seeton, still musing on his cryptic utterance, frowned, and said, "Although why they should feel obliged to praise an insect, of course . . ."

"Ah," said Sir George, with relief. "Tea!" How was he to know that Miss Seeton believed him to have uttered not two words, but three—to have talked of the *djinn's* "paean" of praise to the humble domestic ant?

"*Hymenoptera,*" said Miss Seeton, after the briefest of hesitations. "*Formicidiae.*" And she smiled, thankful for this proof that her memory seemed as sharp as ever, even for the complicated Latin names by which naturalists classified the various species.

Lady Colveden, carrying the tea tray, smiled back without comprehension, and struggled to find a quick and noncommittal reply to her guest's unorthodox salute. "I'm sure you're absolutely right, Miss Seeton. It sounds most interesting—but never mind all that now, if you don't think it rude of me to say so. I'm longing to hear how you enjoyed the Highlands—but you didn't bring your sketchbook with you. What a shame."

Miss Seeton murmured of finishing touches, and unpacking still to be done. She did not say—possibly she did not remember—that she had done some more sketching since she'd come home, and been slightly unnerved by what she'd drawn. Miss Seeton's memory for those instinctive and unusual artistic efforts for which her services are so prized by the police has always been elastic, in order to accommodate a natural reluctance to acknowledge her unique talent. "Perhaps another time," she said; and Lady Colveden, the perfect hostess, did not press her, and with a light laugh changed the subject.

"Has George told you the truth about yesterday evening, or did he fluff round it the way he tried with us? Is that too strong, by the way?"

Miss Seeton accepted her cup, saying that it was exactly how she liked it, and smiled again. Lady Colveden winked.

"I'd never heard of the gin pennant, until George came rollicking home at some unearthly hour last night positively reeking of rum and singing 'Heart of Oak' out of tune. But it seems it's a really old Naval custom—the gin pennant, I mean. If a ship flies the thing, or whatever the technical term for running it up the flagpole is, then any officers who see it are entitled to assume they've been invited to a party—and," with a grin, "they do. And they party—until the wee small hours, given half a chance."

Sir George harrumphed, and twirled his moustache, and put sugar in his tea with a determined hand, trying not to wince at the clink of lumps against porcelain. His wife smiled.

"So of course, when the admiral hoisted it—and Major Howett spotted it, and then George—well, no wonder I was without a husband for so long last night. I do think—" she turned to shake her head at her spouse, who was sipping tea with a faint grin on his face—"you might at least have telephoned and told me, so that I could have come to fetch you, rather than have you risk driving the station wagon under the influence—or—" in more heartfelt tones—"so that I could have come to the party as well."

But Sir George shook his head, and—so potent is the restorative power of tea to those with English blood in their veins—did not wince as he shook it. "Impossible," he said firmly. "Need to be an officer, m'dear. Charming company, but other ranks—not the done thing at all."

A remark to which his helpmeet would have responded with suitable scorn, had not a sudden sound of voices in the hall prevented her. She cocked her head to one side, listening. Sir George twirled his moustache again.

"Talk of charming company," he said, "and here she is— Nigel's latest fancy. Miss Annabelle Leigh." And he frowned. "Wonder why that name sounds familiar?"

# chapter

# −10−

MISS ANNABELLE LEIGH appeared shyly in the wake of a delighted Nigel, who introduced her with a broad smile.

"Miss Seeton," he added to Annabelle, "is an artist, too—I bet you'll have lots to talk about. Come and sit down, and have some tea." He ushered Miss Leigh across to one of the deep and comfortable chairs within easy reach of the occasional table, in another of which sat Miss Seeton. Who, her eyes bright, smiled warmly at Nigel's new young friend, and looked forward to a pleasant little talk at some time in the future: for of course one would not wish to discuss matters not of the general interest among one's friends, who might well be less interested than oneself. Annabelle, her blue eyes alight with her own warm smile, took her seat near her fellow artist with a fluid grace of movement that made Nigel catch his breath, while his father twirled his moustache and decided that his hangover was completely cured.

"Guess what Annabelle's been doing?" Nigel demanded of the assembled company as his mother poured tea and he passed plates. "When I was so afraid she might have forgotten—she was right outside in the drive, drawing the Hall! And it's jolly good— spot on. Won't you let me show them?" he begged, as Annabelle blushed discreetly and murmured that it was the very roughest of sketches: notes and impressions for an idealised English Village painting she planned as a project for the winter, when travelling by bicycle would be rather difficult.

Miss Seeton's attention was caught by Annabelle's talk of cycling, for she herself, though an indifferent mistress of that art, practised it from time to time when necessity required. Plummergen regularly shops in one of its three main stores for the basic, and even for some of the more unusual, items; but nearby Brettenden is a larger centre, and to Brettenden, twice a week, Crabbe's Garage runs a bus service to complement the once-weekly county provision. Should any Plummergen shopper have an urgent need for the unusual on one of the non-bus days, the Brettenden trip must be made under one's own power: in Miss Seeton's case, that of the rubber-treaded pedal.

"So very practical, as well as beneficial—one's knees—though the yoga, of course, has really been most . . ."

As Miss Seeton drifted to a halt, smiling again, Annabelle smiled back, with only the faintest flicker of bewilderment in those beautiful blue eyes. Nigel hadn't warned her about Miss Seeton—he would have thought it impolite to make personal remarks about a family friend who was also to be a guest under his parents' roof—but she had, during her travels, met several old ladies—with picturesque cottages, decaying mansions, and stately homes for her to paint—some dotty, some not. She could, she was confident, cope with Miss Seeton.

She seized on the one word she felt sure of. "Are you a practitioner of yoga, Miss Seeton? Don't you find that it just clears your mind wonderfully—makes you see things in a completely new way?"

"Indeed I do. Which is so very important, as I always tell the children—that they should learn to *see* what they wish to draw, for only when they have done so can they communicate what they have seen to others—not, of course, that I would presume to teach them yoga, as I feel that Mr. Jessyp and the educational authorities would hardly . . . and I am still very much a learner, though perhaps not, after seven years, quite so much of a *beginner*. Which is, after all, is it not, the true purpose of art?"

Annabelle blinked, but Miss Seeton hurried on: "Helping others to *see*, as well—sharing our experiences with those perhaps less able to appreciate them fully until they have been shown how. By those who can. See, I mean."

Nigel cast a triumphant look in Annabelle's direction. "You see? If you'll excuse the pun. But Miss Seeton agrees with me, so do let me show everyone your sketch." And Annabelle, knowing that to repeat her refusal would be as discourteous as if she had thrown a full-scale tantrum, smiled again, and nodded, blushing.

Nigel jumped to his feet—nearly knocking his lady's teacup from her hand—and hurried out to the hall for her sketchbook, which he had placed with all due care on top of the carved old mahogany chest which stood beside a row of coat hooks near the cloakroom door. He returned with the book open in his hand, and said:

"Look, Mother—Dad—isn't that the Hall to the life? Isn't she brilliant?" And Annabelle blushed again as Lady Colveden admired her work, handing the book—with a murmured apology to Miss Seeton—to her husband, who held it at arm's length, stared thoughtfully, blew through his moustache, and turned with a twinkle in his eye to Miss Leigh.

"Notes and impressions, eh? Seems rather more than that to me, though I'm the first to admit I don't know anything about art. Except"—with another twinkle—"what I like." And he chuckled, as did Miss Seeton, who knew Sir George's sense of humour of old. Dear Nigel, too, could be such a tease—he had inherited it from his father—such a charming and amusing young man, and devoted to his parents—though only in the nicest possible way. Teasing them, she meant. And always so very susceptible to equally charming young women . . .

Miss Seeton gazed with interest at Annabelle, wondering whether this time Nigel had really found the Right One; and smiling, for she was really a remarkably attractive girl. None but the best, of course, would be right for dear Nigel, of whom his parents—and she herself, with the privilege, she hoped, of an old friend—was so fond . . .

Miss Seeton emerged from her daydream to the sudden realisation that Sir George must have handed over Annabelle's sketchbook without her having noticed, for she found herself leafing through it, looking at earlier sketches and notes—impressions (and Miss Seeton smiled again)—the girl had evidently jotted down on previous occasions. Automatically reverting to her former persona, the retired art teacher studied each drawing in turn, observing the lively penmanship, the quick and confident grasp of outline, the assured strokes and skilful forms that proclaimed the consummate craftsman. There was, reflected Miss Seeton with a sigh and a wistful shake of the head, true talent in Miss Leigh's work. And such an eye for close work, as well as the ability to capture the essence of a scene with fluency and rhythm—there were copious written notes, as well as sketches and details from the larger whole—delicate use of toning and texture and shade, immediacy of vision coupled with a lasting sense of truth, of certainty that, were the buildings thus shown to be removed in their entirety to a crowded city and the viewer asked to pick out one from among a hundred others, it could be done with no difficulty.

Miss Seeton sighed again. One should not so much *envy* as respect and admire the greater gifts possessed by others. She hoped she was not jealous—that would hardly be proper, in the circumstances—but . . .

She became aware that Annabelle was gazing at her in some surprise; and became flustered. Had she made some comment out loud which had sounded—though of course would not have been so intended—improper? Had she inadvertently given Miss Leigh to suppose that she found her work—which would be untrue—of no interest?

"Indeed not," she made haste to assure Annabelle, whose eyes widened with more surprise than ever, since Miss Seeton had not explained her complete train of thought, and by itself her assurance made little sense. "Not true at all, and most improper—as you must surely realise, my dear."

Nigel, gallant as ever, in instinctive sympathy for his old friend's confusion, hurried to save her from becoming yet more confused, and confusing, by saying:

"Well, I know I shouldn't admit it, but I agree with Dad—about only really knowing what I like, in art. And I like Annabelle's work no end, I must say. Though I suppose"—he rather prided himself on this neat diversion—"a few visits to decent galleries and exhibitions would help to educate the pair of us properly." He looked hopefully at Annabelle: would she take the hint?

As she hesitated, Miss Seeton said brightly: "Dear Jack Crabbe, who drove me home from Brettenden yesterday, as you know compiles those clever crossword puzzles for magazines, and was kind enough to give me a copy—because of the extra money, and the chough. But with having to take the mouse to the garden, and then being rather more tired than I expected after my journey, I only read it this morning—such a sad, romantic story, to which it now seems most unlikely we will ever know the true answer. But she might, perhaps, have been comforted at last to learn that it was being turned to some more practical purpose, after so long." She frowned in silent calculation. "How many years is it since the end of the war? Almost thirty—and that poor woman still mourning as greatly as ever, and becoming a recluse, so the article said. She never married again, and her little twin daughters were supposed to have been buried in the rubble as well as her husband, and were dead when they were finally dug out, or so the story goes. There were so many similar tragedies during the Blitz . . ."

Miss Seeton sighed. As a teacher, she had not been conscripted, but had done her fair share of fire-watching and, later, keeping a lookout for doodlebugs when Hitler's forces threw everything they could at London, yet were unable to break that city's spirit. But the spirit of someone who had suffered from the bombing had been broken beyond repair on a night at the height of the Blitz: the spirit of a woman who, after experiencing her horrific loss, had refused ever to consider having the site of that loss disturbed. It had remained as a stark, gaping void between two adjoining Regency houses whose walls were shored up with scaffolding and buttresses, resting on the empty ground between: ground which had become a small haven for birds and other wildlife, where rose-bay willowherb—fireweed—flew its pinky purple flags in graceful memory of the dead.

Lady Colveden, who also remembered the war, said gently: "Indeed there were, Miss Seeton. Though I'm afraid I don't quite understand . . ."

Her smile was kind, and Miss Seeton turned pink. "Dear me, I seem to have . . . it was the gallery, you see. When Nigel was saying because the article says that, now the poor woman is dead, the site has been sold to a—a consortium of oriental art lovers—Chinese gentlemen whose names, I fear, I find myself quite unable to recall. And even if I could"—she smiled—"I doubt if I could pronounce them. A most interesting language, is it not? Pictorial—or rather it was, having become more symbolic over the years, as I understand." Her eyes twinkled. "The symbol for man, when written with *two* of the symbols for woman, represents jealousy, which is most descriptive, is it not? But the article says that they wish to buy the site, and commission an architect to design a new building in the exact style of the one which was bombed—that is, on the outside, since there was not, of course, an art gallery in the house when the family lived there. But the article suggests that luxury flats are to be built on the upper floors—and, though it is perhaps fanciful to think it, one would hope that the people who buy them, living happy lives in their new homes, will lay the *un*happy ghosts for that poor woman at last."

There was a thoughtful pause as she finished speaking. Sir George, who like his wife remembered the full horrors of the war, broke it at last with a harrumph, and—after a quick glance at Lady Colveden—attempted some lightening of the general mood.

"Not the only tale I've heard about those days recently, y'know. Major Howett, now—wouldn't think a woman could spin a yarn with the best, but she did last night." Nigel, on hearing this, choked, and swallowed hastily several times before regaining composure as his mother glared at him. The major-general ignored them both, intent on his story.

"Timber merchant's daughter, y'know—brothers in timber as well. Reserved occupation," he added for the benefit of the younger generation. "Didn't have to go—weren't allowed, even if they wanted to. The Howitzer—er, Major Howett"—and he harrumphed again—"knew everyone round the place, of course. All able-bodied men in the Home Guard, ready for action if Jerry invaded—shotguns, rook rifles—pitchforks, even—keeping a lookout for enemy parachutists in disguise. Nuns, that sort of thing."

"You could tell them by the size of their feet," came the irreverent murmur from his son and heir. Annabelle flashed Nigel a brilliant smile, then turned politely back to his father, her eyes asking him to continue.

Which he did. "Later on, the end of the Phony War—air raids—bombs dropped, incendiaries and so on. Every man Jack on call—no excuses. Major Howett's brothers slipped down to the pub"—he glared at Nigel, daring him to comment—"and the siren went off. Bad show—nobody on duty. The Howitzer took the telephone message—grabbed her hat, went charging down the road, banged on every door she knew and warned it was Action Stations. Bombs dropping round her thicker than hailstones. One landed in the road—blew off her hat, tripped her up over a heap of sand by the gate." He paused and added the further explanation that sand had been a necessary adjunct to wartime life for the purposes of fire safety. Not everyone, he pointed out, had been lucky enough to possess a stirrup pump.

"And even if you did," his wife reminded him, "if there was no water supply because it had been bombed, what use would a hundred pumps have been?"

"Sand," agreed Miss Seeton, "might certainly be regarded as being more *practical* in such circumstances, although not, perhaps, generally as *versatile*—one can, after all, do so much more with water than extinguish fires. I remember how, when my lodgings were bombed out, for three days we were rationed to just one cup a day, with which we could either clean our teeth, or wash ourselves—or, of course, we could drink it."

"Golly," said Nigel, regarding her with awe, and marvelling that she hadn't mentioned cleaning paintbrushes as yet another option. "Which—if it's not too rude, Miss Seeton—did you choose?"

"Oh, I drank it, naturally. The human body, you see, is over eighty per cent water, as I recall. So it seemed much more sensible to stay *healthy,* rather than *clean.* And for three days one could surely tolerate the inconvenience of having to wait until arriving at school before ceasing to be grubby—when our forces were undergoing such privations in the field of battle . . ." She smiled kindly for Annabelle's ill-disguised shudder. "In wartime, my dear, one's priorities are so very different, you see." And the Colvedens nodded gravely at her words.

Sir George, however, was not to be balked of his story, which he resumed with relish. "Anyway, the major survived, the Home Guard did their duty—thanks to her. Couple of weeks later, up comes young Bocking, friend of her brother—driving a lorry full of Christmas trees, of all things. Says he's brought 'em for her as a thank-you for calling out the Guard. Calls the brothers, unloads the lot, and skedaddles! Pinched, of course." Sir George shook his head. "As Miss Seeton said, different in wartime. Had to hide every blessed one of 'em—inspection pit in the tractor shed, the major said. Still there on VE Day, what's more. Christmas trees . . . very rum."

"What's rummer still," Nigel pointed out, "is the idea of any-one as respectable as Major Howett having risked being pinched for receiving stolen goods." He regarded Sir George with some amusement. "The Buzzard must mix a pretty lethal drink for her to have told you, of all people, a story like that." He grinned at his mother. "I wonder what Dad told the Howitzer in exchange? Let's hope he was at least able to reassure her she's not about to be hauled off to chokey—at least, I trust she isn't, though that depends on the book of rules, of course. Want me to hop along and fetch it? My father," he explained to a puzzled Annabelle, "is the local JP—a pillar of the community, in fact." Miss Leigh blinked, then smiled, slowly, as he translated: "A magistrate—a Justice of the Peace. Duty bound to collar every crook he encounters and see that law and order are maintained, no matter how long since the crime. Now, if he'd only had his handcuffs with him yesterday . . ."

"Nigel," said Lady Colveden, with an apologetic smile for Annabelle, who was frowning again as she stared at the baronet's cheerful moustache, "I'm sure your father knows the difference between a . . . a criminal case, if it still is, and a social occasion thirty years after the event." She turned to her spouse, suddenly curious. "George, I don't suppose . . ."

"Nonsense!" The major-general, magistrate, blew forcefully through his moustache. "Statute of limitations expired years ago. Far more keen on catching today's crooks."

"It just wouldn't be sporting," said his son cheerfully. "To take advantage of what you've been told in your cups, I mean." His eyes danced. "In *both* your cups, that is—you and the major. It would hardly be cricket, would it?"

# chapter

# -11-

"CRICKET," SAID LADY Colveden quickly, before Nigel could say anything more. "Now, that reminds me, Miss Seeton . . ."

And she began to explain, in greater detail than when she had talked earlier to her husband and son, the parlous state of Plummergen's pavilion, and the proposals for raising funds for repairing both the roof and the floor.

Miss Seeton approved the idea of an auction, and agreed that Sir George would make a splendid master of ceremonies; she said that Lady Colveden must be sure to let her know as soon as any raffle tickets went on sale, as even if her services were not required in their selling, she intended to buy several books. One wished, naturally, to do one's best to help one's adopted home in whatever way possible.

"Though I fear, however," she continued, with a sigh, "that my ability is such that, really, much as one feels an obligation to offer further assistance, if such assistance is of no *practical* worth then it is surely much more than a waste of time, it is unfair. Indeed, one ought, perhaps, in all honesty to say *inability*. From what I recall of Jack Crabbe's kind explanation, there are only eleven people in the team, and though ours is not the largest of villages, one would have supposed there to be many more persons with a far greater ability than—"

"Nigel," broke in Lady Colveden with a quivering voice, "run out to the kitchen a moment, would you? I, er, have a horrid feeling I left the kettle on the gas." And Nigel, too grateful for her offer of release to remind his mother that Rytham Hall cooked by electricity, uttered a strangled gasp of agreement before bolting from the room to have his laugh out in private.

By the time he felt able to return without risk of bursting into shrieks of hysterical mirth at the idea of Miss Seeton, clad in cricketing whites—apart, of course, from her distinctive cockscomb hat—and carrying her umbrella, striding out to the crease as Last Man In, destined to save the match, the misunderstanding had been cleared up. Miss Seeton, her face wreathed in smiles, was so relieved to find she was not to be co-opted into the local cricket team that she gladly agreed to produce the required painting, trusting that it would reach a suitable sum at auction and promising to bid for it herself, though she knew almost nothing of the game, and could think of nowhere to hang the picture, should her bid be successful.

"Oh, but you'll have to understand just a little about it, Miss Seeton." Nigel was now able to speak without choking on his words, and managed to do so with a straight face. "Before you can paint it properly, I mean. But honestly, it couldn't be easier— and you've got the basics, anyway. You already know there are two teams, and they're made up of eleven people each. And I'm sure you know that the fielding side tries to stop the batting side scoring runs . . ."

Miss Seeton said that this, indeed, she understood—in principle—but that the scoring, she felt, was far more complicated than he made it sound. Nigel paused. He frowned.

He said: "Well, when a team goes in to bat, they try to hit the ball as far as they can so that they can make as many runs as possible before the bowler gets it back. If it goes as far as the boundary, they score four runs without having to run at all—and if it goes as far as the boundary without touching the ground, then they score six. But if it only goes a little way, then they have to use their judgement as to how far they can actually run—how many times they can charge up and down the pitch—that's the dry grassy bit between the two sets of stumps—before the bowler is ready to bowl the next ball of the over."

"Over," repeated Miss Seeton dutifully. Nigel gazed in the direction of his father and signalled for help. Trying to explain a fact of life with which one had grown up was a great deal more difficult that he'd expected it to be.

Sir George beamed. "Doing a grand job, Nigel—couldn't have

put it better m'self. Ah—over to you, old chap!"

Nigel grinned wry appreciation of his father's little joke, and then frowned again. "Oh. Yes, well . . . The ball is bowled from each end of the pitch in turn—to be fair, you see. Sun in the batsman's eyes, that sort of thing. So, to make sure the advantages and disadvantages of either end balance out, the bowling is in groups of six balls—and, well, each group is called an over, because they, er, change over at the end of it. So do the fielders, if they want to. Change, I mean—their positions, which is what they don't tend to do in the middle of an over, because of being another distraction, you see. But when the umpire says it's all, er, over, everyone can move, if they like—and the wicket-keeper positively must, with having to change ends."

"Behind the stumps," announced Miss Seeton, to the surprise of all who heard her: they did not know of yesterday's sketch, and the Chinese cricketers—whose appearance disturbed her less now she had read the article about the proposed new gallery—and the umpire, standing at the wicket, watching. "Three stumps," she said proudly. Perhaps one's ignorance might be less great as one had at first supposed. "The wicket . . ."

"What did I tell you, Miss Seeton? You've got the hang of it—I knew you would. I should think it'll be a pretty good painting, once it's done." And Nigel mopped his forehead, helped himself to another cup of tea, and, having buttered a scone, spread it with a double thickness of jam as his justly earned reward.

It had been, reflected Miss Seeton as she stood unpinning her hat in the hall of her cottage, a most enjoyable afternoon—educational, as well. One felt far more confident of one's ability to achieve an intelligent portrayal of the game of cricket now that dear Nigel had explained so much in such a very lucid way. And what a pleasure to meet Miss Leigh! So young, and yet so talented—Nigel was fortunate to have won her interest. It was obvious, from the way in which she had looked at him, that won her interest he had. Just as, of course, she had won his, which was, surely, *her* good fortune. Dear Nigel. Such a romantic nature. How one hoped he was not to be disappointed by the loss of his own Annabel Lee—though one had to admit that, in August, even in England, the prospect of any wind chilling and killing one so evidently in the full bloom of beauty and health must be thought unlikely. She and Nigel made such a very handsome couple . . .

Miss Seeton sighed with pleasure as she slipped her gold umbrella into the rack, emptied her handbag of the most important items, and carried her hat upstairs. Not a click or a creak from one's knees—really, the modest expenditure on *Yoga and Younger Every Day* all those years ago had been recovered more than a hundredfold in one's general level of fitness and well-being— though one was, of course, glad not to have been required to bat, or to bowl, or to field on the day of the big match. No, all that was required was that one should produce a painting of the pavilion, with a match in progress in the foreground, and, naturally, as many of the players being recogniseable as one's skill allowed, so that they would be far more likely to bid for it—because, of course, it was hardly credible that anyone would venture the large sums anticipated at the auction in order to own an Emily Seeton original. Which sounded—Miss Seeton, even in the privacy of her own home, blushed—altogether too conceited, given one's limitations as an artist. Unlike Miss Leigh. Annabelle. Whose work—one hoped she had not been offended at the interest one had automatically shown in her entire portfolio—was so very, very good . . .

Miss Seeton, for all Nigel's assurances that she seemed to have grasped the principles of the game, decided that it would be as well if she essayed a rough sketch of the cricket painting before everything he had so carefully explained to her had become muddled. She collected pencils, eraser, and sketching block, then headed for the sitting room, where she hesitated for a moment, gazing out through the French windows. It was a glorious evening, and the sun was still bright, the air still warm: an evening for sitting on her little terrace rather than staying inside.

Miss Seeton opened the double doors and stepped out, the afternoon's accumulated warmth radiating from the flagstones of the patio, though not unpleasantly. A table and chairs—all of heavy-duty, weatherproof plastic—stood waiting for her, and she arranged her drawing gear neatly in a spot where she could see the canal at the bottom of her garden, beyond the chicken house and the wall. She sat down, pulling her sketchbook across to rest one end on her knees, the other against the table edge; and she sat, and looked, and thought: about cricket, and other matters.

She found herself turning back the pages of her book in much the same way as she'd leafed through Annabelle Leigh's, and remembered again how surprised the young woman had been at her interest. Neither Sir George nor Lady Colveden had been so, well, so presumptuous, after Miss Leigh had made it very plain she had not wished anyone to look at her work. Modest as well as talented, reflected Miss Seeton, blushing for her own inadequacies as well as her discourtesy, for so it must have seemed to Annabelle, despite one's attempts to explain that it had been the younger woman's remarkable talent which had caused one's apparent breach of etiquette. And Miss Seeton blushed again, and sighed . . .

Good gracious. But this was dreadful! She had supposed herself to be nothing but kindly disposed towards the young artist: to admire her talent, and to feel curious as to her suitability for dear Nigel—in much the same way as (or so she supposed) his parents would feel, until they had come to know her better. Which was, Miss Seeton thought, perfectly natural, in an old family friend. But that beneath these outward and natural feelings should be such— such unsuspected jealousy, such spite, was—was almost wicked, and certainly worrying. Miss Seeton gazed in dismay at the sketch in front of her, the sketch which she had intended should be a preliminary draft for the cricket painting—had she not turned back through the pages on purpose to look at that earlier sketch?—but for the drawing of which she did not, she realised, remember picking up her pencil.

It was clear, however, that she had. Here was the proof before her very eyes, in black and white—and mostly black. How dreadful! That glorious golden girl, with her blonde hair and those lovely eyes—seldom had Miss Seeton encountered a pair more lovely—and her honey-coloured skin, the picture of youth and health—why, oh why, was she shown here as a dark, sinister, crooked creature, her eyes slits, her mouth twisted, her hands, those hands which had produced the pictures Miss Seeton had so admired, like grasping talons?

Miss Seeton felt faint, and dizzy. Her eyes blurred as they filled with tears. That she, who had always encouraged the development of even the most feeble talent, who had been proud if her pupils excelled their teacher, visiting exhibitions and rejoicing to find red "sold" stickers on canvases signed with names she knew well . . . that she should, unknown to herself, be so eaten up inside with envy that she could produce a drawing like this! It was horrible— frightening. To find that her innermost thoughts were not as calm and quiet as she'd believed them, that a dark side of her character which she'd never before suspected was revealing itself in all its cruel clarity . . .

She would destroy the drawing—tear it to shreds, burn it to ashes. But she knew she could never erase it from her memory— that her happiness would never again be complete, be safe. She had lost her peace of mind, most precious of possessions—and she foresaw no easy way in which it could be restored. She would try—it would be foolish, as well as self-indulgent, not to try—but she very much feared . . .

"Oh, dear—that one could be so malicious," said Miss Seeton, with a sigh. "I can hardly believe it . . ."

"I can hardly believe it, Eric." Mrs. Blaine was on duty at one window, Miss Nuttel at another. They took turn and grudging turn about, each afraid the other would spot something of great interest that her friend, if she'd stayed ten seconds longer, would have spotted first. "That Man is out in the garden *again*! Though it isn't bricks this time."

Miss Nuttel came galloping down the stairs and into the kitchen, which overlooked the rear of the admiral's property. She had been listening to sounds of hammering emanating from inside Ararat Cottage, and craning her long neck, and holding mirrors in either hand, in order to see into the Buzzard's downstairs windows. He was not a man for net curtains—Mrs. Blaine thought it too careless of him, lowering the tone of The Street this way; Miss Nuttel was inclined to believe it just showed how brazen he was prepared to be—but then, without net curtains it should have been possible to maintain a closer watch on the man than was in fact the case. It was evening; the sun was setting; and, as it sank through the heavens, it cast a fiery light over all below—including the walls and windows of buildings in The Street. Walls and windows which gave off reflective gleams that dazzled the eyes, and shone on Ararat Cottage, and rendered its interior invisible to an exterior observer.

And so Miss Nuttel galloped down the stairs to take her place at Bunny's side, peering out into the admiral's garden and seeing him walk over, carrying a strange timber contraption, to a place beneath an apple tree where, earlier, he had been observed setting out bricks and paving stones in a series of rectangular areas. Mrs. Blaine, convinced he must have been digging there without her knowledge, opined that these paved areas were covered graves; Miss Nuttel, whose ears—she maintained—were sharper than Bunny's, insisted he hadn't, and they weren't. What they were, however, she had no idea.

And she still had no idea, even as she watched the admiral set on each of his prepared paved areas one of the timber frames on which, she realised, he had been working as he hammered. Having placed the first frame fair and square in the centre of the rectangle, he went back indoors to fetch another—then another. In all, there were four.

"Oh, Eric," bleated Mrs. Blaine. "More signals—it must be! But who is he signalling *to*, from the back of the house like this, where nobody can see? It's positively too sinister! Do you suppose"—with a fearful look at the darkling sky—"he's signalling to, well, to people . . . *flying?*"

Her horrified shudder was followed by one equally horrified from Miss Nuttel, who cast an anxious look over her shoulder in the direction of Sweetbriars, and turned pale. "Broomsticks, you mean," she gasped; and Mrs. Blaine moaned. Miss Nuttel gulped. What other explanation could there be? Miss Seeton, they knew, was a witch: the admiral was most likely a warlock; both were too cunning to reveal their association—that party, about which Sir George had been (rumour had it) so cheerful, had been a blind; what better way of announcing their plans to the other members of the coven than by leaving the strange geometric shapes out all night, for easy visibility in the moonlight? "Move them every day or so, I expect," said Miss Nuttel, equine teeth chattering. "Mean something different each time."

Mrs. Blaine was on the point of moaning again, but stopped. A sound from the front of the house had caught her attention. "Voices!" hissed Miss Nuttel, who'd heard them first. "Must have come in the lorry! Heard it drive up not two minutes ago—didn't realise it was coming here."

Bunny looked at Eric, eyes wide with fright. "The other war-locks—oh, it's too terrible! How many of them can you see? The admiral must have been expecting them—look!"

For Buzzard Leighton was walking away from his mysterious brick-and-timber signals towards the approaching voices, with a smile on as much of his face as could be seen behind the ginger beard, and his hand outstretched in welcome to the newcomers.

# chapter

## -12-

THE WINDOWS OF Lilikot, though open, were still too far from the admiral and his guests for either of the Nuts to be able to hear what was being said; and the dusk was coming on too swiftly for them to be able to see exactly what was being done. There are no street-lights in Plummergen; the moon had not yet risen; the sun had disappeared behind a bank of low, looming cloud. The mysterious and heavy shapes carried by the admiral and his fellow warlocks from the lorry parked outside, down the front path, round the side of Ararat Cottage, and across to the sinister brick-and-paving rectangles, were shrouded in shadows. The Nuts, desperate to discover the mystery and what was proposed for these, its mani-festations, were beside themselves. Miss Nuttel insisted that the shapes gave off a low, regular humming, as if four small genera-tors were being installed in the admiral's garden: Mrs. Blaine said she heard no humming, but, if she had, it would obviously mean yet another manifestation of Occult Powers, since neither she nor Miss Nuttel had observed any wires or electric cables running from those squat, square shapes, had they?

Miss Nuttel was forced to agree that they had not; and the watch was resumed. But, after delivery of the fourth humming—or possibly not—heavy shape, the warlocks from the lorry van-ished, at the breezily audible invitation of the admiral, indoors: there, no doubt—as Mrs. Blaine reminded Miss Nuttel—to drink their dread potions and conjure up who knew what horrors from the Other Side.

But Miss Nuttel was more interested in the Other Side of the fence. In the Lilikot menage, she played the more practical part:

Bunny attended to the house, Eric to the garden and the various odd jobs about the establishment Mrs. Blaine found too difficult—changing fuses, climbing ladders, putting up shelves. That hammering, and now the low humming, bothered Miss Nuttel. Her curiosity, always acute, had been all the more pricked in that she was starting to suspect—though she had no idea what had made her change her mind—that, on this occasion, there might be a rational explanation for everything. If, for example, the admiral should turn out to be a Brilliant Inventor, who had secretly perfected a method for cheap, do-it-yourself electricity . . .

"Oh, Eric," begged Mrs. Blaine, "don't you see, that's just how they work! Trying to corrupt you—too despicable, pandering to one's *baser instincts*—money, I mean," as Miss Nuttel turned an astonished look upon her. "And money," Mrs. Blaine misquoted in ominous tones, "is the root of all evil. Besides, if the admiral really *has* done anything like that, doesn't it only go to prove he's a Mad Scientist? And we all know—" in even more ominous tones—"about *them*." The Nuts seldom went to the cinema, regarding the silver screen and its artificialities as seductions from the simple life: but, on one occasion when they'd been caught in torrential rain while shopping in Brettenden, and Mrs. Blaine had complained of burgeoning bronchitis, they had abandoned their principles for the shelter of the Picture Palace, which was then showing a rerun of *Dr. Strangelove*. They had not stopped to read the poster in detail, and thus missed the film's subtitle *or: How I Learned to Stop Worrying and Love the Bomb*. They emerged from the cinema emotionally exhausted, and brewed their herbal teas at double strength for a fortnight afterwards.

"Hadn't thought of that," acknowledged Miss Nuttel, with a frown. "All the same—while he's busy indoors . . ."

"You're not to go alone, Eric," Mrs. Blaine said bravely. "Just let me fetch my bundle of herbs from the kitchen, and that copy of *Ghosts and Go-Betweens* we bought when Brettenden Library had a clear-out . . ."

Five minutes later, well to the rear, Mrs. Blaine stood watching as Miss Nuttel, balanced on the small stepladder, leaned over the admiral's fence and shone a torch in the direction of those four humming generators beneath the apple tree. Under her breath, Bunny mumbled prayers, clutching the witch-herbs to

her ample bosom and ready to run for her life if the door of
Ararat cottage opened and the admiral—chief warlock? crazed
inventor?—appeared. Under the moonless sky, stars casting pale
and glittering light, the world had a truly unearthly look, and
almost anything was believable. Panic clutched Mrs. Blaine's
heart as an owl swooped, hooting, overhead. Her terrified eyes
followed the beam of Miss Nuttel's torch as it stabbed, a sword
of righteousness, into the blackness of the sinful night, over the
other side of the admiral's fence.

And then Miss Nuttel, with a sudden exclamation, leaned forward—the torch wobbled in her hand—the owl, a ghostly gliding
form in the night, swooped again. The warlock's familiar! Mrs.
Blaine let out a squeak as the torch waved wildly and Miss Nuttel
staggered backwards—flung up her arms—dropped the torch on
her toes—tumbled off the ladder to the flower bed below.

All thoughts of a Mad Scientist vanished entirely from the mind
of Mrs. Blaine. "Oh, Eric," she moaned, as the form in the flower
bed uttered a curse, groping for the torch—the light had gone out.
Sinister powers? "Oh, Eric!"

"Bulb smashed," announced Miss Nuttel, scrambling to her
feet. "Never mind—saw all I needed." And she began to head
back towards the house, dusting herself down as she did so. Mrs.
Blaine, after a few stunned moments, collected her scattered wits
and scuttled after her.

"You could see? Before it all went dark—you saw what it was?"
Miss Nuttel grunted an affirmative as she flung open the kitchen
door and stalked inside.

"Then—oh, Eric, it's too cruel of you to keep me in suspense!"
Mrs. Blaine reached the kitchen, panting, and slammed the door
shut behind her. "Eric, tell me    what did you see in the admiral's
garden?"

In Ashford police station, three mornings later, Detective
Constable Foxon was at work bright and early, sticking coloured pins into the wall map which loomed over the desk
of Superintendent Brinton. Foxon whistled to himself as he
worked, enjoying the patterns produced by the arrangement of
rainbow shades. He might, he reflected, try to find, or to coax
his mother to make him, a tie with markings like these. It would

give his appearance a touch of—

"Foxon!" The young man had been so intent on his work that he'd failed to hear the approach along the corridor of Superintendent Brinton, whose voice suggested that today, at least, he proposed living up to his nickname. Old Brimstone stood in the doorway of his office, fulminating. "Foxon, do you have to make that horrible noise—or that ghastly mess on the wall? What the hell d'you think you're doing?"

Foxon's expert eye deduced a slight hangover, which was indeed the case. Brinton's brother-in-law and his wife had paid an unexpected visit last night, and Mrs. Brinton's fondness for her family had made her pull out all the stops—and the stoppers. Bottled beer had preceded, then rounded off, a meal at which wine flowed like water at a Holdfast Brethren "Drink: the Demon Destroyer" festival day. Brinton wouldn't go so far as to say that destruction felt imminent—this feeling had worn off at around three o'clock in the morning—but he was definitely not his usual cheery self.

He trod wearily round his desk, pulled out the chair, and collapsed upon it with a faint groan. "Foxon, stop hovering behind me like that, laddie—you make me nervous. Come away from that wall, and let me take a proper look at you—and siddown," he added with a snarl, as Foxon stood in front of his chief, his variegated tie on a level with Brinton's bloodshot eyes. Foxon sat.

Brinton leaned his elbows on the desk and glared at his subordinate. "Foxon, who is the boss around here?"

"You, sir." Foxon looked puzzled.

"So far, so good." Brinton glared again. "Foxon, whose office is this?"

"Yours, sir." Foxon looked as if light were beginning to dawn. In his hand, the packet of pins rattled gently as his shoulders began to shake. Brinton glared some more.

"Foxon, why are you sniggering? And why the hell were you sticking pins in the office—*my* office—map without permission?"

"Sorry, sir." Foxon choked back a full-blown laugh and gesticulated in the direction of Brinton's in-tray, using the hand that held the pins—which rattled again. "I read the overnight reports, sir, and couldn't help thinking . . ."

Brinton winced as he heard the rattle, then glared even harder before a sudden suspicion dawned in his eyes. "More burglaries," he breathed. "Don't tell me, Foxon—let me see the ghastly truth for myself. Not one word, laddie!"

He swung round in his chair to stare at the pin-dotted map behind him on the wall. He stared—sat upright—gave a snort, and swung round again to fix Foxon with the eyes of a man who has seen the scaffold being built, then learned at the last minute it is to be used by someone else.

"Foxon, I ought to demote you for this! What d'you mean by playing the giddy goat and letting me think there's been a burglary in . . . in . . . Foxon, I hate you!"

"In Plummergen?" supplied Foxon brightly. "But surely I didn't give you that impression, sir! I never meant to do anything of the sort, believe me—"

"I don't." Brinton's glare would have nailed his insubordinate subordinate to the wall, if that young man's eyes had met his own; but Foxon was staring thoughtfully at the map, allowing a slight frown to crease his brow.

"No burglaries in Plummergen last night, sir. Potter's report says everything's nice and peaceful—apart from a few complaints about the admiral's bees. Miss Nuttel wants to do him for daylight robbery, sir—says they fly into her garden and slurp the nectar out of her flowers, and she'll sue him unless he cuts her in on the deal. Sir."

Brinton looked at him. "I'll buy it, laddie—I won't know a moment's peace until I do. Tell me the rest, and let's get it over with. Then we can carry on with the real business of the day . . ."

"He's agreed to build another fence, sir. Bees only fly in straight lines—they'll go up and over something rather than round it, so Potter says the admiral's found out. He'll put a row of wattles on the Lilikot side of his hives, then the bees won't bother the Nuts any more because they'll be going somewhere else. Easy once you know the answer, isn't it, sir?"

There was an ominous silence, Brinton broke it at last. "And is that, Foxon, why you were so abominably cheerful as I arrived? Because nothing much is happening in . . . places where we'd rather it didn't? I suppose"—grudgingly—"there could be something in that point of view, but . . ."

"But that's not the reason, sir. Not really. Only, if you look at the map—the different colours of the pins—it does seem, sir, as if they're working to a pattern, aren't they?" All frivolity had vanished from Foxon's expression. "There's method in these burglaries, sir—last night's crop just bears out my theory—and I have to admit"—with a wry grin—"that I've a feeling it won't be long before they hit Plummergen, sir. There aren't too many places left they've not had a go at—places of the right sort, I mean. It's a well-organised operation; we've already seen that. And if—when—they turn up on Miss Seeton's home ground, with her back from Scotland and her batteries sort of recharged after her holiday—well, I reckon our chances of nobbling the lot are going up by leaps and bounds, sir. Don't you? It'll be just a matter of waiting for 'em, and then, well, pouncing, sir. Because the good old Battling Brolly—"

"Shuttup, Foxon!" Brinton turned to study the map with a jaundiced eye. He squinted at the coloured pins, making the distribution of burglaries blur and swim in out-of-focus sight—and was forced to admit that Foxon might just have a point. Whoever was behind this current outbreak of skilful crime—so skilful that frequently householders did not even suspect they'd been burgled until their neighbours mentioned it could be worth checking their belongings—was good at his job.

"There's a pattern there, all right," murmured Brinton. "Someone's gone to a lot of trouble to organise this little caper . . . but I wonder if it isn't just a bit too pat, now. To be able to predict the Plummergen connection so easily . . . could be they're trying to lull us, laddie. Making us think all we need to do is hang around eating fruitcake with Miss Seeton and the whole boiling lot of 'em will fall into our hands—while all the time they're getting up to their tricks somewhere else, and we're left with egg on our faces." Then he brightened. "Could be they've grown over-confident, of course. Careless. They know it's worked in the past, so they aren't so bothered about the future—and if that's the case, Foxon, we'll bag the blighters pdq. But if you don't stop smirking, laddie, I'll send you out into the danger zone, and pretty damn quickly, too. Being seconded to Wild Country with PC Potter should wipe that horrible grin from your face."

"A watching brief, you mean, sir?" Foxon frowned. Essentially a man of action, he didn't much enjoy sitting about doing nothing. On the other hand, he not only had a great deal of faith in Miss Seeton's abilities, he was also very fond of her. They had once, as she herself had cheerfully told a pair of startled newspaper reporters, spent the night together—in church, she'd added, on observing the reaction to this innocent remark. Which had made it seem rather peculiar, she'd enlarged. The reporters—Thrudd Banner, star of World Wide Press, and Amelita Forby of the *Daily Negative*—had evidently known MissEss of old, since neither, after the first few second's goggling, had turned a hair. Just as Miss Seeton herself had never turned a hair when, single-handed, she'd uncovered a phony religious sect and a gaggle of local witches . . .

Witches. Foxon frowned. He hadn't got round to telling Old Brimstone about that part of Potter's report just yet. Perhaps this wasn't the time—

"Stop scowling, Foxon—in fact, stop pulling horrible faces altogether, can't you?" Brinton didn't even bother to glare, this time. "What's wrong with you now?"

Foxon thought furiously. He coughed. "Well, sir, I was just wondering—if maybe they're not as bright as we're giving them credit for being. I mean, it might not be over confidence *or* double bluff that's made Plummergen look a likely bet for a future outbreak—maybe they're just, well, stupid, sir. With good basic organisation, but no real idea of how easy they're making it for us the longer they carry on working to the same plan. Sir."

Brinton grunted. "Could be, could be. I don't see why you needed to pull faces, though—and I'd rather not find out," he added hastily. "Something tells me I wouldn't like the answer if I asked the question, Foxon—and you know as well as I do what that something is. Or rather, that some*one*. Now we've brought her into all this, heaven alone can say where it'll end—and don't ask who I mean, laddie! You shouldn't have to be a detective to work it out . . ."

And Foxon nodded, his eyes on the pin-patterned map: the map with coloured points clustered about various villages and small towns, showing where the burglars had struck, and where it was probable they might strike next. At the current rate of progress, it wouldn't be long before they favoured Plummergen with their attentions: and everyone in the police force knew who lived in Plummergen.

"Miss Seeton, of course, sir," said Foxon, cheerfully twisting the knife in the wound.

And Brinton, cursing him, closed his eyes, and groaned.

# chapter
## ~13~

SUPERINTENDENT BRINTON'S GROANS would have been even
more heartfelt had he known that PC Potter's report was not
as thorough as in normal circumstances it would have been.
But these were not normal circumstances. The coming Saturday
would see the annual cricket match between Plummergen and
Murreystone; and Potter, a keen member of the home team, was
spending rather longer practising at the nets, and rather less time
policing the area, than would have met with Brinton's approval—
had he known.

But he did not know. What the eye didn't see, Potter's comfortable philosophy maintained, the blood pressure didn't rocket
over. He could, if asked, justify his apparent dereliction of duty
during the few days' run-up to the match by pointing out that
if he—not just a keen, but a key member of the team—played
badly, then Plummergen might lose; and, if they did, trouble
would undoubtedly ensue. Murreystone, victorious, would go on
the rampage: to which Plummergen was sure to take exception.
Potter could still recall the fight which had filled The Street when
the Ashford Choppers decided to liven the place up a little—
and the skirmish with the Murreystone saboteurs at the time of
the Best Kept Village Competition—but these incidents would
be mere horseplay when compared to the slaughter that must
follow a defeat for the larger of the rival communities in the
matter of the cricket cup. Potter had done his best to drum up
unofficial support—dropping hints to Bob Ranger, mentioning
his anxieties to Sir George Colveden, hinting in previous reports
to his Ashford superior that a spare man—Foxon, he knew, was a

good scrapper—might come in handy if the burglars struck closer
to home than they had until now—Foxon, after all, was CID,
whereas he was uniform branch . . .

So PC Potter felt a glow of virtue as he composed his latest
weekly report with due care and attention. It went without saying
that, had anything too untoward occurred, he would have obeyed
Brinton's standing orders and informed him at once: but he
hadn't, because it hadn't. Not really. You couldn't count the
rumours that were going round about Admiral Leighton, who
seemed a decent sort of bloke: half the village was naturally going
to suspect a newcomer—and especially if he wore a beard—of
being Up To Something. And of course they'd bring Miss Seeton
into it somehow, though anyone with any sense could tell she
was nothing to do with the man—why, she'd been in Scotland
when he moved into the old Dawkin place, for a start. As for
signalling to spies, or witches, or whatever—well, he'd had to
tip Sir George a warning wink that he'd better not try to drive
the station wagon, when he'd happened to pass the place as the
party was breaking up, and learned about the gin pennant, and
ended up offering Major Howett a lift back to the nursing home.
But it'd been, from what little he'd heard of its final stages, a
perfectly ordinary—if a bit tipsy—housewarming, and as far as
he, PC Potter, was concerned, Admiral Leighton was out of the
same mould as Sir George—and you couldn't say much better
than that about anyone.

The two former serving officers had indeed found themselves
to be kindred spirits. Their careers had run on similar lines,
given that one had been at sea, one on land; the paths of the
two had not directly crossed, but it turned out that they had
one or two acquaintances in common. The admiral's former
first lieutenant—from the days when the Buzzard had been an
up-and-coming captain—had skippered the troop ship which
carried Sir George and his battalion to Italy for the invasion—
a voyage about which the major-general preferred, even more
than thirty years later, not to reminisce unless so fortified with
alcohol that his descriptions of the wartime weather, and its effect
on his men, didn't make him feel as ill as everyone else had
felt in 1943. The admiral, a member of several London clubs—
including the In and Out (more formally the Naval and Military

Club) in Piccadilly—claimed to have met several of Sir George's fellow Welsh Guards officers in that popular establishment, and to have swapped stories with them on more than one occasion.

"Seems a decent sort, Leighton," said Sir George, as the breakfast *Times* was finally folded away. "Sound head on him—Naval training, of course. Good organisation. Those bees—got all the building work done before having 'em brought from his old home. Very sensible." He buttered toast and spooned jam. "Promised us a pot or two, once he's settled. Vibration," he added, before crunching.

"Yes, of course." Lady Colveden smiled as, without having been asked, she refilled Nigel's cup and motioned to him to pass his father's along for the same treatment. "Don't you remember Alicia Eykyn telling us about when they tried to keep bees, and Bill had just bought that new mower, and every time he wanted to use it they all came buzzing out and stung him? He was never sure whether it was the petrol they objected to, or the noise."

"Both, probably." Nigel returned his father's filled cup and appropriated the jam for his own use. "They moved the hives in the end, didn't they? Jolly sensible, if they wanted to stop Alicia being stung"—young Lady Eykyn had roused Nigel's Galahad instincts some years ago, and it was obvious to him that her husband the earl would take all possible precautions to protect her—"but I'm blowed if I'd be dictated to by a lot of insects, honey or no honey. Let the blessed things swarm off to somebody else's garden, that's my view—unless you're doing it commercially, of course." Absently, he buttered a second slice of toast before he'd finished the first. "If there's no money in it, though, it wouldn't be my choice for a hobby."

"Head screwed on the right way—I told you," Sir George reminded his son. "The Buzzard, I mean. Talked to friends, read all the books—been sharing one hive since the spring, he said. Sent 'em all off to the Yorkshire moors for the whole summer—heather honey, y'know." He cocked a thoughtful head in his wife's direction. "Man needs a hobby. Hens do well enough, but—"

"No, George." Meg Colveden, under whose care the Rytham Hall chickens pecked and squawked and laid their contented lives away, was firm. "Absolutely no bees. There's already more than enough for you to do on the farm with Nigel, and I know what would happen the first time things became hectic—you'd ask me to dress up in gumboots and with a motor veil over my best hat and go squirting smoke all over the place the way Bill Eykyn used to with poor Alicia. And she was so thankful when they swarmed off to somebody else's land, you have no idea. I'm sorry, I agree with Nigel—it's not as if we need the money."

Sir George, who would normally have snorted at so naive a remark, instead looked downcast. It was left to his son to say, in cheerful tones:

"Farmers always need money, Mother—why else do we work all the hours God gave? But even if a working man *does* need a hobby, you're right—I can't see Dad possibly having time to run beehives here. Mind you"—for he was fond of his father, and regretted the drooping, even for an instant, of that normally brisk moustache—"there's a good chance the admiral'd let you go shares, isn't there? If he's done it before." The baronet's eyes brightened. His son's gleamed. "And just think," he added, "of how it would shut the tabbies up if they knew the pair of you were partners in crime! Because nobody could ever dream of accusing you of being a . . . a burglary mastermind, could they?"

"Nobody with any sense," agreed his father, while his mother said quickly:

"But, George, that's what they're saying in the village. Not about you, but about the admiral, since they heard about the latest burglaries. They say it's getting closer, and it must be being organised by someone who knows what he's doing—and, well, you know what they're like," she concluded, a faint gleam in her own eye. "Seeing burglars under every bush, and that sort of thing. It seems to me it's a pity we ever gave up the idea of the Village Watch, because—"

"H'mm," said her husband. He frowned. Nigel said:

"Everyone thought things would quieten down now the Best Kept Village competition's finished, and I suppose they did, for a while. Especially"—a grin for his mother, a wink in his father's direction—"with Miss Seeton on holiday. But, now she's back—and with burglars popping in and out of houses all over Kent, so rumour has it . . ."

"H'mm," said Sir George again. His wife said:

"The Night Watch Men did a splendid job before, everyone says so—when all those things were being stolen from their gardens, and, well, everything else . . ."

"H'mm," said Sir George, for a third time. "Old Buzzard was asking me about the Watch, y'know. Now, if a chap like that thinks it's a good idea . . ." Nigel suddenly opened his mouth to speak, but his mother caught his eye, and he subsided. His father went on: "Think I might just have a word with Jessyp—ask his opinion." Martin Jessyp, Plummergen's head teacher, had been Sir George's second-in-command on the last occasion the Village Watch had patrolled the Plummergen streets. "Catch him now, before he buries himself in those timetables again . . ."

Sir George rose from the table, heading out to the telephone in the hall, and closed the door behind him.

"H'mm," said Nigel, as his mother smiled fondly in the direction of her disappearing spouse. "I suppose it was as well I didn't say anything while Dad was around, but has it occurred to you that the tabbies might be right, for once? About the admiral, I mean. It didn't hit me until just now, but if he was really pumping Dad about the Night Watch Men—good heavens, there must be heaps more interesting things to talk about at a party! So it could just be he was trying to find out whether anything was being planned that might put a spoke in his, er, burglarious wheel."

"What a horrid imagination you have." Lady Colveden shook her head sternly at her son. "I'm sure you're wrong about the admiral, and so is everyone else. I expect he was just interested—you know, as one staff officer to another. Comparing notes. Different techniques, that sort of thing. He's bound to have heard people talking about it all in the shop, and been, well, interested when he found out that one of his guests was the person who arranged everything. Organisation skills, isn't that what they need in the forces? And they do so like to stick together—it always surprises me your father doesn't belong to more clubs, except that he hates going up to Town more often than he has to . . ."

"I can't say I'm too keen on London myself. We farmers like fresh air, and there's not much of that in a city—but you're trying to change the subject, Mother darling. Don't finagle—it doesn't suit you. I know officers are supposed to be good judges of character, because that's how they get to be officers, but once in a while they must make a mistake—sheer law of averages. Which reminds me," Nigel said, as the door opened to admit a beaming Sir George, "net practice this evening—Dan Eggleden's going to bowl lots of bouncers for me to get my eye in. My batting average last season was twenty-eight, remember, and I'm trying for thirty this time. And if Murreystone turn up on Saturday with that demon bowler they fielded last year . . . That chap bowled bouncers, and I do mean bounce. Someone ought to invent a crash helmet for batsmen, with people like him around—but I did, if you recall, take fifteen off him before Potter walloped one right back at him, and knocked him out."

Sir George snorted, and cleared his throat. Lady Colveden tried hard to look disapproving, but failed dismally.

Nigel chuckled. "Yes, well, one 'accident' like that is more than enough, if you ask me. Still, if I don't get off to work now, I can hardly justify spending tonight at the nets, can I? Demon bowler or not, there's no peace for the wicked. Coming, Dad?"

Following the exit of her husband and son to their cherished fields, Lady Colveden's smile faded. She couldn't help wondering whether Nigel had been right about the admiral, after all. Perhaps the Buzzard had managed to pull the wool well and truly over everyone's eyes . . .

She made herself another cup of coffee and sat brooding as she drank it. Normally, she would trust George's judgement every time—but these were hardly normal times. A clever crook would naturally have a good cover story . . .

Then her smile reappeared, and she sighed with relief. There was one person, she'd remembered, whose judgement was never at fault, whose instincts always told her the truth about people, though she seldom seemed to know how, or why, they did—but they did, which was all that mattered.

"I think," announced Lady Colveden to the bottom of her coffee cup, "I'll just slip down to Sweetbriars and have a word with Miss Seeton . . ."

# chapter
## ~14~

MISS SEETON HAD been unusually quiet these last few days.
Martha Bloomer had noticed this, and been concerned, though
she'd been able to rationalise the quietness—to some extent—
when discussing their employer with her husband Stan, who
had noticed the same phenomenon when tending Miss Seeton's
garden, volunteering the occasional remark as they encountered
each other about the flower beds and shrubbery. Overtired after
her holiday, poor little soul, said Martha; only too glad of the
chance to rest at home without Things Happening, she must be—
which there was no denying they did, where Miss Emily was
concerned. True, she'd been tired at first—said Stan—but then
she hadn't really perked up, not even after tea with the Colvedens,
and her so fond of them—seemed worse, if anything. To which
Martha had sighed her reluctant agreement. You could almost say
poor Miss Emily was brooding—though about what Martha had
no idea, and not being one to pry, saw no way of finding out.
Anyone would think, if they didn't know Lady Colveden better,
there must have been something said or done at tea that Miss
Emily had been upset by, and she such a happy little soul, most
times. Course, the weather was hot, and with having spent two
weeks in Scotland where—so Martha firmly believed—it rained
every day, poor Miss Emily probably felt uncomfortable with the
contrast, so to speak . . .

When Miss Seeton announced to Martha that she was going
up to London for the day, the first instinct of Mrs. Bloomer was
to advise against it: August in Town was hardly the best idea

for anyone feeling under the weather. Martha held her tongue, however, and was glad she'd done so when she saw how Miss Emily's mood lightened, how her eyes brightened at the thought of going up to visit one or two art galleries—and perhaps, she added, take a look at the proposed site for the new Gallery of Chinese Art about which she'd read in dear Jack Crabbe's crossword magazine.

"Went off an hour or so ago, happy as Larry," Martha told Lady Colveden after opening the front door of Sweetbriars to the latter's knock. "Almost her old self again, so she was. Going round looking at pictures, bless her, and a little shopping too, she said, if she had time . . ."

Martha Bloomer had worked at Rytham Hall for almost as long as she'd worked at Sweetbriars, and her employers could recognise one of her Moods every bit as quickly as Stan, if not more so. Lady Colveden saw that somehow Martha held her to blame for Miss Seeton's *not* having been "her old self" until that morning; she ventured to ask, in the discreetest possible way, what the trouble might be—but was answered with an old-fashioned look, and a pointed change of subject. Her ladyship still expected Martha at the Hall two days from now, didn't she? Oh, no reason—just checking. Which warned Lady Colveden that, unless she behaved herself, one of Mrs. Bloomer's famous Grand Slams could erupt in her kitchen, when cupboard doors were banged, heavy pots and pans clattered, brushes dropped, drawers rattled in their tracks.

Lady Colveden made her excuses, smiled, and left, trusting that things would have calmed down in two days' time. Martha was the most loyal of employees, she knew well, and was far more solicitous of Miss Seeton's welfare than ever Miss Seeton herself thought it necessary to be. Better, in the circumstances, that the little spinster should not be asked—no matter how indirectly—her opinion of the admiral, thereby—possibly—being given further cause to worry: if today's trip to Town worked as well as Martha seemed to think it should, then Lady Colveden would not be the one to upset Miss Seeton a second time, when she hadn't meant to upset her the first . . .

And it was with a guilty conscience that Lady Colveden went home again, hoping that Miss Seeton's self-prescribed solution was working as well as it ought.

• • •

Miss Seeton had begun her day's excursion with a visit to that part of the British Museum where Chinese pottery, porcelain, and paintings might be seen. She had marvelled at the delicate green glazes of the Han Dynasty, the exquisite underglazed decorations of the Tang, the jade-like effects achieved with celadon in the Song. She contemplated the remarkable perspectives of landscape, the superimposed planes and varying viewpoints, the balance of mountains with water, animals with trees; she admired the monochrome handscrolls with their hundred dragons in flight, their hundred birds; she frowned as she tried to grasp the concept of the "three perfections" of poetry, painting, and calligraphy, tried to comprehend this artistic form and rhythm quite outside her normal experience.

She had to concentrate hard, which pleased her greatly. In concentrating, she had managed to forget, or at least to diminish, those anxieties about her own humble artistic efforts which had troubled her for the past few days. One had not, of course, allowed oneself to *dwell* on that unpleasant little sketch of Annabelle Leigh, but one had to admit that it had been harder to dismiss it from one's thoughts than one would have wished. Last night's sudden inspiration that a day in London would help to clear one's mind had been a happy one. Just as oriental landscapes had a perspective very different from the western, so now had Miss Seeton a very different perspective on her own work.

One had obviously been still tired from the journey—a little too . . . scratchy to be as comfortable in oneself as one would have wished; perhaps one should have stayed away from company until one was not. Scratchy, that was to say. Miss Leigh's great talent, her fresh and blooming good looks—as well as dear Nigel's obvious interest in her—had made one conscious of one's passing years and mediocre gifts, in a way which, in normal circumstances, wouldn't have troubled one at all, because one hoped one was honest enough to admit that they were. Passing, that was to say. And mediocre. Both of which, being true, one had surely always seen quite clearly—an artist, however mediocre, must learn to *see* before anything else—and neither of which—one having not only seen, but, being realistic, acknowledged to oneself—had ever previously caused one any concern—although perhaps one had not often before been quite so tired . . .

Miss Seeton, wondering at just how tired she must have been to have responded in such a puzzling way, felt an unexpected yawn coming on, and put up a hasty hand to stifle it. With a clatter, her umbrella slipped from her grasp, landing on the glass of the display case over which she had been poring. Miss Seeton blushed.

The uniformed attendant in the corner cried, "Oy! Watch it, ducks!"

And Miss Seeton, apologising profusely, picked up her brolly and hurried, still blushing, away.

She felt so hot and bothered by this little mishap that her thoughts automatically turned to the sovereign remedy for all English ills, a cup of tea. And, as her still-warm cheeks would cool down so much more quickly after a walk in the fresh air, she decided to go in search of some suitable café, where there would be no glass cases to risk cracking by accident, where she could have a nice sit-down and perhaps a pastry or two before deciding where to go next.

Still musing on the examples of oriental art and crafts which she had seen, Miss Seeton found her feet taking her in a direction she did not at once recognise. London, as one knew, was not so much a city as an amalgamation of villages and towns: Hampstead, of course, one knew well, from one's teaching time at Mrs. Benn's school—and the museums and galleries—and certain of the shopping streets. But there were so many byways and shortcuts—all, naturally, of great interest to one who had not walked them before. Miss Seeton gazed about her at unfamiliar shops housed in buildings of various styles, old and new, medieval and modern, side by side: Georgian and Victorian, plate-glass and Tudor brick, concrete and stucco. Perhaps rather too much plate-glass and concrete for one's own taste, but then— she sighed—it had been the war which robbed London of so many fine old buildings, and the pressure to rebuild in times of peace had been great. No doubt the architects of the mid–twentieth century believed their efforts to be every bit as attractive as those of previous generations . . .

Miss Seeton turned a corner, and stopped in her tracks, narrowly missing a collision with the nimble-footed man who was hurrying a few steps behind. "Oh, I do beg your—"

But he was gone, leaving her to stare at the huge white hoarding, lettered in boldest black and red, which confronted her as she stood stock-still, startled to find that her feet had brought her to the very place about which she had been reading only three days ago.

*Dosset: Superior Builders,* proclaimed the hoarding's top line, with a telephone number underneath, both in black. At the bottom of the hoarding, in smaller letters—also black—was the legend *Architects: P.B. Bossiney, Ltd.,* with not only the firm's telephone number, but also the address. It must be supposed that P.B. Bossiney the architect was as yet less well known than Superior Dosset the builder, and had chosen this method of advertisement to redress, in part, the balance. Miss Seeton nodded. Balance, indeed, was the correct term in this particular case: the black letters at top and bottom neatly sandwiched—if *that* was the correct term—the far larger letters in red, which told of the site's proposed dedication to the world of oriental art, in the form of the new museum. Someone with a good eye and a sense of proportion had designed this hoarding, Miss Seeton decided with approval. A scarlet-and-black sandwich . . .

Which reminded her that her original plan, on leaving the British Museum, had been to find herself a cup of tea and a snack. She really must try to—oh. Oh, how very fortunate. Miss Seeton smiled. Almost exactly opposite the building site she could see, now that she looked, a small café with—she hurried along the pavement to peep in at the glass-fronted door—one or two empty tables, though it was nearly time for lunch. The café, for all it was so close to the dust and commotion and, yes, the noise of the building site, seemed both popular and clean. She made up her mind. Fascinating though it might be to stand watching that huge crane manoeuvre steel girders and blocks of concrete delicately between those two tall buildings either side of the bomb site— rather dilapidated buildings, Miss Seeton observed, her quick eye noting brown stains on the stucco suggestive of blocked gutters or leaky pipes—she would, if she could obtain a table near the window, be able to continue watching from the comfort of the café's interior, while at the same time quenching her thirst. She was, she now realised, very thirsty. Builders' dust was dancing in little puffs and eddies about the base of the enormous crane, swirling wherever anything was disturbed, drifting into the street.

Miss Seeton coughed, then blinked, as a piece of grit blew into her eye. She blinked again to bring tears to wash the grit away, and remembered *Brief Encounter* as she fished in her handbag for her pocket handkerchief, smiling as she did so. Perhaps, instead of visiting another museum after lunch, she might go instead to the cinema.

Restored to her normal bright-eyed self, Miss Seeton trotted into the café, ordered a pot of china tea and an egg—poached—on toast, took her seat at a newly vacated table by the window, and continued to watch what was happening opposite. One did so enjoy seeing an expert at work, and the driver of the crane—so very large—handled it with remarkable skill, in so narrow a street, lifting such awkward weights and shapes. Miss Seeton shuddered as she imagined what might happen if the mighty jaws of the crane slipped open, releasing their load to the ground . . .

"Don't fancy your egg after all, love?" The waitress, unnoticed, had brought Miss Seeton's lunch and set the plate in front of her. "Rather have something else?" And a weary sigh escaped her as she pulled out her notepad and pencil.

"What? I mean—oh, dear, I do beg your pardon. I was so busy, you see, wondering—worrying, I suppose one might say—and quite unnecessarily, I feel sure. Because one can hardly imagine he would be allowed to drive it, if that is the word I want, if he was not an expert, can one?"

The waitress followed her gaze, and replied after only a few seconds' thought. "Albert, you mean? You've no need to worry about him. One of the best, is Albert—or says he is, when he comes in for his elevenses." She looked pointedly at Miss Seeton's plate. "Usually has a poached egg on toast, same as you—if that's what you're having . . ."

Whereupon Miss Seeton, blushing, applied herself to her meal without another word, resolving to leave a sensible tip for the poor girl, who was obviously so busy and found customers who couldn't make up their minds so troublesome.

"And no wonder," murmured Miss Seeton, sprinkling a few grains of pepper over her meal, and slicing a neat triangle of toast on which to balance a portion of egg. After a sip or two of tea, she was beginning to feel hungry. She glanced across the road to the building site and wondered whether Albert the crane driver enjoyed his mid-morning snack as much as she was enjoying hers . . .

From thoughts of the unknown Albert, Miss Seeton turned to musing on the new museum of oriental art, and on the exhibits she had seen earlier in the British Museum. She recalled a still life she had once encouraged her class to draw, and how they had mischievously eaten the fruit, though afterwards some had produced good likenesses of the Chinese vase, and—

But Miss Seeton's happy reverie was rudely interrupted by an outburst of sudden, piercing screams all around the little café.

# chapter

# ~15~

MISS SEETON, ASTONISHED, set down her knife and fork neatly on her plate and surveyed the room with a startled pucker between her brows. Memories of school were all very well, but even in their wildest moments during end-of-term dinner her pupils had never . . . Why was everyone making such a loud and—or so it seemed—unnecessary noise? Above the sound of the building work outside, it was impossible to hear oneself think. Though one could not, of course, be prevented from noticing. And wondering, for instance, why so many of the ladies present were jumping up and down, clutching at their skirts—and why (Miss Seeton's eyebrows arched high in disapproval) so many were climbing on their chairs—some even on the tables—with their skirts wrapped tight about their knees.

Miss Seeton shook her head. One did not expect such behaviour from grown women when one would certainly not tolerate it in younger ones, for whom one always tried to set an example of quiet and ladylike deportment. Which one could hardly claim was being shown now by—

"Good gracious." This really was not good enough: even the waitress—so unhygienic—was clambering up on a nearby table, shrieking with the rest. Miss Seeton gazed about her for the cause of all this hysteria.

She saw it. Them. Scuttling about the floor, too many to count, grey and brown and with long tails trailing, black eyes gleaming, whiskers twitching. Miss Seeton, shaking her head again, stood up, seized her umbrella, and thwacked it on the table, twice. Her egg wobbled off its toast, her knife clattered to the floor, her tea-pot lid danced a tarantella inaudible above the continuing squeals and cries. She thwacked the table again, then tried to add her own voice—the voice, one trusted, of moderation—to the rest.

"Ladies—ladies! These are nothing more than mice . . ."

As reassurance, this information achieved poor results. Although those nearest Miss Seeton had been so surprised by her actions that they had fallen briefly silent, and had thus been able to hear what she said, her calm confirmation of what they had feared served only to make matters worse. And as their outcry redoubled in pitch and volume, so, by some strange alchemy, did that of the others.

Miss Seeton was about to employ her brolly for a third time when she saw something which made her stay her hand. Through the door of the café came a man—young, grinning, a shoe box under his arm—who darted to the nearest table on which a ter-rified woman had taken refuge, and snatched her handbag from beside her plate. Slipping it over his arm, he ran to another table, and seized another bag—to another, and seized two—ran again, and again, until he must, Miss Seeton guessed, have had a doz-en handbags—stolen handbags—in his possession. Then, as those who had been robbed in such a . . . mischievous way were coming to their senses, he threw down the shoe box—the lid fell off—and a further scrabbling, scurrying, bewhiskered overflow of mice poured out all over the floor.

Which made remonstrating with the young man, Miss Seeton realised, even more difficult than it had been before. She would not from choice have stood so idly by as he robbed her fellow din-ers, but her progress towards him in order to . . . to do *something*, she knew not what, to prevent this robbery had been hindered by her wish not to tread on any of the mice as they scampered to and fro in panic—panic, one could not help but feel, every bit as great as that of the women whose shrill cries must hurt their ears, whose great leaps would crush horribly if they landed upon the poor crea-tures.

One could not, however, allow that impudent young man to escape the consequences of such wrongdoing. Miss Seeton, the point of her umbrella sweeping to and fro before her to clear a pathway through the rampaging rodents on the floor, reached the café door perhaps eight seconds after her quarry, who had run out less swiftly than he had run in. Twelve handbags will hamper anyone, no matter how long his arms may be, how tight his grip.

It was not, however, the hampering handbags which had so slowed the young man's escape that Miss Seeton now stood a fair chance of catching up with him as she emerged from the café, fully expecting him to have vanished with his booty in some waiting car. She had hoped to hail a passing taxi, or to encounter a policeman on his beat who would radio full details of the criminal to . . . to whoever needed to know them. Miss Seeton's grasp of constabulary procedure, for all her long acquaintance with Scotland Yard and other forces, was vague; but she knew that a policeman was the right person to approach, and had been prepared to do so.

What she had not been prepared for was to find the young man still within sight, dancing frantically back and forth as he sought a passage around the swinging rear end of an enormous skip now being unloaded from a delivery truck which had just driven down the street, unnoticed by those in the café—understandably unnoticed, as they had all had more pressing matters on their minds. Especially the young man, who was now looking in fury at the skip and the truck—the truck which, as the winch slowly cranked its load towards the ground, almost entirely blocked the road, and completely blocked the pavement on one side of it. And the other pavement was blocked by a crowd of interested spectators . . . For it was, as Miss Seeton had earlier established, the hour for lunch. Office workers were shopping; shoppers, thinking of food, were heading for various cafés and snack bars. The street was a local thoroughfare, popular and busy at certain times—of which the midday break was one.

Which fact seemed to have slipped the mind of the young man when he first released those myriad mice on the café floor. Miss Seeton, forging her slow passage through the throng, found herself, for one wild moment, even admiring his original scheme—one's respect for an expert at work—and feeling some fleeting regret that careless planning had caused it to misfire. The skilful playing on so many foolish women's fear of the harmless mouse—the cool judgement he had shown in waiting for the café to be sufficiently full of customers to make it worth his while . . . and then, his bad luck in not knowing the skip would arrive at the exact instant he planned to escape, coupled with his original failure to time that escape before the surrounding offices emptied of their workers . . . the fatal error which, as one had read somewhere—or had it been mentioned by dear Mr. Delphick, or by Mr. Brinton (such a sense of humour) or dear Bob—that Fatal Error which every criminal always made.

Miss Seeton, breathlessly buffeted by the crowd, which surged backwards from the skip as the chains by which it was being lowered screamed a last metallic warning, gave herself a sharp mental shake, and, having restored her normal common sense, nodded approvingly. For, if they never did, it would perhaps not be so easy for them to catch them.

"Make such errors," announced Miss Seeton in firm tones, reinforcing her return to normality after that inexplicable lapse into sympathy with a wrongdoer. "Criminals—and, of course, the police . . ."

The winch had stopped turning; the chains had stopped screaming. The skip, with a final, resounding clang, had safely reached the ground—and Miss Seeton's words, clearly audible, fell into the sudden silence.

"Who wants the police?" demanded an overweight man with a gold chain stretched across his waistcoat. "Is something wrong, madam?"

Others nearby had caught, if not Miss Seeton's original words, then those of the overweight man. "What's wrong?" "There's something wrong!" "There's been an accident!"

The comments, increasing in wildness, rose all around, and Miss Seeton, still wedged in too-close proximity to that plump waistcoat, found herself in danger of being trampled in the crush as the crowd surged even farther back from the skip. Albert the crane driver, caring little for anything but the job in hand, had cranked the mighty jaws downwards to pick up his first load of rubble and swing it round to feed it into that yawning metal mouth. There was a general feeling that something was about to go wrong . . .

Londoners are connoisseurs of construction. They view with expert eyes the gyrations of bulldozers, diggers, and demolition balls as they transform the face of the city; and they are always

curious to know what will happen next. Like Jerome K. Jerome,
work fascinates them; they can sit—or, as it usually goes on in
the street, stand—looking at it for hours, whether behind wooden
hoardings or not. Memories of wartime queues mean that, where
one or two Londoners are gathered together, several more will join
them, as curious as they. Raise the cry of accident or some other
emergency, and they swing together into action.

"Get a doctor!" "No, she said the police!" "Somebody dial nine-
nine-nine!"

There was too much noise now for Miss Seeton to make her
breathless pipe heard above the clamour of the crane, the cries of
the crowd. Too much noise, from too many people—people who
were pushing and shoving, all trying to see what the fuss was
about, blocking her path to that young man who, burdened with
so many handbags, was trying to look as if he carried business
samples. And he really—Miss Seeton found herself thinking—
ought to have emptied them and then thrown them away when he
had the chance—except, of course, that he'd never had it, because
the street was already too busy when he ran out into it from the
café. As she herself had run out—oh. Her heart missed a beat.

"Oh, dear—my poached egg!" She had run out without paying
for it. Was this, she wondered, theft? Would it be sufficient excuse
that she had only left the café in such a precipitate fashion in order
to pursue—

"I'm a doctor!" came a voice in the near distance. "Is somebody ill?"

"No, no, there's been a mistake!" cried the fat man with the
waistcoat, who had moved, far more quickly than from his bulk
would have seemed possible, as far from Miss Seeton as he could.
"This poor lady seems to be a . . . a little unwell, but . . ."

Indeed, Miss Seeton, still struggling to make herself understood, anxious about her act of unwitting larceny, did look far
more red in the face and flustered than anyone fully *compos
mentis* would be: but it was unfair of the fat man to suppose
she had been thinking of herself as a poached egg, whether
or not such supposition is said to be the sure sign of a
deranged intellect. And his sideways whisper that anyone
who had a straitjacket ought to bring it quickly was decidedly
uncalled for.

"That young man!" Miss Seeton had wriggled free of the press about her and was pointing with her umbrella over the heads of the crowd towards the handbag thief. "Stop him!"

The young man, who had been trying to look as nonchalant as anyone with a dozen handbags under one arm can be, turned his head quickly in the direction of that accusing voice—shrugged—turned away, and made one last effort to thrust through the hordes of shoppers, lunchers, and sightseers who had been trapped by the delivery of the metal rubbish skip. But the truck which had delivered the skip was revving its engine, prior to driving off: he could see a suitable gap—rather too near the café for comfort, but a gap nonetheless—into which, if his luck held, he might dodge . . .

"Stop that young man!" came the frantic pipe once more, and Miss Seeton, gesticulating wildly with her umbrella, was able to clear a space around her as those who had overheard the fat man's muttered explanation to the doctor of an escaped lunatic moved hurriedly out of ferrule range. "He must be stopped! Those handbags are stolen!" Miss Seeton informed the crowd; and the crowd, encircling her at a safe distance, cast nervous glances in every direction in case her keeper should come panting up in search of her. And the young man, observing the crowd's attention focussed elsewhere, prepared to melt, together with his handbags, hastily away.

Everything had happened so quickly up until now that there had been no time to think about what was happening in the café. The screams had started to die down as the mice, finding the door open as Miss Seeton had left it in her hurry, began to run through it to the more peaceful atmosphere outside. The gradual departure of the mice helped to calm the table-bound screamers, the boldest of whom clambered down and darted out into the street in search of their stolen property. They had little hope of finding it, though they intended to give the young crook, if they spotted him, a run for his money; and they were annoyed to find their way blocked by a large and slow-moving builder's lorry which was hooting at some vehicle or other trying to come in the opposite direction, and by an excited crowd evidently watching a street magician with an umbrella instead of a magic wand . . .

"Hey! She was in the café!" Miss Seeton was recognised—a general cry went up—and the young man, who had almost made his way round the edge of the crowd to freedom, hesitated as he saw his intended path blocked by the lorry—which was trying to avoid not only the overspill of the crowd on the road, but also an impatient car coming the other way—and—which made him stop dead in his tracks—by a furious group of his former victims. He knew them—he heard their outcry, or at least their final words— and, knowing he had been spotted, he panicked.

Any passing pigeon, sparrow, or other avian overseer must have dined out for the rest of its life on its bird's-eye view of what happened next. Everything was so confused, to those on the ground caught up in it all—who included in the first rank Miss Seeton, the crowd surrounding her, the angry group of women from the café, the young man with the handbags, Albert the crane driver, the man in the lorry, and the driver of the car he hit—not to mention (in the second rank) the unfortunate beat bobby who struggled to make some sense of what everyone was saying at the same time as he tried to clear the traffic jam, plus his colleagues from the ambulance and fire services called to deal with all those in the building when it collapsed . . . everything was so confused that nobody ever really knew the whole story.

Not even Inspector Borden.

# chapter

## -16-

INSPECTOR BORDEN OF the Fraud Squad sat in his office at New Scotland Yard, drinking his umpteenth cup of strong, sweet tea. This had been prescribed for him by his sergeant, a former Marine who had seen service in the Second World War and knew all about battle fatigue. If Borden had been a reformed smoker, the sergeant would have urged him to give up giving up—but he wasn't, so the restorative powers of nicotine were denied him. He would have to win through this crisis on his own, with the help of a sympathetic listener.

The sympathetic listener was present, though it was not Borden's sergeant, who cowered now in another office working off some of his own stress by typing a preliminary report. The rattle of the keys sounded rather like machine-gun fire, and the sergeant kept telling himself things could really be a great deal worse. He wasn't sure he believed it.

"Even now, I'm not sure I believe it." Borden gulped a frenzied mouthful of tea and reached for a fourth sugar lump. His companion did not prevent him. "I mean—we've had a few hairy cases in the past, Oracle. The depths to which human nature can sink when it's after something for nothing might surprise your average member of the public, but not yours truly—and I'd rather prided myself on being, well, immune. Hardened to it, if you like. Cope with anything—anyone. You name 'em, we've seen 'em, in Fraud—gangsters, protection rackets, swindlers in all shapes and sizes—and we've put a fair number of 'em away. Tidily," he added, a fifth lump of sugar going the same way as the fourth, "and without too much mess. But this . . ." He gesticulated helplessly towards the litter of photographs, newspapers, and handwritten statements spread across his desk. "All this—it's . . ."

"It's not exactly Miss Seeton's fault," Delphick said, trying to sound as if he really thought so. "She has a very tidy mind. She certainly didn't mean anything like this to happen—"

"She never does! And that's the trouble—it's the . . . the horrible contrast between what any normal person might expect and what she actually delivers that makes life so damned difficult for your average humble copper. I read the papers, Oracle"—Borden thumped the scattering of evidence on his desk with an anguished fist—"and I hear the rumours—*and* I'm not going to forget what happened on that nightclub case a few years back, when the racecourse gang had that punch-up in the car park, and my man Haley was knifed, and there was that so-called bomb in the dress shop, and a real bomb in her cottage—for which"—and he glared accusingly at Delphick, who made haste to change a chuckle into a cough—"I can't say, right this minute, I'd blame anyone for attempting, for the sake of the resultant peace and quiet . . . Well, okay, I'm being unfair," as Delphick looked shocked. "Unfair, and ungrateful—we've been after the blighters for weeks, so I suppose you might say MissEss deserves a medal for handing 'em to us the way she did, even if she"—he gulped—"*didn't mean to . . .*"

"At least," Delphick soothed him, "nobody's badly hurt, which has to be almost a miracle." Several bystanders were in a state of shock, and Albert the crane driver was in hospital wondering whether or not to have a nervous breakdown; but, because the arm of his crane and its counterweight had fallen at such a remarkable angle from their height of one hundred feet, they'd caused far less damage than might have been feared, whether to the building on which they'd fallen, or to the people in and around it. Delphick hadn't visited the scene of the crime—or crimes—in person—he'd been too busy responding to frantic requests for assistance in dealing with Miss Seeton and in understanding enough of what she said to be able to extract her statement—but he'd heard several highly coloured descriptions of the aftermath of his friend's activities, as well as being shown—by yet more anguished police officers, most notably from Traffic Division—not only the official photographs, but also those on the front pages of every evening newspaper in London.

Brooding on the disruption to city streets for a considerable distance around the incident—the falling crane had gouged out a large slice of the road surface, thus severing the electric cable which fed several vital sets of traffic lights (*gridlock* was being used as an expletive by the most mild-mannered men)—Delphick helped himself to another cup from the outsize teapot he had instructed the canteen to provide, full to the brim with a double-strength brew. He refrained from adding sugar: it wasn't, he reflected in wry amusement, really his case. Extreme reactions such as those of poor Borden would be no more than self-indulgence on his part—but he certainly couldn't blame the inspector. Despite his proud boast, the man obviously wasn't as hardened to his work as he'd liked to think he was . . .

"And all because of Miss Seeton," the Oracle murmured, stirring his tea with a thoughtful spoon, sugar or no sugar. He felt it might help his concentration. "The handbag thief was captured by the crowd—"

"With concussion," interposed Borden grimly; then a grin appeared on his face. "Serve him right, too—he deserved all he got, working a smart-alec trick like that. And he'll have had a few nasty moments before that brick brained him, realising he'd been sent right into the thick of a Women's Institute on the warpath—enough to freeze anyone's blood. And if you're daft enough to freeze right in the firing line of a crane with an overloaded grapple—"

"A metallurgist would no doubt be able to explain why it buckled in quite so spectacular a fashion," said Delphick, fishing out from the pile a photograph showing miscellaneous steel writhing amid brick and concrete wreckage. "One may suppose, of course, that the driver was so intrigued by what was happening below him that he picked up too much at once, or too quickly, or something of the sort."

"And what was happening was Miss Seeton brandishing that damned brolly of hers and having 'em all think she'd just hopped over the wall from Colney Hatch. Poached eggs," said Borden, a quiver in his voice. "Why that woman *doesn't* end up in the loony bin, I'll never know . . ."

"But if she hadn't been brandishing it, remember, the crowd wouldn't have been concentrated near her—they'd have been all over the place along the road, and when the crane fell some of them could have been seriously hurt. Top marks to MissEss for foresight, I think." Delphick fixed Borden with so stern a gaze that the inspector failed to notice the logical flaw in this chain of reasoning, and nodded meekly. Delphick hid a smile. "And bonus points, of course, for her having uncovered the coiners' den for you . . ."

"And none of *them* was badly hurt, either." Borden shook a marvelling head. "*Miracle* is about the size of it, Oracle—which I reckon's about par for the course, where MissEss is concerned. Rabbits out of hats every blessed time—it's just a pity she leaves everybody's nerves in shreds afterwards—"

"Miss Seeton," Delphick reminded him sharply, "has suffered as much as anyone in all this, remember. That falling crane missed *her* as narrowly as it missed the other people in the road, and brick dust is no respecter of persons. Her hat and coat, she informed me, will never be the same again. I have told her," he added hastily, before Borden could make the obvious retort, "to indent for any cleaning costs and repairs as necessary, and that Fraud will be only too happy to pay. She must, I'm sure you will agree, be considered as having been on duty at the time of the, er, occurrence—albeit unofficially." Borden, once more transfixed by the Oracle's menacing eye, nodded again. "Though I believe," said Delphick, in an attempt to lighten the mood, "she would prefer payment to be by cheque rather than in coin of the realm—just in case."

Borden managed another grin. "There won't be any more snide from that particular source, true—and I'll admit we have Miss Seeton to thank for it—but there's still what's already gone into circulation to worry about, though now the whole boiling lot's ready to sing like canaries—and I love the way they're all blaming one another for bumping off that poor devil who made the dies—it shouldn't be long before we know their distribution route. And once we know it, we can block it." He balanced another lump of sugar on the end of his spoon, dipping it into his by now cooling tea, watching it change from crystalline white to mushy brown. The sight soothed him. He looked at Delphick, and grinned.

"Did I say a medal? If the Black Museum boys collar the coiner equipment after the trial, I'll have 'em run off a Seeton Star, with a gold-plated citation for having unearthed a gang so incompetent, apart from coining, they never had the sense to lose the murder weapon after wasting that die-caster chummie. For services rendered, with grateful thanks—and one for yourself as well, for having coped with her when I couldn't." Borden regarded his colleague with an odd expression. "I'd hate to worry you, Oracle, but it's just struck me. If MissEss is as off-beam as everyone knows she is—which she is—then anyone who's even slightly on the same wavelength as her's got to be off-beam as well, haven't they? And as you and Bob Ranger are the only ones—"

He broke off, and blinked. "Yes—Ranger. Where's your gigantic sidekick this evening, Oracle? In hiding?"

"In Plummergen." Delphick smiled at the dawning look of horror on the inspector's face. "No, he's not psychic, he's on holiday. A long weekend with his in-laws, starting last night—he and Anne drove down after work. Fortunately, I was able to get hold of him at the nursing home and explain what had happened—some of it, anyway." He smiled again. "I'd be surprised if any one individual will ever make sense of everything that went on today but Bob understood enough to know he'd better meet MissEss from the train and escort her home via the Knights' so the doctor could take a look at her, just in case. Anne's father, you may recall, was one of London's leading neurologists before retiring through ill health. Miss Seeton, remember, did have rather a nasty shock this afternoon, and I'd value Dr. Knight's opinion of her mental and emotional state more highly than any of the Casualty doctors in Town—not that they aren't a fine body of medicos (if that isn't"—and Delphick smirked—"too grim a collective term for doctors), but they don't know our MissEss of old, and Dr. Knight does. He'll check that everything's as it should be . . ."

Delphick drifted into a brooding silence, watched by a bright-eyed Borden who said, after a pause: "But everything *isn't* as it should be, is it? What've you heard that's got you hot and bothered, Oracle?"

"It may be nothing. I hope it is."

"I bet it's not, if Miss Seeton's anything to do with it—and you said *Plummergen*, so she must be." The inspector chuckled. "Fair exchange, Oracle—I've been bending your ear for the last I-don't-know-how-many hours, and you've put up with it like a regular Trojan. Fancy a swap?"

Delphick emitted a faint sigh. "I think not, thanks—there's such a thing as tempting Fate. Which is probably why Bob mentioned it in the first place, of course," he added, half to himself. "As an insurance policy—making sure it doesn't happen after all"—he frowned—"whatever *it* might be—though, goodness knows, I don't see how she can get up to anything too outrageous at a cricket match, even if the team's star bowler *has* been . . ." A thoughtful pause; then a smile suddenly brightened his face. "However, *nil desperandum*, Borden—things may not be as bad as at first they appear. Bob suggests I should pop down to Plummergen for the weekend to watch, and I believe I shall. If Miss Seeton's on top form, I would really hate to miss all the excitement . . ."

Superintendent Brinton barged in through the double swing doors of Ashford police station and nodded a greeting to the officer on the desk. He was about to continue his breezy way down the corridor to his office when something made him halt in his tracks and stare hard at Sergeant Mutford. What was different about the man, for heaven's sake?

"Mutford, you're smiling!"

"Am I, sir? Sorry."

Brinton's eyes narrowed. "Mutford, you're not. Neither sorry, nor—on reflection—smiling. *Smirking* would be a better word for it, Mutford—and I don't like it. It makes me nervous to have you grin at me the moment I walk into the place. The last time I saw you look so cheerful . . ."

There was a furious pause. Mutford cleared his throat deferentially. "Yes, sir?"

Brinton goggled at him. "I've *never* seen you look this cheerful before, Mutford—never, in all the years you've been stationed here!" He glanced at the clock on the wall above the desk. "The pubs shut hours ago, so that can't be the reason—"

"Sir!" Desk Sergeant Mutford drew himself to his full height and frowned in a way that, in anyone less obviously determined to remain deferential, might have been better described as an insubordinate glare. "I'm a member of the Holdfast Brethren, sir. Strictly teetotal, we are, as you ought to know, and the demon drink is anathema to us, sir." Mutford raised his eyes in pious invocation. "Drunkenness, sir, as Jeremy Taylor says in *Holy Living*, is an immoderate affection and use of drink; and *Proverbs*, Chapter Twenty—"

"I didn't ask for a temperance lecture, Mutford, I asked why you were grinning in that ridiculous way!"

The sergeant primmed his mouth. "Strictly speaking, sir—holding fast to the literal truth, as you might say—you didn't in fact ask me—"

"Shuttup, Mutford!"

The desk sergeant lowered his eyes and fell silent; but a keen observer would have observed the corners of his mouth twitch.

Brinton was a superintendent. Superintendents do not achieve such rank if they are unobservant. "You've got ten seconds, Mutford, before I put you on a charge—or on market day traffic duty for the next six months, if you'd rather. The choice is yours, and you'd better make it quickly. Stop playing silly bees with me, or—"

But he didn't need to start timing ten seconds by the wall clock, as Mutford—who'd been longing to tell him anyway—cleared his throat, raised his eyes again, and drew the Occurrence Book towards him, turning to the section in which Official Business was recorded. The smirk hovered very close as he read, in his best pulpit tones:

"Report from Police Constable . . . Potter, sir"—and the pause was infinitesimal—"received this afternoon at—"

"No!" Brinton leaped for the book, snatched it from the sergeant's hands, and slammed it shut, breathing hard. Mutford gave vent to a sigh that embodied sympathy, tolerance, and understanding—so much of it that his tormented superior uttered a heartfelt groan, swore once at him, and stamped away in the direction of his office without another word.

He flung open the door with such force that his nameplate fell off, but he ignored its clatter—and the crack, when he trod on it—as he stood on the threshold glaring at the long-haired young man who sat with his arms folded, his eyes closed, and his shoulders gently shaking, behind a desk piled high with paperwork. One item of which was clearly, to the superintendent's wrathful gaze, the report from Plummergen's own PC Potter which—Brinton greatly feared—contained something he would far rather not know.

He took a deep breath, gritted his teeth, breathed out, and walked across to his desk without a word. Detective Constable Foxon, meanwhile, had opened his eyes and clambered to his feet. "Sir?"

Brinton ignored him, pulling out his chair and sitting down at his desk as wordlessly as he'd entered his office. He looked at Foxon, and waved a hand towards the visitors' chair. Foxon, startled, hurried to sit down. Still Brinton did not speak. "Sir?" ventured Foxon, who hadn't seen his chief like this before. "Sir?"

"Foxon?" said Brinton at last, mimicking the young detective's tones. Foxon looked at him, then leaned forward as if by accident and breathed in carefully. Brinton's fist slammed down on the desk, missing his nose by an inch.

"I'm not drunk, laddie—I'm desperate! I'd been crazy enough to hope it was just Mutford winding me up, but I knew the moment I saw you he wasn't—and now I've got to know, even if it drives me completely round the bend. Tell me the worst, Foxon. What has Miss Seeton been doing?"

# chapter

## -17-

"I'VE NO IDEA, sir." Foxon gazed at his chief with a wide-eyed innocence that could—just—have been genuine. "Were you expecting her to have, er, done something? If you're interested, we could always tele—"

"Shuttup, Foxon!" Foxon shut up. "And let me see that report, laddie—now!"

Foxon pushed back his chair and went to retrieve the report over which he'd been chuckling; and returned, head hung low, discreetly tiptoeing, to the superintendent's desk. "Excuse me, sir, but is it in order," he enquired in hushed tones, "for me to say *here you are, sir*—or, er, isn't it safe just yet?" And he ducked nimbly as Brinton grabbed a paperweight and hurled it at him. It missed.

Grinning, Foxon bounced back to his seat, sat down, and waited while his seething superior perused the report from Plummergen's PC Potter. Brinton's breathing was loud and irregular; his chest heaved with strong emotion. He uttered not one word as he read through to the end, then turned to Foxon with a dangerous light in his eye.

"What has she done that nobody's told me about? There's not one mention of Miss Seeton in this entire report!"

Foxon contrived to look wounded. "Well, sir, I'm sorry if you're disappointed, but I never said there was, did I? Sir. What I *did* say, if you remember, was that we could always telephone . . ."

He caught Brinton's expression, and again shut up. Some moments passed while the superintendent struggled with himself, and Foxon tried to look as if he weren't there. In the end, Brinton said, very mildly:

"A remarkable place, Plummergen, wouldn't you say?"

"Er—yes, sir. I suppose I would."

"Like going there, do you, Foxon?"

"Er—it has its moments of interest, sir."

"Such as Saturday's cricket match?" demanded Brinton, in accents that were still very mild. Foxon blinked.

"I enjoy a good game of cricket, sir, yes."

"Good game? Are you out of your tiny mind, laddie? Is it you and not me that's gone crazy? That won't be any ordinary game of cricket on Saturday, Foxon—as you and Potter and probably everyone else but me has suspected right from the start. This, laddie, will be a massacre!"

"Oh, Murreystone aren't such a bad team, sir—I think it'll be a reasonably even match, if—"

"Not now they've nobbled your star bowler—what am I saying? *Your* star bowler? I *am* going crazy!" Brinton was too despondent even to clutch at his hair as he usually did when life became too much for him. Foxon regarded him with some concern. "Have a peppermint, sir," he suggested.

After emitting a hollow groan, Brinton picked up the report he'd flung down in the heat of the moment, and began to read selected passages aloud. "Wilful damage to a blacksmith's portable forge . . . set of wrought-iron gates, property of Mr. and Mrs. Farmint of Glenvale House, in for repair . . . one bicycle, property of Major Matilda Howett . . ." At this, he gazed at Foxon from tormented eyes. "If it had been *her* bicycle, I could've understood it all, but . . ."

"I must plead not guilty on Miss Seeton's behalf, sir, in her absence."

He was ignored. The mournful litany continued. "Flood damage sustained by house next door, belonging to Miss Wicks . . . fire damage to roof of same . . . cost of supplying tow truck to Brettenden Fire Brigade . . ."

"Crabbe's Garage," supplied Foxon, helpfully. "Jack did it cut-price for 'em, seeing as—" He shut up again.

"Injuries sustained: one broken arm, two cases of shock, assorted cracked ribs, one broken toe—*and the fire-engine side panels where the horse kicked them in!*"

"Jack says they can do those cut-price too, sir," Foxon informed him brightly. Brinton had often wondered whether the young man had any rubber planters in his ancestry. But the superintendent felt too weak to glare, or to groan, or to throw anything: he had passed through the fire and come out the other side. He said at last:

"I never knew horses could get drunk."

"No, sir, I don't think many people do. It's hardly the sort of thing you'd expect, is it? I mean, take your average horse. Hangs about in fields all day chomping grass, and every now and then you bung a saddle on its back and jump over fences with it—or you shove a harness round its neck and ask it to pull a cart . . . Pretty big, those Shires, sir. Can weigh over a ton, so I'm told."

Brinton said nothing. Foxon gazed at the ceiling. "You have to hand it to 'em, sir—Murreystone, I mean. Think of how much planning must've gone into the idea—the hundreds of apples they had to collect to have enough ferment for the horse to eat and get tiddly on . . ."

Still Brinton said nothing, though his look was eloquent—as was Foxon's tongue, as he warmed to his theme. "It was clever, sir, you must admit. Dan Eggleden's a big, tough bloke—there's an awful lot of power behind those balls he pitches down—and if they'd tried to nobble him in what you might call an ordinary way, sir, he'd have smashed 'em to a pulp. Whereas . . ." Foxon chortled. "Whereas the only *pulp* around was from the fermented apples, sir, and all of *them* were inside the horse . . ."

"No wonder Mutford was reading me the riot act about the demon drink," muttered Brinton. "And goodness only knows why the fool thought it was amusing—those Brethren have a damned peculiar sense of humour, if you ask me."

"They'd be shocked to hear such strong language, sir—"

"Hard bloody cheese!" Brinton thumped his fist on the desk, scattering papers. "It's a miracle I don't say something a good deal stronger, in the circumstances. You've asked for the day off on Saturday, haven't you? To go to this horrible cricket match where Lord knows what is likely to happen, after this little effort . . . but I suppose," he added thoughtfully, "they may well rope you into the team, now they're a man short. Which means the Murreystone bowler might use your fat head for target practice—which would save me a lot of future heartache, Foxon. I think," Brinton announced to his startled subordinate, "I'm taking Saturday off as well, laddie—the afternoon, anyway. If there's any excitement due, I don't want to miss it."

Foxon shot him a wary look. "As a matter of fact, sir, Plummergen already have a twelfth man—two, if it comes to that. They sort of take it in turns at the tail, sir—a bloke called Scillicough, and another called Newport. So Potter tells me. Their wives are sisters, and they've got seven kids between the pair of 'em, Potter says. I'm surprised either of them's got enough energy left for crick—"

"Foxon!"

"Sorry, sir." Foxon shot him another wary look. "You, er, serious about Saturday, sir?"

The superintendent sighed. "Ever heard about the sheep and the lamb, laddie? If things really are going to go over the top—which my instincts tell me they are—then I may as well be on the spot when they do. Otherwise, it'd be just my luck to break my neck crashing the car haring over to Plummergen when the balloon goes up . . ." Inspector Borden's ex-Marine sergeant was not the only policeman to whose mind the images of battle seemed eminently suitable.

Foxon nodded. "Of course, sir, I understand. Er—any chance of a lift?"

"Don't push your luck, laddie. Neither of us is going anywhere if there's an emergency—or if the paperwork's not up-to-date," he added, surveying the chaos on his desk with some dismay. "I suppose we'd better get on with the rest of it—I'm sure Potter's report wasn't the only one that came in while I was out, was it?"

"No, sir." Foxon was all seriousness at once. "There's been another burglary outbreak, sir . . ."

And, resolutely pushing Plummergen and its cricket match to the back of his mind, Brinton settled down to read.

Paperwork is paperwork the whole world over; liked by some, loathed by others less mentally attuned to its demands. Nigel Colveden, for instance, had relished the practical part of his course at agricultural college, coming a respectable third in his year—and had passed his written exams with less than respectable marks. After graduation, he had sighed with relief at the thought that he would never again have to take any sort of test . . .

Yet here he was, sitting with his father trying to sort out Plummergen's cricket team now that Daniel Eggleden was unable to play. The bad news of the blacksmith's broken arm and the drunken Murreystone carthorse had scorched its way round Plummergen as fast as any news had ever done: helped, of course, by the fact that there had been so many witnesses to the perfidy of the rival village. The high-speed advent of the Brettenden fire engine with its bell ringing at full volume had drawn almost all who heard it into The Street to watch what was happening: only those who were housebound ignored its summons, especially since the distance between the forge and Sweetbriars may be measured in yards. General opinion, before the full facts were known, unwittingly echoed that of Superintendent Brinton: what was Miss Seeton doing this time?

"Well, I think it's jolly unfair of them to blame Miss Seeton for the horse," said young Galahad Colveden, as his father frowned over the list of names and pencilled in a few tentative changes to the batting order. "How could it possibly be her fault when she's been in London all day?"

"But she hasn't," said Annabelle gently, as Sir George huffed through his moustache, swapped Jack Crabbe's name for Mr. Stillman's, and added a question mark. Miss Leigh had been invited to supper after her day's journeying was done, and was delighted to accept. She sat with her sketchbook on her knee, jotting down impressions of what she had promised Nigel would be a portrait of himself, though her preference, he knew, was for buildings. He hadn't known whether to be pleased or embarrassed at her tentative offer to draw, perhaps paint, him, but when he learned that it would be unnecessary for him to pose, he agreed, silently reasoning that in order to achieve the series of rough sketches Annabelle said she needed, she would have to spend lots of time with him. Which suited Nigel very well . . .

"Harrumph!" Sir George broke into his son's reverie with a sympathetic, though forceful, cough. Couldn't blame the lad for admiring the girl, but work came first. "Team to be picked, remember. Sorry, m'dear," to Annabelle. "You were saying?"

Annabelle flashed him her most brilliant smile. "Only that—begging your pardon, Nigel—Miss Seeton hasn't been in Town *all day*, if it was Miss Seeton I saw as I cycled to Brettenden earlier, which I'm pretty sure it was. We artists don't often forget faces—and she smiled at me as if she knew me, so it must have been her. In a tiny car being driven by a most enormous young man, turning into the nursing home."

"Bob Ranger!" Nigel grinned. "What a stroke of luck—I hadn't heard he was coming for the weekend, but I'm jolly glad he has. We might well have found our substitute for Dan Eggleden—all thanks to Annabelle." And his admiring glance made her blush.

To cover her confusion, she said: "I'm glad I seem to have been of some help, though I really don't understand how—or why, if it comes to that. Nigel thinks I'm awfully ignorant," she confided to Nigel's father, "but cricket just isn't something that's interested me. Until now." And it was Nigel's turn to blush, as Annabelle looked at him.

"Oh, gosh," said Nigel; adding hastily: "I mean, suppose Bob *doesn't* play cricket? I know he's in the police football team—he looks as if he could be a handy bowler like Dan—but if we're wrong, we'll be back to square one." He shuffled the papers with a dismal finger. "We can't really afford to mess around with the tailenders and twelfth man unless we really must—they're nowhere near good enough. You're doing a grand job, Dad, when I'm not even sure it's the umpire's job to sort out the players, but . . ."

"Jessyp's busy with his timetables again," his father reminded him. Martin Jessyp was captain of the Plummergen team, with Nigel as his deputy, an arrangement which generally worked well. The schoolmaster was acknowledged to be the best paper shuffler in Plummergen, while Nigel was the best bat, always going in at Number Four, after things had settled down. Mr. Jessyp would open the batting, his partner being Charley Mountfitchet from the George and Dragon; Three was usually Mr. Stillman from the post office. He and Nigel could be trusted to put on a fair number of runs together, though it was his spin bowling for which he was most valued. Young Len Hosigg, Sir George's shy farm foreman, made a good stonewalling partner for Nigel once the postmaster's wicket had fallen, followed by PC Potter, Bert the postman—who had at last managed to win the Plummergen round for his own and was regarded as a local even though he lived in Brettenden—and, at Number Eight, Daniel Eggleden, whose broken arm had caused such consternation among his friends . . .

"I'll give the Knights a ring, shall I?" Nigel was on his feet, eager for action.

"Is someone ill?" Lady Colveden, who had refused Annabelle's offer to help with the washing up, had rinsed and left to drain the last of the dishes, and now came to join the rest of the company. "Has worrying about the team driven your father to distraction? I don't need to ask," she added, "whether you, Nigel, have survived the ordeal. I'm sure you've delegated it all beautifully."

"To my elders and betters." Nigel grinned. "I think Dad'll pull through, though—which is more than can be said for us, if we don't find another bowler. But Annabelle says Bob Ranger's in town—at least, how many other enormous men driving Miss Seeton about in tiny cars do you know who're likely to take her to the nursing home—"

"The nursing home? Oh, dear. Perhaps she's not well." Lady Colveden frowned. "Wasn't she going to London for the day? I hope nothing's wrong—Nigel, if you're phoning, do ask, won't you?" And her son, who hadn't thought of anything so unfortunate as illness or accident requiring Miss Seeton's visit to Dr. Knight, promised he would report back as soon as possible.

During his absence, Sir George took it upon himself to answer Annabelle's shy query as to the importance of someone so large as Bob Ranger, or a blacksmith, to the cricket team in preference to Nigel, and why Nigel himself was in such a state about it all.

"Muscles, m'dear." The baronet twirled his moustache in Miss Leigh's direction and allowed his eyes to twinkle as he enlarged: "Not that Nigel hasn't his share, of course—working farmer—but big, beefy chaps like that—fast and deadly, y'know. Knock 'em down like ninepins if they get it just right—stumps, that is, not players."

"The wicket," said Annabelle, who'd learned a lot over the past few days. Nigel's devotion to herself had almost equalled his devotion to the national game. He had spent those moments when he wasn't gazing into her eyes, or paying her compliments, in explaining the strategy he and Mr. Jessyp had worked out between them for Saturday's big match; and, whether or not she'd been deeply interested, the young woman now knew far more about cricket than she had before. "Three stumps," she said with a faint smile, "with two bails balanced on top, and if they're knocked off by the ball when it's bowled, or when the wicket-keeper catches it and hits them, or by the batsman if he's clumsy with his bat, then he's out."

"Or l.b.w.," said Sir George, the umpire. "Leg before wicket," as she turned wondering blue eyes upon him. "If the ball hits the chap on the leg—out. Why you wear pads when you're batting," he added. "Ball can fairly whistle down at you sometimes. Why you wear—harrumph! No, never mind—you wouldn't." And he reddened behind his moustache as he realised how close he'd been to embarrassing the young lady by mentioning the batsman's vital little plastic box. He caught his wife's warning eye and changed the subject.

"Ranger's a sporty type—wouldn't surprise me if he bowled. Hitter, too, probably—different, of course, from a batsman. Just as likely to be out as to hit a six, y'know—but a batsman like Nigel, now . . ."

Annabelle smiled faintly at her swain's father's casual compliment to his son, and Lady Colveden, who knew how susceptible her menfolk were to a pretty face and didn't think overkill was a good idea, remarked:

"You and Nigel and Mr. Jessyp seem to have sorted it all out wonderfully, George. I'm sure Murreystone don't stand the ghost of a chance—but I can't help thinking, especially after that business with the horse. It really would, you know, be rather a good idea to go ahead with the revival of your Village Watch scheme . . ."

A suggestion which, after a few twirls of a thoughtful moustache, Sir George was moved to discuss with the assembled company for no more than a few token moments before agreeing that it was a thundering shame the blighters couldn't be trusted, but, since they couldn't, he'd do his best to settle their hash for them.

Starting that very night.

# chapter

## ~18~

HAVING EXAMINED MISS Seeton with all due care, Dr. Knight was able to reassure Bob that she would, after a day or so, be back on top form without any lasting effects from the day's little adventure.

"Miss Seeton," he said, waving his stethoscope beneath the startled nose of his son-in-law, "is a walking marvel, as you and your precious Oracle really should know, by now. I'm concerned about the quality of policing with which England must be burdened when so-called detectives can trust neither the experience of years, or the evidence of their own eyes. Some people never learn."

Bob grinned. "She's a marvel, all right—but you can't help wondering if she isn't going to push her luck too far, one day."

"Well, she hasn't today. And if it's any consolation, I doubt if she ever will. Just goes to show what yoga can do for you, plus an overactive guardian angel, of course. Better ring Delphick at the Yard and let him know what I said, to stop him having kittens about his protégée."

When Bob returned at last from the telephone, he found Miss Seeton taking a late-afternoon-tea-cum-early-supper with Anne, her parents, and Major Howett. The cakes—left over from the patients' earlier meal—were delicious, the tea itself just right, and the company, as ever, delightful—so said Miss Seeton with one of her brightest smiles, as if collapsing cranes and handbag thieves and coiners' dens were no more than hiccups in an otherwise orderly existence—which (thought Bob with a secret chuckle) to Miss Seeton they probably were. He accepted a cup of tea

133

from his mother-in-law, suppressing a grimace as he realised how weak, in deference to their guest, it had been made; and ate three cakes in quick succession.

"Got to keep up my strength for Saturday," he explained to Miss Seeton, who was twinkling at him as she refused to pass the plate a fourth time, after hearing Anne's protests that he wasn't to be encouraged. He sighed and turned to his father-in-law. "You know Nigel rang just after I spoke to the Oracle? He's asked me to play in the Murreystone match—asked if I could bowl at all, and I said I hadn't been too bad at school. So he said I could take Dan Eggleden's place at Number Eight."

"Ah, yes. I patched up the poor chap's arm before they took him off to hospital." Dr. Knight shook his head. "It's a bad business, for a self-employed man like a blacksmith. Those silly bees from the Marsh deserve a good kick in the rear end."

Miss Seeton was the only one present who didn't know the full story of perfidious Murreystone, and was properly distressed when she heard it. "Poor Mr. Eggleden—it looks so splendid, and has been much admired, though Miss Wicks's ornamental balustrade is his *pièce de résistance,* I believe. My wrought-iron fence. And one has to be so careful, with fire. One cannot help but feel that the Murreystone people have a . . . a less than responsible attitude . . ."

"Load of silly bees," repeated the doctor, with a snort. "Potter says, and I agree with him, that things are getting completely out of hand over this feud nonsense."

Major Howett offered a somewhat stronger opinion before recalling that Miss Seeton was not, perhaps, accustomed to her bluff military manner, and barked an apology, her cheeks pink. Miss Seeton assured the major that she had known dear Sir George for some years now, and moreover sympathised with the feelings of those who, labouring to care for the sick, must feel their time was likely to be wasted by those whose misfortunes, to a greater or lesser degree, might be regarded as having been their own fault, and thus unnecessary.

"Except, of course, poor Mr. Eggleden. And—oh, dear." Miss Seeton looked suddenly more upset than she had when the crane collapsed. "I had forgotten dear Miss Wicks, who can hardly be blamed for the flooding of her home any more than one can blame the fire brigade—who were, after all, only doing their duty. But he will be unable to work for so long—and she is so prone to arthritis, poor soul, that one cannot help feeling anxious . . ."

A general chorus, in which the voice of Dr. Knight became rapidly dominant, hurried to explain that Miss Wicks was even now upstairs, taking a well-earned nap, and Miss Seeton had no need to feel any anxiety for her friend's welfare. Miss Wicks would remain in the Home until full repairs had been carried out on her cottage. Which, in such warm weather, shouldn't take too long.

"And she has everything she needs," he added, as Miss Seeton continued to look anxious. "Anne went down with me to help her pack, and they've made a list between 'em of what's what for later in the week. But don't worry about her," he said again. "Let her keep quiet for a day or so, and she'll be her old self again. Sit on the boundary with you watching Saturday's match, if she likes."

"Oh, dear, yes." Miss Seeton was looking anxious again. "The match—and I promised Lady Colveden . . ."

Ten minutes later, Miss Seeton was waving good-bye to Bob Ranger, who had driven her from the Knights' in Anne's tiny car despite her protests that she would enjoy a walk in the evening air. She had been, Bob reminded her, walking round London most of the morning, so how much more fresh air and exercise did she want? Besides, he was under orders to take good care of her: not just from Dr. Knight, but also from the Oracle—who was coming down on Saturday to watch the match, and would give him hell— he begged Miss Seeton's pardon—who would be annoyed with him if Scotland Yard's favourite art consultant gave any appearance of not having been properly looked after.

Miss Seeton had no wish to get dear Bob into trouble, of course. She smiled and accepted his escort without further demur; and realised, as he drove away, that she was indeed a little more weary than she had supposed. Another cup of tea would do no harm, she thought, though one felt one had been drinking it all afternoon. But so much dust . . .

She sighed as she removed her hat and set it on the hall table. She very much feared that it would never be the same again after having been knocked off and, one had to suppose, trodden on when the building fell in and all the bricks were sent tumbling into the road. How very fortunate that nobody had been hurt. And

how distressing for the poor driver, who had kept saying over
and over again—the shock, of course—that he hadn't meant to,
but he couldn't believe his eyes. Miss Seeton hadn't understood
what he'd meant, but, knowing how important it was that one
should be able to trust the evidence of one's eyes, and to see
properly, had hoped the poor man would visit an oculist as soon
as possible. Should one, perhaps, have suggested such a visit to
him? He might have regarded it as an impertinence from one
who was, after all, a complete stranger. Which was no doubt
why he had been so very insistent upon travelling to hospital
for his checkup in one of the other ambulances: he would
naturally not wish a stranger to observe him in a moment of
weakness. Male invalids, as Miss Seeton understood—and as
her experience with generations of schoolgirls had led her to
believe—were far less courageous in matters of health than
females, though nobody could doubt their courage in battle and
time of war . . .

"Oh, dear." She sighed again, thinking of Murreystone, and
poor Daniel Eggleden, and Miss Wicks . . . One accepted ordinary mischief, such as schoolchildren might accomplish, but
there was also, one regretted having to say, the rather more
malicious variety. To which Murreystone, one feared, seemed
to be inclined. Poor Constable Potter . . .

While Miss Seeton was sighing over PC Potter's problems, he
himself was wondering whether he'd done the right thing in letting Ashford, and Superintendent Brinton, know about what had
happened. He'd hoped to maintain a discreet silence in the matter of his reports until Saturday's match was over: a laudable end
he thought he'd safely achieved, until that Shire horse had gone
berserk and, almost literally, kicked over the traces. After which,
he really didn't see there was any way he could've kept it quiet, no matter how much he might want to. His occurrence book,
for one thing: drunk in charge of a horse was the sort of crime
you didn't get much of, these days. The first time the superintendent checked through the pages to see how the other half lived,
he'd hit the roof. Besides, he was bound to find out long before
that—next week's local paper'd have it written up for sure. Front
page, most like, seeing as it'd happened in Plummergen, home of

Miss Emily Dorothea Seeton, the nation's favourite Battling Brol-ly. Potter didn't even bother wondering how *The Brettenden Tele-graph and Beacon* (est. 1847, incorporating (1893) *The Iverhurst Chronicle and Argus*) would find out: he'd lived in Plummergen for too long to doubt the efficiency of the tom-tom network. If the fire brigade didn't tell everyone, the hospital staff who'd set Dan Eggleden's arm, and treated the cracked ribs, the shock, and the broken toe, would. Bound to be in the *Beacon,* then—and when Old Brimstone spotted it he'd want to know why he hadn't been told before. But at least—which made a change—nobody could blame Miss Seeton, could they?

Miss Seeton remained, as ever, oblivious to all thought that any-one might blame her for anything, in just the same way that she was able to remain oblivious of the momentous service she had, yet again, rendered to the police. Inspector Borden had thanked her: she had thought it perhaps somewhat excessive for one who had merely been doing her duty in preventing a thief from run-ning off with so many handbags, but she didn't know him very well—perhaps it had just been his normal manner. But dear Mr. Delphick's talk of coiners had really been . . . rather muddling. Naturally, there had been coins—money—in the handbags: one kept a five-pound note and a limited supply of small change in one's own bag at all times, for emergencies, and it wasn't to be supposed that other ladies would have less foresight. No doubt it was the—yes, one had to admit it at last, in the relaxing privacy of one's own home—it was the shock of having been so near to the building that collapsed under the weight of the crane which had slightly addled one's wits . . .

"A cup of tea, I think," said Miss Seeton firmly, leaving her damaged hat on the table without another glance and heading for the kitchen. The kettle, as ever, was full and waiting. Within ten minutes, she was in her sitting room, a laden tray on the table at her side, and a feeling that she still lacked for something . . .

It was instinctive for Miss Seeton to reach for pencil and paper when in pursuit of a certain degree of relaxation. First thing in the morning, and last thing at night, she made a point of following her yoga routine: during the day, however, she rarely chose this way of quietening her restless mind—which, all too often, was accom-panied by a restless body. One's hands, in particular. They might,

if one was of a fanciful turn—which, sadly (for the gift of imagination is, to an artist, of the greatest value) one was not—almost be
considered as having a will of their own. They would sometimes
fidget and dance on one's lap in a way which was, well, uncomfortable. One felt as one might have done with a class of children
who simply could not be persuaded to keep still, when often the
only way to cure the problem was to take them out into the play-
ground and persuade them to jump about, or to run races, to work
off their excess energy. Miss Seeton had no inclination either to
jump, or to run: neither would calm her dancing hands, she knew
well. Whereas drawing—especially as one so much enjoyed, even
if one did not, alas, excel at it—she found often helped. Besides,
one had promised Lady Colveden a painting of the Plummergen
cricket match, for the pavilion auction: it would do no harm to
make a few preliminary notes before—

"Oh. Oh, dear. I had forgotten . . ."

Miss Seeton stared at the strange sketch of the Chinese
cricketers she really did not remember having drawn. Then
she turned to another page and was even more startled. Her
sketch of Annabelle Leigh—how had the young woman aroused
so much envy in her heart? With hindsight, of course, and a sense
of distance—the British Museum artefacts had been a humbling
experience—one did not feel so disturbed by Miss Leigh's abilities as one evidently had before—but things, Miss Seeton told
herself with a sigh, were very . . . strange, just at present—one
was still, no doubt, suffering from a sense of anticlimax after
one's holiday, although one would have supposed that a day
out in London—but it was of no use to look back. One must
always look forward. To Saturday, and to watching dear Nigel,
and Jack Crabbe—and dear Bob, of course, because of poor Dan
Eggleden's broken arm—how fortunate that Dr. Knight had been
so quick on the scene, and how one wished broken bones could
set as quickly . . .

When Miss Seeton emerged from her idle dreaming, she was
not surprised to find that she had doodled a strong likeness
of dear Anne's father, brandishing bandages and splints, and
busily wrapping a brawny arm belonging to a large man in
a leather apron—the village blacksmith, without a doubt—and
with a cricket bat in his other hand. Behind him, a heavy horse

with waving feathers about its huge feet, reared up on its hind
legs, hooves flashing, nostrils flaring, eyes wild—and a circle of
dots whirling above its head. Miss Seeton peered more closely.
No, not dots. She could hardly help chuckling. One should not
mock the afflicted, but really it did look most comical. Not dots,
but tiny creatures—some with tusks, and trunks. Elephants! She
had a strong suspicion that, had she used coloured rather than
black graphite pencils, the elephants would have been decidedly
pink in hue—but perhaps not the other creatures, which weren't.
Neither pink, nor elephants. Miss Seeton peered more closely.
Winged, and rounded of body, and striped—yellow and black,
she somehow knew the stripes would have been, had she used
colour. Bees—bees and elephants. How very . . .

"Strange," murmured Miss Seeton, rubbing her eyes and looking again at the likeness of Dr. Knight. "Oh, of course—those
mischievous persons from Murreystone." And the dear doctor so
careful of her feelings that he'd referred to them as silly bees.
The people who'd fed it fermented apples and let it kick poor
Mr. Eggleden, that was to say. The horse. How considerate he
was, and dear Anne, too—packing her belongings and letting her
stay in the Home for as long as was necessary for the roof to be
repaired . . .

Another swift likeness appeared on the paper from Miss
Seeton's pencil, this time of Miss Wicks. She was wearing
gumboots, which surprised Miss Seeton, who'd never dreamed
of her old friend as owning anything other than galoshes—gumboots, and carrying a suitcase in her hand. No doubt on her way to
stay with Dr. and Mrs. Knight, and the dear Major, Miss Seeton
told herself with a smile; the boots, of course, because of the flood
from the fire engine. One could make out the cottage in the background—and those must be the firemen inside, glimpsed through
the window in silhouette, though they were not wearing helmets.
One must suppose that—like policemen—they doffed their hats,
or rather helmets, when entering a private residence. One knew
that firemen played their hoses on burned-out buildings for some
time after the fire had been extinguished, and therefore—since
it had been clear, as dear Bob drove down The Street, that the
damage had been minimal and Miss Wicks's cottage still stood—
one assumed they must here be playing, or rather plying, their

pumps, to remove the water they had been previously at such pains to introduce to put out the fire on the roof caused by the wayward sparks from Daniel Eggleden's overturned portable forge. Which made her think of Murreystone once more, and sigh for the weaknesses of human nature . . .

# chapter

# ~19~

THE HIGHER THE rank reached in HM Forces, the greater the organisational ability of the officers concerned: a rule to which Sir George was no exception. He it was who had instigated, and supervised, the Village Watch scheme during the most recent flare-up of rivalry between Plummergen and Murreystone; he it was who had—so successful did the scheme prove—filed away the lists of volunteers and patrol timetables in case they should be of future use. Plummergen and Murreystone, he knew, had been in dispute at least since the Civil War, when Plummergen took the Royalist, Murreystone the Puritan side. The feuding had if anything increased rather than decreased in intensity over the past three hundred and thirty years; it would take more than the efforts of Major-General Sir George Colveden, Bart, KCB, DSO, JP to stop the villagers trying to score off each other at every opportunity, though discouraging them as far as possible struck him as a sensible notion. Accordingly, he retrieved his files, brought them up-to-date with a few judicious telephone calls, and issued a number of new orders concerning the cricket ground, in case of a sneak attack.

"Pity the fire brigade had to be called," he explained to Lady Colveden, as Nigel set about warning Annabelle of the likely dangers of that lengthy half-mile trip down Marsh Road from Rytham Hall to the George and Dragon, insisting she should abandon her bicycle until the morrow and accept his escort in the MG—just in case. "Wouldn't put it past the blighters to flood the pitch—one or two retained, remember. Know their way around."

As in many country areas, Plummergen and its neighbours are served by a retained—that is to say volunteer—fire brigade. It is not so many years back that they were summoned to the fire station from work, from home, or wherever they might happen to be by means of the old air-raid siren. The introduction of bleeping personal pagers, however, meant that volunteers could be called from farther away than within immediate earshot of the siren, and one or two of the Murreystoners with fast cars had promptly signed up. Always providing they were never on the same duty roster as the Plummergenites—which the chief officer took great pains to ensure—all tended to go smoothly; but, as Sir George now pointed out, they knew as well as any how to operate the appliances: filling them with water, driving them, and pumping the water out through the hoses . . .

"Flood the pitch? Surely they wouldn't do that!" Lady Colveden was suitably shocked at the suggestion. Sir George shook his head.

"Can't be too careful, m'dear. As Nigel"—with a twinkle in the direction of his son—"knows, of course. Better safe than sorry, every time." And Annabelle Leigh smiled at this gentle hint, promptly agreeing with Sir George's son and heir that perhaps the distance between the Hall and the hotel might be a little unsafe for a solitary female; she would feel far happier traversing it in company.

"George," warned his wife, as the MG roared away, "don't overdo the hints, will you? Nigel's old enough to do his own courting."

"Pretty girl," said the old warhorse, twirling his moustache. His wife smiled doubtfully.

"Yes, I know, but at Nigel's age the last thing he wants is his parents' approval of his choice—at first, anyway. He still wants to be Romeo, or someone like that—carrying off the girl in the teeth of all opposition. If you make it too obvious you like her, you'll put him off. And you'll almost certainly frighten *her.*"

The moustache was still, as bristling eyebrows twitched. "Jealous, m'dear? Notice you said if *I* liked her, not you."

"I never said any such—well, I suppose I did, but I certainly didn't mean it like that. I think. I mean, all I meant was . . . Oh dear, I'm *not* one of those terrible, possessive mothers, am I, George? When Julia married Toby, you can't say I made a fuss, now can you?"

"Cried half the time," her husband reminded her, adding, as he caught her eye: "Not the same at all, anyway, mothers and sons—different from daughters. Very." A mischievous glint appeared in his own eye. "Never been absolutely sure . . . Daphne Carstairs, y'know. M'mother liked her. Often wondered—if she hadn't, maybe . . ."

Whereupon Lady Colveden, though tempted to throw something at him—not once in twenty-four years had she ever needed to ask herself where Nigel's dreadful sense of humour came from—contrived that her eyes should widen and fill with wounded tears; and the conversation which then ensued was of an entirely private nature.

Lady Colveden having duly forgiven her husband his teasing, she prepared sandwiches and flasks of coffee, despite the protests of her menfolk—Nigel had returned in a blissful state from driving Annabelle to the George—that they were supposed to be on patrol, not having a picnic; and sent them out on that patrol with stern warnings that nobody was to act the hero, because there was still the rest of the harvest to get in, and they'd be no good to anyone if they were laid up with bruises or broken arms, like poor Dan Eggleden, would they?

Her husband and son poured a chorus of scorn on this argument. "Visible deterrent," explained Sir George, as Nigel cried that really, Mother, surely it was obvious that was the whole point of patrolling. His mother widened her eyes once more and contrived to look bewildered.

"If they know we're on the lookout, they won't try anything," her son kindly enlarged, while his father unscrewed the top of his flask to sniff at its contents. A sign of Lady Colveden's true forgiveness would be a ration of rum against the chilly autumn night . . .

"Oh, George, really! It isn't even September yet." His wife watched him in some amusement. "I'll leave the bottle out for when you get back, if you like, but I'd have thought you'd had enough rum the other night, at the admiral's."

Sir George fingered a thoughtful moustache. "Talked about the Village Watch then, as I recall. Wouldn't like to think he was, well, pumping me."

"I'm sure he wasn't. I'm sure he's much more interested

in those bees of his than in feeding horses with fermenting apples . . ."

And Lady Colveden hurried her menfolk out of the door, so that they might set a good example by arriving early on parade.

A few yawns next morning were the only signs to distinguish the assorted groups of Night Watch Men, who had been on duty from the fall of Thursday's darkness to the rise of Friday's sun, from their fellow Plummergenites. The night had been, they congratulated themselves, uneventful; Murreystone had put in no appearance; those vital twenty-two yards of greensward making up the cricket pitch were as level, firm, and dry as they had ever been. Flushed with virtue and success, the Village Watch went about its normal business of the day.

Others, who had not been patrolling Plummergen at two-hourly intervals, also began to go about their business. Red-haired Cockney Bert came bowling down The Street in his scarlet GPO van, whistling between his teeth as he parked neatly outside Mr. Stillman's post office and prepared to deliver the mail. Nothing much of interest, today. Mostly letters, and none of them airmail, or looking like unpaid bills or final demands; a few postcards from people holidaying later than their friends, trying to make them jealous; various magazines of assorted interest; and two or three parcels, one of which had to be signed for.

Bert crossed the road to Lilikot, and pushed *Psychic News* through the letterbox with as much commotion as he could legitimately manage, holding the parcel clearly in sight of those net-curtained windows. With a nicety of timing developed over the two or three years he had been on the Plummergen run, he delayed his walk away from the house until the Nuts, now certain the parcel must be for them, were opening the front door to collect it.

"Morning!" Bert turned round with obvious surprise to wave at Miss Nuttel and Mrs. Blaine, privately christened by himself the Long and the Short of It. "Nice day, innit?"

And he trod on purposefully down the path without another backward look, whistling a tuneless air.

"Well!" Miss Nuttel and Mrs. Blaine scowled after Bert as they ignored *Psychic News* on the mat, watching where he might go and wondering who was to receive that parcel . . .

With another wave, and a wink, Bert opened the gate of Ararat Cottage, and marched, still whistling, towards the admiral's door. Craning their necks, the Nuts strove for a view of the little porch's interior, so that—

"Bugger!"

Two pairs of eyes looked at each other in shock. "Well, really!" said Mrs. Blaine. "Typical," snorted Miss Nuttel, as a further selection of picturesque language floated over the fence. Bert, it seemed, was unhappy about something: before he had started to curse, he had stopped whistling, though there was no hint now as to what had caused his altered mood, or how long it was likely to last. Miss Nuttel began to wonder whether a little judicious gardening in the front might be a good idea, when:

"Spot of bother, old man?" The voice of the admiral could be heard over the fence, every bit as clear as that of Bert had been before falling silent as the door was opened. There came a Cockney murmuring of which Miss Nuttel and Mrs. Blaine were quite unable to distinguish the words, though they could hear well enough Admiral Leighton's brisk reply: "Bicarbonate of soda—come on in!" And every sign of life vanished from the front porch of Ararat Cottage.

Miss Nuttel looked at Mrs. Blaine. Mrs. Blaine looked at Miss Nuttel, her eyes wide. "Bicarbonate of soda? Oh, Eric—too dreadful, at this hour of the morning, for the man to be suffering from a *hangover*. Driving that van all over the place *under the influence*——it's disgraceful! *And* dangerous—we should report him to someone at once."

But Eric shook her head for the utter innocence of her friend. "No, Bunny, no. Code, of course. Bicarbonate of soda—*white powder*—think about it . . ."

Mrs. Blaine, with a horrified squeak, thought about it. Her eyes lit up. "Oh, Eric, you're so right—cocaine, of course. Too, too dreadful!"

And when Bert emerged from the cottage ten minutes later minus the parcel, but with a bandage round his finger, the Nuts knew what he had been doing. Miss Nuttel preferred the term *drop*—Mrs. Blaine thought *handover* more apposite—but both Nuts knew, beyond all doubt, that Bert had just delivered the latest consignment of drugs to the self-styled Rear Admiral Bernard Leighton, RN (retired).

They knew yet more. Bert drove off down The Street in a series of grinding gear changes and bunny-hop starts which not only convinced them their drugs theory was correct, but proved to their satisfaction that Bert was no simple pusher, he was an addict, too—an addict who had just received, as his reward for delivering the dope, another fix. Hadn't he driven off decidedly under the influence? Alcohol, cocaine—they were both drugs, weren't they?

It was not until he reached Rytham Hall that Bert, after his irregular progress down The Street, gave up the unequal struggle and rattled the front doorknocker to ask for further aid. When Martha Bloomer—it was one of her days—opened the door, he waved one hand glumly under her startled nose, even as he produced the Colvedens' letters with the other.

"Stung by a bloody bee," he said, moaning now that sympathy was in sight. "Just my luck an' all—be like a balloon before the day's out."

Martha clicked her tongue, studying the bandage. "Well, I allow it looks neat enough—but you're right, swollen's not the word for it. You really did ought to get that seen to properly, Bert."

"The admiral give me some bicarbonate—"

"Bicarbonate? Trust a man! Bicarb's no good for when it's as bad as this. A blue-bag's what you need, and if her ladyship's not got one in the kitchen I'll be surprised, so you come on in this minute while I look."

Bert went on in; and Martha looked; and a blue bag was found, and duly applied. But the bee poison was already circulating merrily round his bloodstream, and, though the swelling was arrested, it did not diminish.

Bert regarded Martha with a worried expression. "Reckon I'd best have a word with young Nigel," he said. "Seeing as how I've already been to Mr. Jessyp—him being vice captain. Nigel, I mean. But it looks as if they'll be one man short tomorrow for the Murreystone match . . ."

And he waved his blue-bagged finger glumly in the air.

# chapter

## –20–

MARTHA HAVING USED the last of Lady Colveden's blue-bags on Bert's finger, more were needed. Mrs. Bloomer had been busy in the kitchen making up a list of domestic requirements when Bert interrupted her, and blue-bags were duly added to that list, which she handed to her employer when Lady Colveden announced that she was just popping to the shops, if Martha wanted anything.

She arrived at the post office in time to overhear an excited Norah Blaine advising everyone that not only was Admiral Leighton a suspected warlock, and In League With Miss Seeton, but a drug dealer, as well. "Bicarbonate of soda—too ridiculous," she scoffed, while Miss Nuttel nodded confirmation at her side. "As if anyone would believe such an idiotic story! What other explanation could there possibly be, except drugs?"

This was too much for Lady Colveden, who was moved to interrupt the general murmur of thrilled agreement by speaking in that fashion which Nigel—though her family seldom heard it—called her "ladyship" voice.

Aristocratic hauteur combined in unison with ice-cold anger and disdain. "I for one, Mrs. Blaine, am prepared to believe what you are so careless as to call the admiral's *story*. There are laws of slander in this country, remember—and may I suggest you should also remember that bicarbonate of soda is a noted remedy for anyone who has suffered a bee sting? As are blue-bags. Which I—and I trust that no suggestion of *idiocy* on my part is thereby assumed on yours—have come to buy now because Mrs. Bloomer used the last of mine in trying to help the postman, who was stung by one of Admiral Leighton's bees while delivering his letters

147

earlier today. And if such information, Mrs. Blaine, does not convince you that you should be very careful about what you say in public, then may I point out that the admiral is crossing The Street at this moment, and heading this way."

Collapse of stout party. Mrs. Blaine gasped, and uttered a little squeak; Miss Nuttel's nostrils flared, and her face assumed an attitude of disinterest she was in truth far from feeling. Everyone else tried to look as if they'd had nothing to do with any accusations against anyone . . .

And by the time the Buzzard came through the door, the post office was once again a normal village shop—even if a few of the shoppers had a decidedly stupefied appearance.

Lady Colveden thought it no more than her duty to force home the message of the admiral's innocence by repeating, in his presence, the story of Bert's little mishap. She was as unprepared as anyone for his dismay.

"The cricket match? Too bad, too bad. Can't blame the bees, of course—instinct to sting, as I told Bert—self-defence, though just as painful, of course. But far worse for her than for him—they die afterwards, you know. Sting gets left behind as they pull away—unpleasant. And all my fault," he added, stroking his neat ginger beard and frowning. "What number did he play?"

The suddenness of his question took Lady Colveden by surprise. "Why, I really can't say—Mr. Jessyp and my son are responsible for the order, you see. With some help from my husband," honesty made her add, as she thought of Thursday evening. "As far as I recall, somewhere in the middle—but Mr. Stillman would know. He's one of our star bowlers—the only one, at the moment." And she introduced the admiral to the postmaster, who had been, from behind his metal grille, a delighted spectator of all that had previously been going on.

The two men at once became involved in a highly technical discussion which left their female audience almost totally baffled. Mr. Stillman, the admiral elicited with a little prompting, prided himself on his googlies; Admiral Leighton, as Mr. Stillman was delighted to discover, had been noted—when not at sea—for his chinamen.

"Best let Mr. Jessyp know, then, or young Nigel," said Mr. Stillman, with a grin. "Nigel usually carries his bat and makes a good score—hey, your ladyship?—but there's allus room for another good bowler, especially with Dan Eggleden out of things on account of his arm." And the admiral, with a modest smile, stroked his beard again and muttered that, as he was partly to blame for the loss of a man—and as redheaded men really should stick together—he might just follow Mr. Stillman's advice . . .

Mr. Jessyp, timetabling frantically, had taken his telephone off the hook, and Admiral Leighton hardly liked to arrive unheralded upon the doorstep of a man he'd never met. Nigel Colveden's parents, however, he already knew: and thus it was the Rytham Hall telephone which rang while Nigel was at lunch, Martha having earlier taken a message and told the Buzzard to ring back when Mr. Colveden was sure to be in.

Nigel bounced back to the table in high spirits. "Gosh, if he's even half as good as he says, we ought to wipe the floor with Murreystone tomorrow. What with Mr. Stillman's googlies, and the admiral's chinamen, it should more than make up for losing Dan, because he may be *fast*, but he's never been what you'd call *cunning*, has he? Fast bowling just wears the opposition down, but a good googly . . ."

"I think," said Lady Colveden, as her son pushed aside his plate and prepared to hunt out pencil and paper, "you'd better give me a translation. It all sounds faintly . . ." She groped for the *mot juste*, then remembered Mrs. Blaine. "Faintly ridiculous," she concluded. "Googlies, indeed!"

Nigel shook his head at her. "Just goes to show how wrong you can be. A googly is a special sort of leg-break—a slow-paced ball with a spin on it—that fools the batsman by looking like an ordinary leg-break till he's on the point of hitting it, when he realises it isn't, it's an off-break. So then he plays it wrong, and misses it, and the wicket-keeper stumps him."

"And he's out," supplied Lady Colveden, feeling pleased she'd understood something, at least.

Nigel grinned. "That's the intention, yes, but you have to be able to bowl genuine leg-breaks as well, otherwise the surprise element is lost. Mr. Stillman's jolly good at both sorts, luckily. Pretty good, when you consider—er, that is . . ." He caught his father's eloquent eye. "Well, it's pretty good, anyway."

His father, whose moustache had bristled as alarmingly as his eye had gleamed, subsided. Sir George was five years younger than the postmaster, but had less hair; not that he was sensitive about his age—of course not—but there was no need for the boy to carry on as if everyone over thirty had one foot in the grave. The Buzzard, now—bowled chinamen, did he? Should be a useful addition to the team. Best put Mr. Stillman on first, though. Just in case.

Nigel grinned at this display of military caution, but acknowledged there could be some sense to it.

Lady Colveden gave up trying to look as if she knew what they were talking about, and asked a direct question, which Nigel took it upon himself to answer. "A chinaman? Same sort of thing as a googly, but left-handed instead of right. Either of them works equally well, because the spin makes them more awkward to hit, with most people batting right-handed. So they can be jolly useful ways of getting them out." He scribbled a few arrows on his list of names and frowned. "We'll have to change the batting order *again*, Dad—the Buzzard says he's a hitter rather than a batsman. I'm bowling a few overs at him after supper to see how he shapes—but it's as well to have a contingency plan . . ."

And, despite all Lady Colveden's efforts to enjoy a civilised meal, her menfolk were too busy emulating the England Test selectors for these efforts to be worthwhile.

Saturday morning dawned bright and sunny, encouraging everyone to look forward to the afternoon's match whether or not they were playing, and whether or not they had reason to be busy. The Bloomers, among others, had. Martha, who'd spent the whole of the previous afternoon baking cakes, chivvied Stan up The Street with his whitewash almost before he'd finished breakfast. It was his job to mark out the cricket field's boundary line and creases, those distinguishing marks on the grass near which the stumps would stand, and from between which the bowler would deliver his ball. Stan, who took his job very seriously, marked everything with two coats; but some whitewash still remained at the end of his marking, so with his creasing brush he used the leftovers to refurbish the sight-screens, those large white boards at either end of the pitch, against which the red ball shows up in clear contrast as it hurtles towards the batsman. Satisfied with a job well done, he put the lid back on the empty whitewash bucket and headed for home.

Here he found Miss Treeves, the vicar's sister, discussing with Martha the best way to transport the tea urn to the pavilion, and where it should be plugged in to avoid water dripping—given the poor state of the roof—on the electric flex, if by some misfortune it should rain.

"It won't," said Stan, countryman born, farm worker and Plummergen sage. "Tomorrow night at the earliest . . ."

Which reassured both ladies: who nevertheless continued making plans at such a rate that Stan was glad of the chance to escape across the road to see to Miss Seeton's chickens.

Miss Seeton, who had to be in the right mood to read the newspapers because she found so much of what was printed rather dispiriting, was busy poring over the sports pages of the *Daily Negative,* which she had deliberately ordered that morning after Nigel told her it was sure to carry a report of the current England-Pakistan Test Match at the Oval. She wanted, she told Stan with a puzzled smile, to be in the right frame of mind.

"But I fear," she said, and sighed, "that it is somewhat beyond me—so many technical terms. And such strange names—the fielders, I mean. At least, I think I do, from what I understand, even though in another sense I know most of the words already." She shook her head as she peered at the newspaper. "Slip, and gulley, and backward short-leg, and silly mid-on, and deep mid-off—really, quite remarkable. And short third-man, which makes me think of the film . . ."

Stan, whose contribution to Plummergen cricket had never involved playing, nodded in sympathy for her confusion, and spoke of chickens, and the garden: whither he now went.

Miss Seeton was left to her study of cricketing terms, but soon realised she was achieving very little for all her hard work in trying to memorise them. She would—she decided—do just as she always did—sit happily watching from a deck chair near the boundary, enjoying the sunshine and the good company and the sheer comfort of belonging. She would take a sketchbook and pencils with her, and make notes of what she saw; and she was sure—at least, she hoped she was sure—that in due course she would be able to produce the required painting, which she would of course ask dear Nigel, and Sir George, to inspect before she finished it, so that they could tell her if there were too many errors of procedure in it—if that, brooded Miss Seeton, were the correct term. But it was too pleasant a day to brood for long . . .

Lunchtime came; and went. Those who planned to play ate less than the rest of their families; those who had jobs to do worried more. Would there be enough cakes, enough sandwiches? Would the sandwiches curl at the edges before anyone had time to eat them? Had extra milk been ordered—plenty of clean tea towels commandeered—the immersion heater for the washing up turned on?

By half past one, everybody with any business to be up at that end of the village was in the vicinity of Plummergen's playing field, at this season the cricket ground, in winter the football pitch. Deck chairs were set up by keen observers about the white-lined perimeter; people sat with wide-brimmed hats shielding their faces, and their rugs, which had been in other years all too often wrapped about their legs, underfoot, or forgotten in their cars. Miss Seeton, staking her claim to a convenient mid-field view, laid out a new sketchpad and her pencils on the grass, and prepared to relax in the sun, even if a deck chair—so kindly lent by Lady Colveden—was less comfortable, perhaps, than an ordinary folding chair might have been. One's spine—so little support—but the yoga, of course, had helped so much . . .

Because his son was otherwise engaged in the pavilion, it was Jack Crabbe's father, Very Young Crabbe—whose father, killed in the war, had been known as Young Crabbe; and whose grandfather, now in his nineties, was Old Crabbe—who drove the family coach in its familiar red-and-green livery into the parking space at the edge of the playing field and tootled the horn. Out poured the Murreystone team, their umpire, their scorer, their supporters. Plummergen eyed the invasion warily. Murreystone eyed them back.

Sir George produced the gold half-sovereign with which the home team always tossed; Mr. Jessyp bowed to his opposite number; the Murreystone captain voiced the ritual grumble that it might be double-headed, he'd just check, if it was all the same to them . . . tossed—and lost. And muttered.

Plummergen elected to field first.

"Play!" from the Murreystone umpire before Sir George could draw breath; and the match was on.

# chapter

# -21-

"THIS IS GOING to be exciting, isn't it, Aunt Em?" Anne had left her parents—the nursing home, in their absence, being under Major Howett's command—at the pavilion—Dr. Knight was one of the scorers, his wife helped with the teas—and come across to join Miss Seeton. The fact that Bob, fielding at deep mid-wicket, was easily visible from where his wife now elected to sit had nothing to do with this election: the adopted niece had promised yesterday afternoon, when taking tea with Bob at Sweetbriars, that she would be happy to lend moral support during the game, though if Aunt Em expected any detailed explanation of what was going on, she would be disappointed. Bob, after all, was a foot-baller and not a cricketer, though just as used to running around. She must watch his calorific intake at lunch very carefully.

Because Mr. Stillman of googly fame was bowling first, Mr. Jessyp had arranged a split field. "Just think of all the exercise they'll get," Anne said, with a chuckle. "Chasing after balls to the boundary—dashing from one side to the other at the end of each over when it's PC Potter's turn to bowl—they'll need their tea when the time comes!"

"Did somebody mention tea?" enquired a pleasant baritone voice from over her shoulder: and Chief Superintendent Delphick stood smiling down at Miss Seeton in her deck chair, at Anne curled up on her travelling rug. "Are we too late to watch Bob distinguish himself at the wicket?"

Anne and Miss Seeton looked beyond the Oracle to where Superintendent Brinton, smiling grimly and bearing a flask, and Foxon, struggling with three folding chairs, made their way towards the little group. "Mind if we join you?" Delphick enquired; and the ladies, naturally, said they did not.

Bob observed his colleagues' arrival from the corner of his eye and risked a quick wave before returning his attention to the play. Mr. Stillman, bowling from the pavilion end, was expected to have a few of the usual tricks up his sleeve once he'd got into his stride, and conscripted Bob didn't want to let the side down.

Foxon, who was starting to wish he'd come to Plummergen under his own steam instead of scrounging a lift, dropped his burden with a clatter, sighed, and observed Brinton's gleeful smirk. Trust Old Brimstone not to let him get too uppity, pub lunch with his superiors or no pub lunch. But they were all, he reminded himself as he unfolded the first chair, off-duty this afternoon . . . He hoped.

The game progressed as games of village cricket always do: a slow start, runs mounting one by one in PC Potter's overs, the occasional four when Mr. Stillman lost control of his off-break, a man out to a splendid catch by Nigel, at cover. Miss Seeton's pencil dashed across the paper so fast she had no time to join everyone else in the applause which rippled round the boundary as the Murreystone player tried hard not to show his disappoint-ment, marching back to the pavilion with his head held high.

Number Three fell four overs later to a mistimed swing at the ball, when he was smartly stumped by Jack Crabbe. Seventeen runs for two wickets. Plummergen began to look hopeful.

Mr. Stillman, however, began to look tired. He was con-scious that his responsibilities to the team were far greater than usual. PC Potter, when he bowled, was uninspired but steady, invariably producing medium-paced balls which were generally blocked, though sometimes yielded singles; Nigel, on a good day, might take the occasional wicket with a lucky leg-break. But Daniel Eggleden had always been Plummergen's other bowling mainstay, his blacksmith's arm complementing admirably the cunning tricks of a skilled off-break bowler, such as those perfected by the postmaster long before he perfected his even trickier googly. And Dan was out of this game . . . And being tricky all the time—knowing you had to be, that everyone relied on you to do so—was a serious matter for a man in his early sixties. Mr. Stillman had watched the admiral bowling to Nigel at practice, and been impressed; but how he would fare in real life remained to be seen. Mr. Stillman felt he must last as long as possible before asking Mr. Jessyp to put the Buzzard on, just in case; and Mr. Jessyp, who had only Nigel's word for it that the newest member of the team was no passenger, intended to err on the side of caution. When Mr. Stillman started to turn pink in the face, the captain called for Nigel to bowl in his place, and to alternate with PC Potter, happy to plod on from over to over, for the next half dozen.

A six! The Murreystone batsman struck a mighty boundary off Nigel's second ball. Young Mr. Colveden pulled an apologetic face: he had never been more than a competent bowler, even at school. Dan Eggleden glared at his plaster-casted arm and brooded on past glories when the speed and power of his delivery had terrified the opposition. Twenty-eight for two: and Murreystone cheered.

"It sounds to me," Delphick said, as Nigel's third ball was snicked between short and square legs for two, "as if we weren't the only ones to stop off in a pub on the way here."

"I *thought* Very Young Crabbe looked rather fed up when the bus arrived," said Anne. "The silly chumps! If they've spent all lunchtime drinking . . ."

"Presumably, Potter would consider it hardly cricket to breathalyse such supporters as arrive under their own steam, but I trust Murreystone intends to take no unfair advantage of his good nature." Delphick's glance travelled over the cars which were still entering the ground and being parked a convenient distance from the white line of the boundary, to give the occupants a clear view of the field. "Some of the newcomers appear to be a little on the, er, lively side."

Brinton muttered something; Foxon secretly rejoiced that he hadn't worn his smartest clothes, then changed his mind as a perfectly gorgeous girl—blue eyes, long blonde hair, golden skin—walked by, stopped, backtracked, and greeted Miss Seeton with a smile. Annabelle Leigh had come to watch Nigel's afternoon of glory—if such it was to be, though he had modestly warned her there were heaps better players than himself—and, like Miss

Seeton, carried her sketchbook with her. Miss Seeton returned the greeting and introduced her to her companions as an artist friend of young Mr. Colveden.

Foxon, gallant in disappointment, nevertheless offered Miss Leigh his chair, but she thanked him, glanced at his superior officers as if to emphasise the courtesy of their subordinate, and said she would prefer watching from nearer the pavilion, whither she was now bound.

"Just a moment, Miss Leigh!" Delphick's quick warning startled her, and she almost dropped her sketchbook as she halted in her tracks. "No movement, please, in the vicinity of the sight-screens until change of over—it distracts the batsmen." And Annabelle's blushing apology was one of the prettiest Foxon had ever seen.

Nigel's three overs were done, with a loss to Plummergen of another eight runs, but without a wicket: the sight of Annabelle had inspired—or possibly distracted—him. And PC Potter likewise had allowed Murreystone to score eight off his bowling, for no wicket. Forty-six for two.

Murreystone were becoming ever more vocal, and one or two car horns sounded. Plummergen faces were downcast. Mr. Jessyp made up his mind. He altered the field, and crossed mental fingers.

The admiral rolled up his sleeves, took the ball, flexed his physical fingers, ran up, bowled . . .

Forty-six for three. "Good man!" from Sir George, forgetting umpirical impartiality, above the claps and cheers of Plummergen. Murreystone murmured, and consoled itself with the flasks and bottles brought by its supporters in picnic baskets and carrier bags.

Fifth man hadn't expected his innings to start so soon and was still buckling on his pads in the pavilion when his predecessor marched up the steps. There was a pause, during which Plummergen regarded the Buzzard in a new light. Could he perform the miracle it seemed Mr. Stillman was, for once, unable to work?

Number Five took guard. Twice, to a warning frown from Sir George; but the admiral ignored this feeble attempt at gamesmanship. He bowled again.

Plummergen sat up. Murreystone scowled. Forty-six for four. Number Five turned to gape at his spread-eagled wicket, observed Sir George's signalling finger and the glum face of his own umpire, and trudged back to the pavilion.

A longer pause, while Number Six nerved himself for the Ordeal by Admiral. Plummergen began to cough, loudly and in meaningful tones. Murreystone murmured, more loudly. Number Six strode to the wicket . . .

"A hat-trick!" All save the ranks of Tuscany cheered as the Buzzard's third wicket in succession fell. "And off his first three balls—good man!" Delphick said, clapping as loud as anyone.

"And in the first match he's ever played for Plummergen, what's more." Anne was bouncing with glee. "Didn't I tell you, Aunt Em, that this was going to be exciting?"

"Indeed you did, my dear." Even Miss Seeton, who understood so little of the game, realised that village history had just been made—could hardly help but realise it, from all the commotion, the clapping and cheers, around the field as the admiral tossed the ball in the air with a nonchalant action, turned to face the score-board, and bowed as he watched the numbers being changed. Miss Seeton's pencil flew again across the paper.

Delphick had heard in the pub something of the admiral's romantic last-minute membership of the Plummergen eleven, and was curious to know how this newcomer to the village appeared in the eyes of Scotland Yard's tame art consultant. Miss Seeton, so much shorter than he, so absorbed in her work, was unaware of his interest, and did not notice him leaning quietly to one side to look over her shoulder at the sketchbook on her knee.

The Buzzard's acknowledgement of the applause for his hat-trick had clearly caught the artist's fancy. A beaming, bearded face looked out of the paper, attached to a body obviously about to bend at the waist: a waist across which the folded arm displayed a proud anchor—a tattoo, it seemed to Delphick. It was curious that Miss Seeton had drawn the pavilion and scoreboard behind the admiral, instead of in their proper place: but this, the chief superintendent decided, must be because she wanted to show a flag—the White Ensign, he thought, emblem of the Royal Navy—flying from a flagpole on the roof—a flagpole the pavilion did not possess. And what else seemed to be flying in

Miss Seeton's imagination and not in real life? Small, winged, rounded, striped insects . . .

Delphick had just made up his mind that these were honey bees when Miss Seeton, having completed one sketch, turned to a fresh sheet ready for her next. Out on the field, the admiral was bowling again, and Number Seven looked apprehensive; but he managed to block the ball, and for the rest of the over no more wickets fell. As the admiral tossed the ball to PC Potter, the pencil darted again across the paper: action sketches, rough and swift but full of life, thought Delphick with interest. The admiral leaning forward, poised on one foot, one hand outflung, fingers spread, the ball just released; the admiral preparing to bowl, his arm swinging up and round for the delivery, a glint in his eye. Was this, the Oracle wondered, the satisfaction of a man who had done a good job well, and planned to do still better—or was there some hidden cause for satisfaction in the smile of Admiral Leighton? It was hard to be sure. The paper was very white and glaring in the hot August sunshine . . .

Miss Seeton looked up, observed Delphick's eyes on her, and blushed. Hurriedly, he begged her pardon, and sat back to watch PC Potter's next over: which was as uneventful as most of his others had been. No wickets, a few runs, restless murmurings from Murreystone . . .

Miss Seeton dabbed daintily at the back of her neck with a lace-edged handkerchief and blinked at the paper in front of her. On such a day as this, perhaps one should have worn a broad-brimmed hat, or brought a parasol . . .

"Excuse me," Miss Seeton murmured to Delphick at her side. "But—the over, you know. I recall that you warned Miss Leigh—and I was wondering—my umbrella—only you told her she should not move, and . . ."

The field was taking rather longer to rearrange itself than usual. It was therefore with a clear conscience that Delphick was able to assure Miss Seeton no harm would come of his taking the gold umbrella hooked neatly over the back of her deck chair, opening it, and balancing the handle under a convenient canvas seam. It would never do, he reminded her, for one of Scotland Yard's favourite colleagues to suffer an attack of sunstroke.

Miss Seeton smiled at him and settled thankfully into the shade. She didn't want to miss a single movement made by the admiral, who was, one understood, so very clever . . .

When the admiral took the ball again, his previous sparkling form seemed to have mellowed a little. Now he bowled nothing but off-breaks, and there were no more wickets. There were, however, no more runs. PC Potter, fired by this example, himself bowled a maiden over: no runs.

Plummergen began to preen itself, Murreystone to mutter. People who had never watched a cricket match in their lives now began to appear, by some mysterious village alchemy, at various points about the boundary, intent on watching: while the admiral bowled his third over, it seemed that most of Plummergen's five hundred-odd inhabitants were positioning themselves about the playing field to watch.

The Buzzard did not disappoint his audience. There was a sneaky Murreystone single—fifty-four for five—and then he produced another chinaman: and another. Fifty-four for six! Plummergen jumped up and down as Len Hosigg at short mid-wicket flung out a hand and caught the ball—might this be the start of another hat-trick?

Everyone held their breath as the Buzzard prepared to run up again. Suddenly, from the Murreystone clique on the other side of the field came a fanfare of car horns that made him miss his step, and drop the ball. As Murreystone tried to appear innocent, and Plummergen muttered, the admiral, bending towards his dropped ball, looked towards the umpires. "Didn't reach the crease," he called. "All right if I just carry on?" Sir George seemed ready to signal yes, but the Murreystone umpire looked set to argue. The two conferred together while everyone waited, and the car horns sounded again: which decided Sir George, who wasn't normally given to riding roughshod over the opinions of others. But gamesmanship wasn't the thing at all, and he was dashed if he was going to encourage it, or to allow anyone to benefit from it.

"Carry on," he instructed; and there came not a syllable of disagreement from the other umpire.

But the interruption had rather thrown Admiral Leighton off his stride. No-ball. He threw an apologetic glance towards Mr. Jessyp, tugged ruefully at his beard, scowled in the direction of Murreystone, and sent down three unplayable balls, though without taking a wicket. PC Potter bowled the next over: two runs more, no wicket, though the batsmen were beginning to look nervous. The admiral bowled another maiden—Potter then gave away four runs, but to his astonishment took a wicket; and the admiral, calculating the likely strength of the Murreystone tail from the next man's apparent unease, suggested to Mr. Jessyp that Mr. Stillman might like to go on again, for a share in the fun. The captain agreed.

The tail-end batsmen weren't the complete rabbits every-one had expected—sheer frustration made them hit harder, and last longer, than any of them had ever done before—but were nevertheless no great challenge. Alternating overs, Mr. Stillman and the admiral, PC Potter and Nigel, dismissed the rest of Murreystone for a grand total of seventy-eight runs, one of their lowest scores in years. Nigel's leg-break, to his delight, accounted for one of these final wickets: he hoped that Annabelle had been watching. But the undoubted hero of the Plummergen hour was Admiral Leighton, whose back was slapped in congratulation all the way back from the bowling crease to the pavilion.

Tea, served by the Plummergen ladies, took half an hour. Delphick, being advised that Martha Bloomer's fruitcake was for players only, shamelessly pulled rank and persuaded Bob to surrender his slice, reminding him that Anne was worried about his weight. With Mrs. Knight watching, poor Bob had little choice but to comply with his superior's demands.

Help, however, was at hand. Nigel, keeping an eye open for Annabelle, observed the entire episode; and, as he came to realise that his lady was reluctant to make her appearance among so many strangers, reverted to his vice captain's per-sona, grabbed an extra plate and a second slice of fruitcake, and hurried across the tearoom to join his friends, handing Bob, with a grin, what he insisted would help to keep his strength up.

"We don't expect a century, but we do expect fireworks," he said, as Bob tried to hide behind him from his mother-in-law's eagle eye. "Brilliant strokes, of course—the odd six, if you feel you can manage it, though a few fours would do. We've seventy-nine runs to make to win, remember."

Bob, swallowing surreptitious crumbs, tried to protest that he wasn't the firework type. Delphick kindly thumped him on the back. "Your favourite adopted aunt, remember," he told his red-faced and wheezing subordinate, "has been commissioned to portray the highlights of this match for the benefits of the Plummergen Pavilion Fund. I should imagine the sight of her nephew in action must inspire her to great things, and Anne—should modesty prevent your own participation—will bid vast sums at the auction in order to gain possession of the prize."

Then he noticed Nigel's expression and chuckled. "Your Miss Leigh, I gather, is of course also an artist. Might one hope for two prize pictures, instead of one, in two distinct artistic styles? If the pair of you," he said wickedly, "feel too bashful to place your own bids, but prefer to be sure of procuring the odd heirloom to hand on to your grandchildren, I would be only too happy to oblige . . ."

At which remark, the number of blushing male faces turned towards him promptly doubled.

# chapter

# -22-

DELPHICK CHATTED WITH his two young friends until the end of tea, when everyone trooped back outside. Charley Mountfitchet and Mr. Jessyp were the traditional Plummergen openers; they could expect to push the score up to the high teens or early twenties before one or other of them fell—the one usually being Charley, who once, in his youthful prime, had made the mistake of carrying his bat and making fifty-two runs, winning the match almost single-handed—and discovering, after he was clapped back to the pavilion, that his teammates had drunk all the cider. Whereupon he vowed never again to run such a risk, saying that twenty would in any future game be the highest he was prepared to reach.

The Plummergen innings opened. Miss Seeton, shaded by her umbrella from the sun, sat with her pencil poised, watching and waiting for something to happen. She did not have long to wait. Mr. Jessyp was clean-bowled for seven; and Bob Ranger, coming in at number three, took the schoolmaster's place. Charley, startled by his partner's early dismissal, was caught off the final ball of the over by the Murreystone slip, running backwards with his arms upflung: twenty-three for two. Out now came the fourth man: Nigel Colveden. And everyone settled down to enjoy themselves.

Everyone from Plummergen, that is. Murreystone knew what to expect from Mr. Colveden, and were reluctant to settle. There was a restless air about the visitors, as if a too-tight lid had been slapped on a pot of bubbling pasta, which might at any moment erupt.

Bob, who'd said all along he'd have a go at hitting but didn't claim to be a batsman, had already made three runs and was relieved there would be no duck marked on his scoresheet. He was even more relieved to see Nigel appear at the other crease. Now he could relax and do as he'd been told when he and Nigel—with considerable help from Delphick—had discussed tactics at tea: try to stick to singles so that the better batsman— here Nigel's natural modesty had been subsumed into his vice captain's persona—could face the bowling as often as possible.

This plan worked well, for the next half-dozen overs. Mr. Colveden made twenty-seven, including two sixes; Sergeant Ranger made another nine—seven singles and a daring two. Perhaps he was getting the hang of it at last. Miss Seeton's pencil captured his look of pleasure as those mighty shoulders powered the ball between two fielders. Anne, watching on the boundary, was pink with excitement.

Bob, too, was growing excited: and excitement made him careless. Towards the end of the partnership's seventh over he hit out harder than he'd intended. Crack! of leather on willow, and the ball flew away. Bob realised he might make another two, if he ran fast. For all his size, he felt he might risk it. "Yes!" he cried, and pounded down the pitch with a broad grin on his face.

He and Nigel crossed, and reached their respective wickets safely. Nigel drew breath—turned to prepare himself to receive the first ball of the next over—saw Bob, to his dismay, already halfway back—knew himself far better able to manoeuvre at speed than his enormous friend—set off on a frantic sprint over those vital twenty-two yards . . .

"Oh, no!" Delphick groaned; Anne squeaked; Foxon cursed his colleague's clumsiness. "Bob, you idiot!"

Scarlet-faced, Bob dropped his bat and gestured in helpless apology as the Murreystone bowler caught the fielded ball and dashed it in triumph squarely on the bails. Nigel set his teeth, shrugged, and walked back to the pavilion as his father raised a sorrowful, the Murreystone umpire a joyful, finger.

"Silly juggins," said Dr. Knight of his son-in-law, as he sat over the score sheet in the pavilion. And against "Colveden" he wrote, sadly but firmly, *"run out."*

Number Five was Len Hosigg, a silent, steady young man who

normally took great pride in his stonewalling partnership with Nigel, leaving him to score all the runs while he blocked every ball at the other end; but Len hadn't expected to be going out to bat so early in the game, and certainly not with somebody other than Nigel as his partner. Nigel grabbed him as he was treading thoughtfully down the pavilion steps.

"Look, Len, Bob's not afraid to hit out, so let him try to go on making runs, and you just, er, act as if he's me. And—and don't worry!"

But Len looked decidedly worried as he headed for the crease and for partnership with the man who'd run out the son of his employer. Not a stranger, no, not with him having married the doctor's daughter: but not someone whose play poor Len knew anything about. He'd try to do as Nigel had instructed him, of course, but . . .

Suddenly, from the opposite side of the field came a commotion which halted him in his tracks. There was a series of whoops and yells from the Murreystoners, and

"Stop that man!" The major-general's command came in the old parade-ground voice as the figure erupted from among the Murreystone supporters to hurtle, pink and panting, between the startled fielders. *Very* pink—flesh pink, with the occasional hirsute shadowing . . .

"Good Gad! A streaker!" From the verandah steps came the booming voice of the admiral. "You! You there—stop!"

Consternation among the Plummergenites by the pavilion, amusement among the Murreystone ranks both on and off the field. The young man with no clothes on was moving so fast, weaving and dodging, that nobody seemed able to pull themselves together to grab him, and indeed appeared to be making little effort to do so. His friends urged him on with ribald shouts and yodelled view-halloos. Car horns tootled. There were whistles and catcalls.

The streaker streaked on. Len Hosigg recovered his wits and threw down his bat, running to intercept him. For some strange reason, he found his path impeded by the Murreystone fielders, who seemed unable to decide on a concerted course of action. Plummergen, seeing this, rose growling to its feet and followed Len. The streaker whooped, and swerved.

"He's coming this way!" Anne jumped up. "Oh, Bob—for goodness' sake, do something!"

"He'd better," muttered Delphick, who considered himself twenty years too old for such goings-on. At his side Brinton, likewise, was unprepared to hurl himself into the fray. He glowered at Foxon.

"Don't just sit there staring, laddie—after him!"

"Er," said Foxon, bemused, as the streaker pranced from silly mid-off to silly mid-on and back again, doubling in his tracks, thumbing his nose at Len Hosigg, easily avoiding the enormous Bob who, like Len, found the fielders very much in his way. "Er, I'm off-duty, sir," said Foxon, stifling giggles. "So's Bob Ranger—and Potter . . ."

Brinton turned purple. "And what the hell—sorry," to Miss Seeton and Anne, "has that got to do with anything?"

"No—no helmets, sir," chortled Foxon, as Len made a desperate lunge, and the streaker slipped from his grasp with a shrug and a wriggle. Murreystone roared approval as Sir George's young farm foreman stared, bewildered, at his hands. "He'll have g-greased himself, sir," said Foxon, choking. "Lard, or s-something . . ."

"I'll lard you, laddie, if you don't get after him this minute!"

"But, sir—we've got nothing to c-cover—to hide . . ." And then Foxon gave up the struggle and collapsed, writhing, on the rug beside Anne: who looked from the hysterical young detective at her feet, to the staring faces of the spectators around the field, to the ominous closing-in of the Plummergen males upon the pale and prancing, jeering figure heading in her direction: and acted.

"Aunt Em, do you mind?" And she snatched the umbrella from its place, gripping it by the handle, spike foremost. She turned, a tiny toreador, to face the onrush of the naked Murreystone bull. She pointed the umbrella directly towards him and twirled it menacingly. The streaker saw her; and for the first time hesitated.

"Bob!" cried Anne, as she ran onto the field; and her husband, jerked out of his trance by her cry, came pounding towards the nude intruder, with other Plummergenites not far behind, Len Hosigg in the van.

"Butter!" Len yelled his warning as Bob prepared to hurl himself upon the streaker, who had realised that Anne's advance now blocked any direct escape, but who had not realised just how many spectators had been arriving to block the Plummergen side of the ground in recent minutes. The streaker dithered—Bob gathered himself together and pounced—an avalanche of Plummergen joined him; and the streaker vanished beneath a heap of shouting, writhing white flannels.

Sir George and the Murreystone umpire were on the scene, trying to restore order. The streaker emerged from the fray far less pink, stained green with grass and brown with dried mud, but bare as he had ever been. Anne rushed up with Miss Seeton's umbrella and positioned it quickly over such regions as required its protection, while the Plummergenites seized the streaker by his arms. All traces of butter seemed to have been rubbed off in the turmoil, for his struggles now to escape had little effect; the episode was over. Once he was marched to the boundary, and decency restored, the game could continue . . .

"Behind you!" Delphick, jumping to his feet, made a megaphone out of his hands, and his warning carried far over the ground. Plummergen looked behind: and saw the Murreystoners, angry at their rakish representative's rough reception, flooding on to the field, while the fielders stood and let them pass unhindered.

And, in a case of invasion, what else could the defending forces be expected to do but retaliate?

Foxon had stopped laughing and was clambering to his feet; Brinton and Delphick were already standing. From all around the Plummergen side, muttering male spectators started to converge on the Murreystone streaker and his friends as they hastened to his support . . .

PC Potter cast an anguished look towards his superiors. Miss Seeton clicked her tongue. The eyes of Sir George met those of the admiral as the noted ginger beard appeared in the throng of later arrivals from the pavilion steps.

"Silence in the ranks!" roared Sir George. "Silence, I say! Halt! Atten*shun*!"

The roar so startled his hearers that, Plummergen and Murreystone alike, every single one stopped dead, exactly where they were. In the subsequent breathing space the admiral, not to be outdone, bellowed:

"Belay there, the lower deck, or I'll keelhaul every man jack of you!"

The breathing space continued for a few tense moments, while all present held their breath. Then Murreystone looked at Plummergen, and began to grumble; and Plummergen looked at Murreystone, and began to mutter again.

And then, above the rising tide of discontent which the quick wits of the two former officers had but temporarily stemmed, the voice of Anne was suddenly heard.

"If this man isn't off the field within half a minute, he'll be *dead*." She twirled the umbrella as she spoke. "Of exposure!"

There was a pause. Not only was the speaker a female—and a tiny female, at that—but everyone in Plummergen knew her for the doctor's daughter, and a nurse. Much of Murreystone was also privy to that knowledge. And something about the way she'd said her piece caught the fancy of the rivals. There was another pause, for baleful eyeing of one another; then the various factions, repeating her remark to savour it better, began to laugh. Those who had the streaker by the arms allowed him to raise them in a victory salute above his head, before grabbing at him again; Anne continued to hold Miss Seeton's umbrella in a strategic position, smiling as she did so; Sir George started to wave the Murreystone supporters back to their places; the Murreystone umpire motioned at Plummergen to follow suit. Those spectators who hadn't stirred from their seats voiced the opinion that it took all sorts, they supposed, though a joke was a joke and they did really ought to be getting on with the game now . . .

It took time for everyone to settle; but, slowly, settle they did. The streaker was escorted towards the dressing room, and a detachment sent in search of his clothes. There was a continuing air of suppressed excitement over the little cricket ground, and Plummergen males bemoaned their lack of eyes in the back of the head to look out for what Murreystone might try next.

"Let's hope," growled Brinton, as he, Foxon, Delphick, and Miss Seeton watched the fielders start to reposition themselves, "the blighters don't try any more daft tricks. It was touch and go there for a while, if you ask me."

"Not quite so easy to *touch*, at first," remarked Delphick, watching Len Hosigg hunting for the bat he'd flung down in his excitement. "It might be considered rather cheering to learn that the old country customs die so hard, even in the nineteen-seventies. Your ancestors, Chris—indeed, all our ancestors, if we trace back to our rural roots—used to grease a pig at fair time and run after the poor creature, grabbing and snatching until, as in this case, enough of the grease had rubbed off for the winner to keep hold of it. No fear of starvation for a while with so much pork to smoke and pickle and cure . . ."

Foxon snorted suddenly. "B-bacon, sir," he gasped, as the dangerous eye of Superintendent Brinton directed itself upon him. "I just thought—when Mr. Delphick said about curing—not so much *streaky* bacon, sir, as streak*er*. Sir." And he hastily stifled further evidence of mirth, though he didn't miss the twinkle in Miss Seeton's eye and the chuckle in Delphick's voice as he replied:

"Mr. Brinton would no doubt wish to, er, *tan* the young man's backside for him . . . But let us hope—" in a more serious voice— "there will be no repetition of the incident, whether here or any where else. The imagination boggles at what would happen if such a scene were to take place, say, at a Test Match." He smiled. "Though I've no doubt the commentators would cope in their own inimitable fashion: one can almost *hear* John Arlott. 'Oh, we've got a streaker down the wicket. Not very shapely, and it's masculine . . .' And a detailed description of the offender's removal from the scene. Arlott, of course, is a former policeman . . ."

But there came no reply. Everyone was too busy watching Len Hosigg, his bat retrieved, take guard. Len's normally equable temperament was roused by what had just happened: so much so, indeed, that he not only managed to block the ball, but even to hit it—and with force. Plummergen sat up. Lily Hosigg squeezed baby Dulcie Rose so hard in her excitement that the infant yelped The sun, brighter than ever, glistened on Len's well-oiled bat and gleamed on the white numbers of the pavilion scoreboard as they were altered yet again . . .

Len made—to his surprise—seven runs before falling at the end of his third over to a vicious—though possibly accidental—high beamer. He returned to the pavilion covered in glory and loudly applauded. Bob, meanwhile, still suffering pangs of conscience about having run Nigel out, found them overcome by annoyance at Murreystone's behaviour, and walloped everything he could, adding another ten before Len was dismissed.

So that when PC Potter headed out to join his colleague at the crease, the score was seventy-six for four.

Three more runs, and Plummergen would win the match.

# chapter
# –23–

THE PLUMMERGEN SPECTATORS began to murmur. The Murreystone contingent was conspicuously silent. Inside the pavilion, Lady Colveden and the rest of the washing-up team—into which Anne, still chuckling at the streaker's behaviour, had been conscripted by her mother—cast aside tea towels and squeezy mops and crowded to the windows to watch.

Potter took guard. The Murreystone bowler, having run out of legitimate tricks, in desperation deliberately sent down a low, fast, potentially lethal bouncer. Breath hissed between Plummergen teeth. Going to play dirty, were they? But Potter could stonewall as well as Len Hosigg, when he had to: and he had to now. He successfully blocked the bouncer, and sighed with relief: no run, but no wicket.

The second ball arrived in similar fashion, and there was increased muttering among the spectators. Bob, at the other end, could have sworn he'd felt the air hiss as the bowler's arm whirled in its delivery arc and the ball missed his ear by less than an inch. He gulped, and blinked, and followed its flight with a horrified eye—an eye then distracted by a movement just out of his direct vision, in the vicinity of the sight-screen. Who on earth knew so little about cricket that they'd wander around in the middle of an over, and at such an important point in the match, as well?

"Miss Seeton," breathed Bob, as the Murreystone bowler began his third run-up. What on earth did Aunt Em think she was playing at, trotting along the boundary in the direction of the pavilion, innocent as Dulcie Rose Hosigg of what was going on? Why on earth didn't somebody . . . ?

Somebody—more than a few somebodies—did. "Miss Seeton!" was hissed from half a hundred throats, and hands signalled furiously as the little spinster, her hat tilted over her eyes, stopped, and turned, and gazed about her at the friendly waves. Smiling, she nodded, and waved back.

But once she'd stopped walking, everyone lost interest in her. All eyes returned to the pitch, where Potter stood bracing himself for the fourth ball of the over. He'd clipped the third past forward short-leg, only to have it fielded by the bowler, who was now polishing it on his trousers, ready to hurl it down again. Bob, rubbing a thoughtful ear, moved even farther from the wicket than he'd been for the earlier balls, holding his breath.

Down came the ball, scorching through the air. Potter automatically flinched as it approached him; Bob winced as he followed its flight—a flight for once mistimed. The ball bounced early, and, much to Potter's relief, shot safely past. Bob watched the dark red dot sizzle across the white sight-screen, presumably to thump to the ground: *presumably,* because he never knew for sure. "Miss Seeton!" he groaned between his teeth, as the little figure emerged from the other side of the sight-screen and continued on its way to the pavilion . . .

"Hey!" Bob's yell startled even himself. "The pavilion!" Bat in hand, he came thundering out of his crease down the pitch, past Potter—who spun round to look, saw what Bob had seen, and galloped, shouting, in his wake—towards the pavilion, on the verandah and steps of which the entire Plummergen team and their supporters sat enjoying the sunshine of an August afternoon, the prospect of an early victory, and thoughts of a celebratory evening in the pub. The tea ladies crowded the open windows, chattering with excitement; even Dr. Knight, scoring with his Murreystone opposite number, had carried score book and pencils and table out of doors . . .

And if everyone was either sitting outside, or clearly visible inside—who were those people glimpsed in furtive silhouette through the wide panes of the changing-room windows?

Even as Bob first yelled, the figures stopped being furtive and began, clearly, to fight. Two, perhaps three, silhouettes struggled and swayed to and fro against the light as the batsmen abandoned

the wicket with a shout and a rush, their cries raising the alarm
even as their fellow players sitting on the pavilion steps started to
suspect that something was wrong, and hurried to find out what
that something might be.

At exactly the same time, however, Lady Colveden and her
colleagues were hurrying from the kitchen in an attempt to learn
what was causing all the uproar. And when too many people try
to charge in opposite directions through the same door at the
same time, the intruders after whom some of the the chargers
might, given the chance, wish to go in pursuit are warned well
in advance of such pursuit, and have ample opportunity to make
their escape through the same back door by which they originally
entered.

Which is what happened on this occasion. Bob, Potter, and the
Murreystone fielders—who had at last cottoned on to the fact that
this was serious—could see, as they drew near the pavilion, the
changing-room windows very clearly, and shouted to those on the
steps and in the doorway that the quarry was making a break for it
and ought to be headed off.

"Tally ho!" cried Sir George, as game as any but twenty years
older than most, his pace slowing. There was nothing, however,
wrong with his hearing: he knew the sounds of a gunned engine
and a retreating vehicle when he heard them. "Tally ho!"

"View halloo!" responded the admiral, to whom the same
applied; and he brandished a ferocious bat, requisitioned from
the general stock. "After them, at the double!"

Delphick and Brinton, joining them some moments later, felt
little difference between themselves and their friends. The senior
branch of the Plummergen Protection League stood panting and
blown as the younger men grabbed cricket bats and spare stumps
and tore round to the rear of the pavilion uttering bloodcurdling
cries. Some of the ladies, inspired by the example of their menfolk,
snatched up serving spoons and other kitchen implements before
rushing after them with these makeshift weapons, although Anne,
who hadn't returned Miss Seeton's umbrella before she'd been
coerced into the kitchen detail, was better equipped than most.

Yet, run as fast as they might, none ran fast enough to catch the
fleeing figures in the car nobody recognised as belonging to either
village—the car which, screeching on two wheels as it scraped

through the playing-field gateway, turned left into The Street and headed south.

"After them!" Sir George's command outroared Brinton, who'd been trying to suggest exactly the same thing. Those who had car keys about their persons veered off at speed towards their individual vehicles, with quick-witted friends following in their wake; cricketers—with keys in mufti pockets in the changing-room—and ladies—with no keys at all, save in the pockets of husbands and sons—hesitated—stared about them—and were gathered up by Pied Piper Jack Crabbe as he sprinted for the red-and-green coach where his father, who had been a bemused spectator of the rout, was clambering into the driver's seat, the keys in his waiting hand.

"Come on!" cried Jack, and they came: car-less cricketers—fleet-footed spectators—tea ladies rattling spoons—and Sir George Colveden, who'd realised what was about to happen and was having none of it.

"No, Meg! Anne, Mrs. Knight—not a show for women." The major-general had found his second wind and cut across to reach the door of the coach just as the last man scrambled up the steps.

"But—"

"No, Meg!" Nimbly, Sir George blocked his wife's path and banged the flat of his hand against red-and-green metal. "Carry on, Crabbe!"

"But—"

"Crabbe, drive on!" The baronet's bellow drowned out his wife's protest and the start of another from Anne, who frantically waved Miss Seeton's umbrella as if bidding with it for the right to participate in whatever slaughter might eventually ensue. Very Young Crabbe—who, though his father died in the war, had enjoyed every minute of his National Service—was deaf to the voice of his son at his side, his ears tuned only to the military tones of Sir George. Former Lance-corporal Crabbe, obedient to command, first pulled the lever which closed the coach door, as regulations required, then released the brake, revved the engine, and began to spin the steering wheel, ready to send the coach chasing after everyone else, grass flying up from beneath whirring tyres as he skidded and for one desperate moment looked like slipping backwards.

The squeal of the tyres, the roar of the diesel exhaust drowned out any remonstrance or argument of the female persuasion; and before they could die away, Sir George was gone, leaping into the back seat of Brinton's police car as Foxon slammed on the brakes and Delphick flung open the door, beckoning wildly.

"Bob, wait!" But her husband ignored Anne's cry as he swept past in their little car with the admiral beside him, and PC Potter squeezed in the back, urging his colleague to keep up with Brinton and the rest. Very Young Crabbe, with Jack still shouting to let him drive because he knew this coach better than his father, finally moved off in juddering slow motion. With a swirl, a rush, and a rumble, the field was almost empty of pursuers and pursued.

Those who remained—tea ladies, older or more cautious spectators, assorted pedestrians—were divided in what to do next. Lady Colveden, after some discussion, led the Domestic Detachment back to the pavilion to find out what on earth had been going on in the changing-room; others hurried to that side of the cricket ground bordering the road, or crowded towards the gate, to see what they could of the chase once Crabbe's coach was out of the way. It was unlikely, some said, that the foremost car, having made—it seemed—a successful escape, would turn round and come back north again rather than lead its pursuers a merry dance around the southern marsh byways: but the unlikely, others pointed out, in Plummergen could not be called unknown.

And then it seemed, from all the noise, the hooting of horns and the screaming of tyres, that the unknown might be about to occur yet again . . .

The Street is wide, more or less straight, and well over half a mile long. If a fugitive car speeds south to warn accomplices still in the area, and passes these accomplices heading north in search of their missing friends, it is not impossible that neatly spun steering wheels will produce convenient U-turns, if sufficiently emphatic warning is hooted as the paths of said vehicles cross.

Which is what happened. The car from the cricket pavilion—a Hillman—speeding to raise the alarm, spotted its complementary Commer van coming the other way, braked, skidded in one of the tightest circles The Street had ever seen, and prepared to follow-the-leader north. The Commer, which had not been expecting anything of the sort to occur, found itself stalled as, responding to the Hillman's hooted warning, it attempted the same manoeuvre in reverse. The Hillman squeaked past the Commer with no more than half an inch between, hesitated, then carried on northwards as the cars from the cricket ground drew closer.

The Commer's engine, with a splutter, started, and the van was wrenched the rest of the way round to the south with seconds to spare. The first wave of cricketing cars was now upon it—was braking, and pulling on steering wheels, and trying to get out of the way—was (in part) safely past. But other cars, in the slower second wave, failed to pass in safety. Even as Foxon and Bob, driving in the more cautious third wave, arrived at the scene, a concertina of cars collided one after the other with the Commer, all with their bonnets facing south, to the shock and dismay of those cars which had continued to the south and, hearing the series of crashes from behind, had turned and were heading back north again towards the giant metallic sandwich which had suddenly spread itself all down the eastern side of Plummergen's Street.

And then the Hillman reappeared from the north, making again for the south because Very Young Crabbe, struggling to complete the turn out of the narrow gateway, had blocked The Street's northern end . . .

Before Bob and Foxon had finished discharging their top-brass passengers in an attempt to control the chaos, the Hillman was upon them—was braking, pulling on the steering wheel, trying to get out of the way—was about to make it—was panicked by the sudden sight of the cars returning from the south, and swerved noisily into the side of the Commer van at the head of the concertina, though there should have been ample room for it to pass in safety. For Plummergen's Street, it must be recalled, is unusually wide . . .

Wide enough for Crabbe's red-and-green coach to lumber safely past the crunch and scream and petrol-smell of mangled metal, because Very Young Crabbe—holding to his overtaking right of way, since the crash was contained to only one side of the road—was slow to take notice of the warnings of his son; and equally slow to apply the brakes, or to pull on the steering wheel. It was

not until the coach had gone well past that Jack succeeded in per-
suading his father to brake, and to turn, and to stop and see what
on earth was going on back there, and did they ought to let their
passengers disembark to join in . . .

It was a good fight, while it lasted.

# chapter
# -24-

WHEN THE DUST had settled, Murreystone and Plummergen found themselves, for the first time in over three hundred years, united. To everyone's astonishment and surprise, they stood intermingled in a menacing circle about the battle-scarred occupants of the Hillman car and the Commer van, with their only feeling towards one another mutual congratulation.

It had been the buckling of the Commer's rear doors when the Hillman hit it which made Plummergen lose its collective temper. After the series of crashes, once the Hill-men and the Commers were seen to have suffered no serious damage—the speed with which they scrambled from their vehicles and tried to flee was taken as proof positive—attention was directed towards the said vehicles, in case there should be risk of fire or explosion.

Risk of fire, no. But of explosion, more than risk, as Plummergen observed in the back of the van an assortment of household valuables, varying in size, but all portable, and certainly identifiable in the open light of day. The sight did more than suggest that previous suspicion of the unknown vehicles had been justified. Wrathful Plummergen, recognising its own property, fell upon the thieves—and Murreystone, rejoicing in the chance to work off some of its bottled-up spleen, waded in as well.

The strangers were hopelessly outnumbered, though theirs was no quick surrender. The doughty Men of Kent hailed the support of their de-coached colleagues as fists flew and the battle surged up and down The Street. Delphick, Brinton, and the others recognised that, realistically, they could do nothing until tempers had cooled a little, and the strangers had yielded.

178

Yield, in the end, of course they did. Odds of more than three to one may sound glamorous in regimental memoirs, but in real life means almost certain, bloody defeat. Major-General Sir George knew to an instant when the time had come to call a halt: and called it.

Chief Superintendent Delphick of the Metropolitan Police looked towards Superintendent Brinton of the Kent constabulary. Brinton had his eyes closed and was muttering to himself: Delphick listened to the low-pitched rhythmic outburst and supposed it to be a string of oaths.

"Handcuffs, Potter, and fast," said Delphick, when it became clear that official etiquette was the least of his friend's concerns. "And you'd better call an ambulance or two while you're about it."

As Potter nodded and hurried off to the police house, Brinton opened his eyes and gazed about him with a disbelieving air. He shook his head and groaned. "Traffic'll have kittens when they see this little lot . . ." A throat was cleared pointedly at his side. He jumped.

"Want me," enquired Jack Crabbe, "to slip along for our tow truck, Mr. Brinton? Not that we're exactly touting for business, me and Dad, but, well, the garage isn't more than a step up The Street, and . . ."

Brinton took another long look at the crumpled cars and the battered van, at the broken glass and smears of burned rubber on the road, and emitted a faint moan. He closed his eyes again and resumed his muttering. Sir George, who had been conferring quietly with the admiral, sized up the situation at once and hurried over as Delphick was starting to think that the mutters, repeated over and over in a monotone, resembled a mantra rather than an outlet for Brinton's undoubtedly strong emotion. The chief superintendent felt a chill finger suddenly caress his spine. Of what—of whom— did the word *mantra* remind him?

"Carry on, Jack—Crabbe." Sir George included father and son in a quick and knowing glance as he observed Delphick's attention focus on something other than the immediate problem. "Leave the pair of you to use your judgement—can't have the place left looking like a scrap metal yard, can we? Sort out the paperwork later," with a nod in Brinton's direction. "More important now to clear

Her Majesty's highway—freedom of the road, and so forth."

Jack nodded, much gratified, then headed north on foot to fetch the tow truck. His father, eyeing the glass and twisted metal on the road, looked back at his waiting coach, and hesitated, brooding on his tyres.

Delphick, having scanned the scene around him and failed to find what—(or rather whom)—he sought, now moved closer to Brinton, ready to utter words of encouragement.

Potter appeared, and with the aid of Bob and Foxon began handcuffing the six prisoners, to an accompanying chorus of jeers and catcalls from the circle of onlookers. Brinton opened his eyes again and watched as the last lock was snapped shut. His lips still moved in anguished muttering. Delphick strained his ears to make out what he was saying.

He nudged his friend in the ribs to bring him out of his trance. "I haven't the faintest idea," he told him sternly. "And I fail to see how you can possibly blame all this on—well, on the person you're obviously blaming—because she isn't anywhere around, is she? Just take a good look!" For Brinton, as Delphick had suspected, had been chanting "Miss Seeton, where the hell's Miss Seeton?" as if everything that had just happened was entirely her fault.

Brinton sighed, raising his eyes to heaven. "Why bother looking? I believe you! She *isn't* anywhere around—but you know as well as I do she doesn't *need* to be. She just sets the ball rolling—prancing about by the sight-screen, scaring the pants off those chummies in the pavilion—then off she skips, all innocence and surprise, waving that damned umbrella." At this, Delphick tried to speak, but was ignored. "We don't," continued the superintendent glumly, "have to know where she's skipped off *to,* because it doesn't matter—the damage is already done . . ."

Above his groan, Very Young Crabbe coughed. "You looking for Miss Seeton, Mr. Brinton? She's most likely still on the coach, I reckon. No place for a female, such a—"

He leaped several inches in the air at Brinton's bellow of rage, then melted quickly into the crowd as Delphick, seizing his anguished colleague's arm, shot him a warning look. The Oracle led the superintendent as far from everyone else as he felt it proper for the nominal boss of the operations to go. "Chris, I'm sorry," he said, in a voice that barely trembled. "I really didn't think she'd had anything to do with, er, all this, and I can't understand—"

Brinton cursed him fluently. Delphick smothered a grin.

"I've no doubt you're right. In which case, why don't we make the best of a bad job, and leave everything in the capable hands of Potter and the rest, and find out exactly what's happened—and what Miss Seeton's had to do with it all? If anything, that is. When I last observed her making for the pavilion, she wasn't carrying her umbrella, as far as I recall, which surely suggests . . . but such speculation is pointless. There's only one way to satisfy our curiosity, so come on—the walk will do you good." And he dragged his friend south past the wide ribbon of metallic wreckage, towards Crabbe's coach.

The coach was empty.

Delphick, startled, called Miss Seeton's name more than once without an answer. Very Young Crabbe, who had followed the police officers, stared down the aisle with a scowl. "She *was* here, sure's the three of us. She was all hot and bothered on account of that business with the sight-screen, poor old duck. Said she'd only just realised why everyone'd started hollering at her, and did I mind if she took a seat for a spell while she got her breath back to apologise properly—only, well, with 'em all suddenly running and shouting like that she could never've got off the bus . . ."

Brinton was all set to groan again when Delphick seized him by the arm, his head cocked to one side. "Chris, listen! Would that, by any chance, be an ambulance heading our way? Ten to one MissEss hopped off home to phone for one when she saw what was going on—they've arrived much sooner than I'd have expected from Potter's call. In which case, she's either still in her cottage, or on her way back here to see if she can help in any way." Honesty made him add, after a pause: "I hope." He shot a glance at his quivering, red-faced friend. "But there's only one way to find out for certain, so come on."

Brinton, still in his trance, followed the Oracle as he strode in the direction of Sweetbriars. Delphick, who had been thinking, started to share his thoughts out loud. "Bob is a good man, of course—and so's Potter—and Foxon, too. I'm sure they wouldn't let him do a bunk, even if he *is* a pal of Sir George's . . ."

Brinton woke up, and stopped dead. "You mean you're expecting the admiral to do a bunk? I don't believe it! Why, the man as good as saved the match!"

Delphick raised amused eyebrows. "Not cricket for him to be a burglary mastermind, you mean? I'd have said it was the best possible cover. As far as I understand it, once Dan Eggleden was out of action, the man pretty well volunteered himself into the team—and he put on a regular firework display, remember, to ensure every single house in Plummergen was empty for his pals to loot at their leisure. What's more, if you think about it, the game isn't over yet. They've got three runs more to make . . ."

Brinton was still spluttering at the chief superintendent's side when, to an accompaniment of ambulance sirens, they reached Sweetbriars, and found the garden gate open: as was the cottage door at the end of the short front path. Delphick, with a look of *I told you so* for Brinton, rapped with relieved knuckles on the frame, and called:

"Is anybody home? Miss Seeton, are you there?"

A pause, a startled exclamation, a hasty rustling, and Miss Seeton appeared from the sitting room with a worried expression which faded as she first recognised her visitors, then reappeared as she greeted them and said:

"Oh, dear, is anyone badly hurt? I intended, you know, to return once I had telephoned, but then I—well, as they have safely arrived, one must assume they are now in better hands than mine. The ambulance, I mean." She blushed and dropped her gaze. "And those poor people in the cars." She tried to sound more definite. "Of course, you know, they faint so very often—girls, that is, at school—and one is naturally accustomed to incidents of that sort—but general first aid is, I fear, rather beyond me, and far better left to those who are more knowledgeable, although one would have wished, of course . . ."

Her cheeks were pink, and her hands danced in the air as she uttered her disjointed excuses. Delphick eyed her sharply. He said: "You meant to go back, and something distracted you, didn't it? Something you thought you'd better put down on paper before you forgot it?"

Blushing, guilty, Miss Seeton could not deny it. Delphick said: "I'd like to see what you've drawn, if I may."

Her hands danced all the more. She raised troubled eyes to his. " . . . not finished . . . dreadful waste of time . . ." murmured Miss Seeton, ashamed. Delphick shook his head.

"Remember, you're under contract," he said, and prodded Brinton, a fascinated observer of the scene, with a brisk elbow.

The superintendent yelped, and nodded as Miss Seeton turned her anxious gaze in his direction. "Under contract," he managed to blurt out, to Delphick's satisfaction and Miss Seeton's confusion. She blushed all the more at his words. Had one appeared reluctant to fulfil one's professional obligation? If, indeed, it was, because there had, after all, been no crime committed, which was when the IdentiKit drawings for which one was retained by the constabulary were required—and therefore no reason to suppose the police would be interested in one's personal impression—especially when it was so, well, uncomfortable—of one who had, after all, not been long in the village. And, as such, surely deserving of the courtesies normal between host—if one might so consider oneself after seven happy years—and guest.

"Guest," murmured Miss Seeton, looking more ashamed than ever. Delphick smiled at her, for once misunderstanding.

"Don't worry about us, Miss Seeton. We can look after ourselves—I've no doubt the superintendent here would welcome a cup of tea for his, er, nerves, but I can always fix that for him. If I don't know by now where everything is in your kitchen . . . We'd both far rather you went back and finished your drawing than bothered yourself with the, er, amenities. Believe me, we won't feel affronted in the least."

He nudged Brinton once more, and the superintendent mirrored his colleague's smile. Miss Seeton, looking startled, found herself smiling back, then dropped her gaze to her still-dancing hands and blushed again. Conscious of Delphick's eyes upon her, she blushed even harder; hesitated . . .

And then hurried back to the sitting room.

# chapter
## -25-

BRINTON WAS ABOUT to follow her, but Delphick caught him by the sleeve. "We'll make tea, just as I suggested," he said. "She'll be glad of a cup if she's on overdrive, the way it would never surprise me to know she was—didn't you see how she was all of a twitch? Which means," said Scotland Yard's Seeton expert, with authority, "that she's going to produce something we'll be very glad to see, once we've persuaded her to show it to us . . ."

Brinton, stumping down the little passage to the kitchen in his friend's wake, rolled his eyes. "She's already shown us, hasn't she? Back there, in the road." He dragged out a chair and collapsed at the table as Delphick tended to kettle and teapot. "A ruddy nightmare, that's what she's *produced*. If you ask me, the only person who'll be *glad* of what she's done's your garage bloke. Wonders for his business, *that's* what she's done."

"And—if you insist on blaming Miss Seeton for what's happened—surely for yours as well, Chris." Delphick shook his head at the injustice of his friend's attitude. "Think about it for a moment. Whose recent daily reports, I'd like to know—unless I've misunderstood completely—have been full of unsolved burglaries?"

"Umph." Brinton scowled, rubbing his chin and rereading in his head six weeks' worth of files. "Yes, well, so that gaggle of chummies Potter's putting the cuffs on might just be the lot we've been looking for—"

"I think I'd bet on it, knowing Miss Seeton."

"—and then, they might not. In which case, *knowing Miss Seeton*'s got nothing to do with it. Remember, you're the one told me back there it wasn't her fault those cars chased each other's rear ends up and down the road—"

"That was before I realised she'd not only been hanging round the pavilion and alerting suspicion to what was going on inside, but had been riding on the bus, as well—and was therefore likely to be . . . shall we say, on her usual form?"

"Oh, do let's." Brinton rolled his eyes again, sighing heavily. "After dropping a hundred-ton crane smack on top of a coiners' lair, and causing gridlock in the city for an encore, why not another little traffic jam right outside her front door, just to round it all off nicely? Usual form, indeed!" He caught Delphick's expression, clutched at his hair, and groaned. "No, you're right, and I'm being unfair—she's done it again, hasn't she? Gift-wrapped the whole bunch for us, even if it *was* in sheet metal instead of fancy paper. That lot out there being carted off to hospital's the crowd we've been chasing these past few weeks, no question." Then he sat up. "Or maybe not—because I know MissEss as well as you do, Oracle. Why's she still Drawing if the case is closed? What's she know that we don't? Or"—a look of alarm darkened his eyes—"is she already planning her next little adventure, and giving us advance warning? I think I'll just go quietly barmy now, and save her the bother. There's a limit to what anyone can be expected to put up with." He shuddered. "I bet they're all a bunch of nervous wrecks like me, back at the Yard."

"Inspector Borden of Fraud and his colleagues have every reason to be grateful to Miss Seeton," said Delphick, raising his voice as his quicker ears caught the opening of a door and the approaching patter of female feet down the passage. "As, indeed, have we." And the feet stopped outside the kitchen.

Delphick called: "Come on in, Miss Seeton, tea's almost ready, And while we're drinking it, you shall show us your picture—or pictures, if you've drawn more than one. That is, if you'd be so kind," he added, as Miss Seeton came shyly through the half-open door and hovered, her hands no longer dancing, beside the refrigerator. "I can tell," Delphick said, "that you've finished, haven't you?"

She nodded, looking unhappy; but, since such was her habitual look when being coaxed or coerced into parting with any of the instinctive drawings for which Scotland Yard so prized her services, Delphick paid no attention. He set pot and crockery on the tray and made as if to pick it up.

"Shall I carry this through for you, Miss Seeton? Or—might there be a chance of some of Mrs. Bloomer's fruitcake? We didn't have such a splendid tea as the players, you know. Sandwiches are no substitute for Martha's cooking, though I won't ask for gingerbread. I'm sure Bob will be along as soon as he can to see you, and you'll want to save it for him. But if we have all the . . . business sorted out before he arrives, why, so much the better, wouldn't you say?"

Miss Seeton, who had looked by turns relieved, anxious, apologetic, amused, pleased, and relieved again as Delphick spoke, now explained that she could, she feared, only offer biscuits, as dear Martha had been so busy, these last few days, baking for the team teas, that she'd had only enough time to make a *small* fruitcake, of which the last slice, she regretted, had been eaten that morning, with her coffee. But they were, she added, with a glance at Brinton's bulk, chocolate; and, she thought, nourishing as well as delicious. If they didn't mind too much, that was to say.

Delphick took three seconds to work out what she was saying, nodded back, smiled, and said that chocolate biscuits—which he knew to be one of her favourite sorts—would suit admirably. And, in all the bustle of hunting out the tin, and the plates, and rearranging the tray, Miss Seeton lost her look of guilty discomfort over what she had just sketched, so that the chief superintendent had high hopes of learning something to his forensic advantage before very much longer: although, after Brinton's remarks, he couldn't help wondering exactly what this might be.

Brinton, deciding that his self-diagnosis of a nervous breakdown abrogated him from further responsibility, followed Delphick and Miss Seeton as they made for the sitting room. The superintendent reasoned to himself that Potter, Foxon, and Bob Ranger were fully capable of dealing with the ambulance, and the tow truck, and the burglars—if that's what they were, and knowing Miss Seeton you couldn't really doubt it. At a guess, she'd disturbed a splinter group of the main gang helping itself to the players' belongings as their colleagues turned over the Plummergen houses, empty while the inhabitants were up at the cricket ground, watching the match . . .

"Admiral Leighton," muttered Brinton. It still seemed incredible. Potter, who'd mentioned the village's newest inhabitant in his weekly report, evidently approved of the bloke. So did the Colvedens, and Mr. Jessyp—you didn't invite people into your cricket team if you thought they were wrong'uns, did you? Still, Brinton was the first to admit you could never really go by appearances. Take Miss Seeton, now. Your typical English spinster schoolmarm, tweeds and lace handkerchiefs and hatpins, and that umbrella . . .

"Bosh!" The ejaculation set the teapot wobbling in his hostess's pouring hand. "Oh, sorry, Miss Seeton." Brinton cleared his throat. "A sneeze—going down backwards, you might say."

Miss Seeton nodded sympathetically. "Dear me, yes, your hay fever, Superintendent. Such a pity, and so inconvenient when visiting the countryside, is it not?" And he breathed a quiet sigh of relief that she didn't seem to recognise the excuse as one he'd used on previous occasions.

He might have expected Delphick—who knew his friend no more suffered from hay fever than he did—to say something, but the chief superintendent appeared to have missed the little exchange. He accepted his cup from Miss Seeton with a murmur of thanks, then returned to studying the sketchbook he had picked up almost as soon as he'd set the tray on the sitting-room table. It wasn't, Brinton observed, the small, almost jotting-sized book Miss Seeton had been using at the cricket match—the one, he realised, she must have left behind when she started all the recent kerfuffle by slipping off to the pavilion . . .

He couldn't bear it: he had to know. And, as Delphick was apparently too busy to ask, then, dammit, Chris Brinton would ask, instead. He cleared his throat again.

"Miss Seeton, I just wondered—why did you leave your chair and go over to the pavilion without telling one of us first? I mean, if you'd spotted the thieves inside—and there we all were right next to you, as fine a bunch of coppers as anyone could want . . ."

Delphick's head went up as he tuned in to his friend's question. He, too, would like to know her reason: and well done, Chris, for asking. He'd been so interested in these sketches he hadn't got round to thinking of it yet.

Miss Seeton turned pink. "Oh, dear—one feels so badly about distracting the batsman's eye—the importance of *see-ing* properly, which of course, as an artist . . . and particularly when dear Mr. Delphick had already . . ." Her eyes fell, and her hands danced another of their unhappy little dances. She gulped. "When . . . when everyone was calling and waving, I thought—so very friendly—I had, I fear, forgotten about crossing the sight-screen, and I felt so . . . and, naturally, one could hardly return to the chair without disturbing them again. And it was so very hot, which is why . . . and when I saw Crabbe's coach, and dear Jack's father resting on the step, I thought perhaps . . . He was so kind, and allowed me to take a seat on the bus while . . . and then . . ."

"Yes, yes, we know all that." Brinton met Delphick's *I-told-you-so* look with a nod and a rueful grin. "But why did you, er, want to cross the sight-screen to begin with?"

"It was so very hot," she said again. "So bright on the paper—the sunlight, you know. And dear Anne had taken it when he ran across the pitch—not that one grudged it for a moment, of course. Nudity," said Miss Seeton, oblivious to the embarrassment of explanation in the matter-of-fact tones of an art teacher, "is all very well, in its place. Which is not in the middle of a cricket match." Even now, there was the hint of a twinkle in her eye. "Such foolish behaviour—but so very clever of dear Anne, though the glare, of course, made it difficult afterwards to see the paper in any great comfort. I thought she might have forgotten, and that I could save her the trouble of bringing it back by fetching it myself . . ."

Brinton found that he was holding his breath. Delphick stared at his friend in some alarm. The superintendent was turning redder by the minute, though references to blood pressure would probably do more harm than good. The Oracle turned to Miss Seeton with one of his kindest and most understanding smiles and said gently:

"Your umbrella, of course. Yes, Miss Seeton, I believe that explains almost everything . . ."

Almost, but not quite. As Brinton let out his pent-up breath with a gasp and quenched his boiling blood in a long, welcome gulp of tea, Delphick turned back to the sketches over which he'd been poring. Miss Seeton regarded him with some anxiety. Had one been too, well, ridiculous—or impertinent? Certainly unwelcoming, in one instance . . .

"You haven't dated these," Delphick said, "but I believe I can guess which are the drawings you've made since your return from Scotland. This, I take it, is the first." And he held up the page covered in wounded birds. "Cranes," he said, with a smile.

Miss Seeton blinked. "Do you think so, Chief Superintendent? I wasn't sure, myself, whether they were cranes or herons, but if you believe them to be cranes . . ."

"I most certainly do." Delphick showed the sketch, with another smile, to Brinton. "What do you think, Chris? Not a doubt of it—injured cranes. Some, quite badly injured—so that they've . . . collapsed . . ."

"Oh," said Miss Seeton, faintly.

"Well, I'll be . . . blowed," amended Brinton rapidly, remembering where he was. "These aren't rocks, they're the rubble from when the coiners' house fell in, of course—and these'll be the fifty-pence pieces the blighters were forging!" He stabbed with a startled finger at the irregular—the seven-sided—circles Miss Seeton had taken for hailstones, and favoured his hostess with a wondering look. "Miss Seeton, you're a ruddy marvel, if you don't mind me saying so. Who'd have thought it? Cranes. Well, well."

Delphick hid another smile as Miss Seeton, blushing, was heard to murmur that she really hadn't meant . . .

He took swift pity on her. "The Chinamen, of course, we understand at once, in view of the performance put on by the admiral earlier this afternoon." He turned to the next page after briefly showing Brinton Miss Seeton's first attempt at a cricket match, and the oriental influence to which she had, unknowing, succumbed. He hesitated, looked from the drawing to Miss Seeton with a frown, then passed without comment to the next page.

"The pink elephants and the carthorse we know about, if even half of what Anne and the others told us is true. But the chap in the leather apron interests me. Would you call it a good likeness of—what's his name? Eggleden? Plummergen's blacksmith, anyway."

"Daniel Eggleden, yes." Miss Seeton beamed. "A skilled and knowledgeable craftsman, Mr. Delphick, and such a pleasure to watch at his work. It is a great pity that his arm was broken—he made my fence, you know, as well as the balustrade for Miss Wicks—her cottage, I mean."

Delphick nodded, turning to the next page. "This, as I recall, is Miss Wicks. Flooded out of house and home, and currently staying with the Knights. But that's not their place behind her in your drawing, is it? It's her cottage, balustrade and all. Who are those people visible through the windows?"

"I've really no idea," said Miss Seeton, reaching for the sketchbook. "She lives, as I expect you know, entirely alone—oh. Well, of course—the fire brigade, I suppose. Because of playing their hoses. After the horse, and the fire, and the flood . . ."

"Yes, we heard about that." But Delphick didn't look convinced that her interpretation was the right one. "You'd recognise the firemen, would you? It is, after all, a local service. Take a good look, now."

And the frown with which Miss Seeton had to confess her ignorance of any of the people she'd drawn was enough for the Oracle. "Then these must be the burglars," he deduced. "Without a doubt." And Brinton's expression was one of awe.

"Oh," said Miss Seeton again. "Oh, dear . . ."

"Two more," said Delphick kindly, "and then we're done. The last first, I think—the one you've just finished. You said that your other drawing is a good likeness of the village blacksmith—of Daniel Eggleden." Miss Seeton regarded him warily, but nodded. "Then, who is this?"

And he showed her a sketch of one who could be nothing but another blacksmith. He wore a leather apron and had broad shoulders and mighty forearms, ending in huge hands. One hand held a hammer, the other a long piece of paper, with what looked like rows of figures on it. To one side of the leather-aproned man stood an anvil, behind the whole scene a fire burned, and on the walls of the vaguely limned room were horseshoes, as well as a shelf of large and heavy spring-bound volumes.

"Ledgers," said Delphick softly, watching Miss Seeton's face. "The St. Leger, as we all know, is a horse race—but I don't believe that's what you were referring to. This man isn't called Leger, or Saint, or Derby—not even Grand, or National," with a chuckle. "Is he, Miss Seeton?"

Puzzled, she shook her head, peering at the sketch and frowning again, ignoring his little joke. "I don't think so," she said. "That is—well, he might be, I suppose, as one could hardly be expected to know his name, although I don't believe I've ever heard of—ever met . . . that is, I'm sure this is just a—an imaginary man. To make up for poor Dan Eggleden's inability to work for so long . . ."

But Delphick, in turn, was shaking his head. "I think not, Miss Seeton. He's *not* an imaginary man, and I believe I can put a name to him, though I do, I admit, have the advantage of you, in that the Yard has its rogues' gallery of portraits, and the good old regulars don't like to try new tricks. Because if this picture shows who I believe it does—I know him, Miss Seeton. And, thanks to you, I know that he's the mastermind behind the burglaries you've been having around here . . ."

And Miss Seeton said faintly, "Good gracious."

# chapter
## ~26~

DELPHICK HELD THE sketchbook out to Brinton. "I don't know whether you've heard of him, but hazard a guess, based on a little prompting from myself as you look at this. A chap in a leather apron, knee-deep in horseshoes and hammers and all the appurtenances of the forge—but cluttered up with what we might loosely call the work of an accounts department: in ledgers and . . . *bills* . . ."

"Bill Smith!" cried Brinton, after fifteen thoughtful seconds. "Burglar Bill, as I live and breathe—good grief, I though he'd been put away years ago!"

"Put away, and subsequently released, I fear, on several occasions. Proclaiming loudly, the last time, that he'd be going straight from now on—to the disbelief of all concerned, though proving it, of course, was another matter. But now . . ." And Delphick looked with some pride towards Miss Seeton, whose expression was still one of bewilderment.

"Congratulations, Miss Seeton. He may be too canny now to do the dirty work himself, but Bill Smith's one of Scotland Yard's oldest friends. One might almost say he's one of the dearest, too, for as burglars go, he's a decent chap. He abhors violence, and refuses even the risk of any rough stuff—he's loyal to fences, and always sells the proceeds of his exploits through regular contacts—he never robs the same house twice, and never makes a mess. Indeed, he takes pride in leaving the place as tidy as he found it . . ."

There came a muffled snort from Brinton, and Delphick's voice quavered as he, too, remembered the mess left in The Street by Burglar Bill's less efficient junior colleagues. "Ahem! Yes, well, Bill Smith will very likely be himself, ah, tidied away before much longer, once he's received a visitation from the force and answered a few questions. He's honest enough, for a burglar. He'll find it hard to deny, I fancy—particularly as we seem to have most of his team already in custody." He looked again at Miss Seeton, then turned back the pages of her sketchbook.

"Most, but not all, I think," he said quietly.

Miss Seeton's quick eye recognized the drawing at which he was looking, and she blushed. Her hands began to dance their unhappy little dance once more, and she lowered her gaze.

"I might," said Delphick, "have expected a picture of the admiral among your sketches, Miss Seeton. But you don't seem to have drawn him at all, until this afternoon."

"Admiral Leighton?" She brightened perceptibly at this apparent change of subject. "Well, of course, one gathered that he was the star of the match—all the cheers, and the comments during tea but I made so many sketches, in order to have a good selection for the final painting, once I have decided how it will be. In my haste to retrieve it, I must have left it on my chair—my umbrella, that is to say. And my smaller sketchbook. If you wish to see those drawings, I feel sure it will be safe until my return—and I will certainly do my best to include . . ."

Delphick was shaking his head, and she fell silent. "It isn't those sketches I'm interested in, Miss Seeton. I was, if you'll excuse my saying so, watching you while you drew them. I was particularly struck by your picture of Admiral Leighton with the pavilion behind him. My first thought, when the burglars were spotted inside, was that there was some connection between the admiral and the pavilion—but then I remembered that you showed a flag flying. The, er, gin pennant, perhaps? I understand that Sir George thinks very highly of Rear Admiral Leighton."

He cocked a quizzical eyebrow at Brinton, who grinned, and nodded. Miss Seeton smiled politely, looking puzzled. Were they not, after all, both senior officers, with distinguished war service? The admiral, and Sir George, that was to say, not Mr. Brinton and Mr. Delphick—who also were, of course, senior officers, and distinguished—but of a very different sort. "Although both fighting," she murmured, "if one might be excused so picturesque a turn of phrase, the forces of . . . of evil." And she signed and shook her head.

"A force for evil?" Delphick regarded her closely. "It does appear that such was your view of her, from this." And he showed Brinton the sketch of Miss Annabelle Leigh, dark and sinister and crooked, her eyes slits, her hands grasping talons. "Recogniseable, and revealing," Delphick said, as his friend first goggled, then stared at the portrait while the artist blushed, knotting her fingers in distress.

"I feared . . . so unworthy—so *unkind*," murmured Miss Seeton, all the old misery returning. "To be so envious of a greater talent—of youth, and beauty . . . when one had always supposed that a teacher's greatest wish would be to see one's pupils excel . . ."

Delphick recalled being introduced by Miss Seeton to Miss Leigh—who had seemed, he now realized, rather more uneasy at the constabulary status of the little spinster's companions that anyone with a clear conscience ought to have been . . . Miss Seeton, in her introduction, had mentioned the younger woman's artistic abilities: and here, on the page of the older woman's sketchbook, Miss Leigh had been portrayed with the full paraphernalia: easel, paints, sketching block. Yes, he could understand how Miss Seeton might suppose this drawing to suggest her own jealously: in a lesser character, such could indeed have been the case . . .

But in this case, no. There was nothing petty or mean about Miss Emily Dorothea Seeton: he was shocked to realise how miserable she'd been making herself since she'd drawn this portrait. He addressed her kindly, but firmly.

"Please, Miss Seeton, don't torment yourself any longer. Miss Leigh is no doubt a skilled artist—but she really should apply her skills to a more honourable cause. After all, someone has been telling the burglars where to go, and the best times to burgle, and the easiest routes in and out of the houses . . . and what better method than for an artist to sketch these houses, and make detailed notes? Nigel Colveden was telling me at tea all about his latest young lady and her self-styled journeyman artistry . . ."

There was a long pause, during which Brinton exclaimed again that he'd be blowed; and during which Miss Seeton's fingers slowly unravelled themselves, and her eyes lost their look of distress. She said at last:

"If Miss Leigh has indeed been advising these . . . these criminals where they might most easily commit their crimes, then that is truly shocking. She must be stopped at once, Mr. Delphick—but oh, dear. Poor Nigel. He seemed so very taken with her, you know, although one might venture to hope that Lady Colveden . . ." She blushed again, though with far less anguish than before, and murmured of respecting confidences, particularly when they were no more than the merest impressions.

"A mother's instinct, no doubt," said Delphick gravely. "And an artist's," with a bow for Miss Seeton. "Feminine intuition comes in many guises—though I must wave the flag for my own sex, and say that I doubt if Miss Leigh would have fooled anyone for long, if she'd remained in the village. Even Nigel, who's so prone to fall in love . . . but this is no time for speculation. As far as we know, Miss Leigh won't have let on, when her confederates were being pursued, that they were anything to do with herself. She'll be anxious to maintain her innocent persona until she can make her escape from the area undetected, and with so many cars blocking the road . . ." He cleared his throat and continued.

"And with so many people wandering about, I don't imagine she'd be able to do a bunk just yet—if, indeed, she even knows what's happened. Sir George was adamant, I could hardly help noticing, about letting none of the fair sex on the bus—and might I guess that Anne and the others were trying to tell us that as you, Miss Seeton, were already on board, they didn't see why they should not be permitted to join in the fun?"

Miss Seeton, thinking things over, agreed that this was doubtless the case, although it had been a great surprise to her when so many of her friends had crowded so quickly into the bus, and dear Jack Crabbe's father had driven it out of the cricket field before she could explain that she didn't really want to go anywhere, because everyone had shouted so loudly she couldn't make her voice heard above the noise, and in any case one had always understood that it was inadvisable to address the man at the wheel. Especially when the man wasn't Jack Crabbe. Because his father, she feared, did not, perhaps, possess the same grasp of the rudiments of driving as his son . . .

Without forcing the matter at all, while Miss Seeton was speaking, Delphick drained his cup of tea, nodded to his colleague to do the same, and set his plate and saucer back on the tray. A good hostess, Miss Seeton automatically followed the gentlemen's lead. Delphick smiled at her and rose to his feet.

"You've been, as ever, most kind and helpful, Miss Seeton—but now I think it's time to put your theories to the test. Or rather"—as she began to demur—"the theories I've evolved, with the help of your sketches. I'd like to take the book with me, if I may." He glanced towards Brinton. "By the sound of things, Potter and the others must be well on the way to clearing up outside—the tow truck's gone up and down The Street at least three times while we've been talking. I think we'll, er, risk it now."

Brinton shrugged. "May as well see the thing through to the bitter end." He cast a wary look at Miss Seeton, who was picking up the tea tray while Delphick's attention was diverted. She smiled before either man could speak.

"I believe that, just this once, one may be excused poor housekeeping, although I am not altogether sure she would agree—but I appreciate that it must be a matter of some urgency. Going back, I mean, to apprehend her. She takes excellent care of me, and is so particular—but if she has no idea I intend leaving them to soak while I accompany you, there can be no cause for concern. The young woman, I mean. Dear Martha—and then, there is her chair, and my sketchbook." She sighed. "He will be sadly disappointed, I fear, though there can be no question that it is the right thing to do—as he will realise, of course, and more so because of his father. Poor Nigel. A Justice of the Peace . . ."

Her words, as they so often did, had left Brinton floundering, but Delphick was better able to work out what she was saying, and assured her that they understood perfectly, and would wait while she carried the tray into the kitchen so that they might escort her back up The Street to the cricket ground, where she could collect both her sketchbook, and Lady Colveden's chair.

"You might even get to sit in it again." He checked his watch. "They must have lost a good hour's play with all the commotion, and if half the players are still off the field taking statements and towing wrecks, the match can hardly have started without them, even though it's not very likely they'd be needed. Once Bob gets going, it shouldn't take him long to knock up three runs . . .

"Well, they may have started, but I don't believe they can have finished yet," he went on as, Miss Seeton having duly carried her tray and locked her front door, the three were hurrying down her front path. "It's too quiet in the pub—I'm sure most of Plummergen would be in there celebrating by now, if it was all over."

There were indeed no signs—or sounds—of life in the George and Dragon just across The Street. There were also no signs of life along The Street, apart from Jack Crabbe, busy attaching yet another of the wrecked cars to his tow-truck. As Delphick and his party passed the wicket-keeper, he gave them a cheerful wave.

"Don't reckon they'll need me to bat, do you? Three to make, and young Bob doing well—shouldn't take long. Be a fine old night in the George once we've won."

"And night, indeed, draws on," murmured Delphick, as the three made their way towards the cricket ground. "It's well past six—Potter and however many of the others went should by now be back from the police station with a selection of crooks safely kicking their heels in the cells. Statements, where appropriate, will have been taken, and solicitors notified—I wonder if any of them has mentioned Miss Annabelle Leigh." He quickened his pace. "A pseudonym, one imagines. For a while, I wondered whether the similarity of the admiral's surname might not suggest . . . but I have every faith in your judgment, Miss Seeton."

Miss Seeton uttered a little squeak of protest, but he ignored it, and smiled at her. "Every faith," he repeated firmly. "I feel sure that, when we compare your impression of Miss Leigh, which I have here, to that of the admiral in the sketchbook we must retrieve before anything else, we'll find no reason to dispute my conclusions. She will be questioned thoroughly, of course, and given every chance to explain, but I fancy that our journeyman artist has journeyed her last, and drawn her final picture for some considerable time."

"Oh, dear," said Miss Seeton, as they neared the cricket ground; and then, as they heard the murmur of male voices, "Oh, good. Surely they cannot have resumed play, if they are all talking? So distracting. Which means I will be able to do some more sketches, particularly if dear Sergeant Ranger is about to score the winning goal—I mean, wicket. I mean, runs," with a blush for her confusion, which was understandable, if not excusable. One hadn't cared to think of that glorious young creature being sent to prison, losing the freedom of body and spirit so necessary for the development of the artist: but there was no doubt, or so it seemed, that she had behaved badly, to say the very least. Dear Mr. Delphick was so knowledgeable—so seldom wrong about such matters . . . And Miss Seeton sighed.

Brinton, too, sighed; the thought of spending the rest of his nominal day off interviewing burglars and arranging bail, instead of enjoying a jar or two with his friends in the pub, had depressed him. Then, suddenly, he perked up.

"Anyway, it's bound to have put a stop to all that daft village feuding, and a good thing too. No more dirty tricks—you can't be on the same side as a bloke when you're chasing burglars together and then not have a nice friendly chat with him the next time you see him, can you?" He added yet another tick to Miss Seeton's credit on his mental scoreboard: three hundred years of hostilities, ended with just a couple of waves from her umbrella. Amazing.

Delphick, who'd been listening to the cricket-ground murmurs, said, "I wonder. They don't sound quite as friendly as I would have expected, in the circumstances. Anyone would think they were about to start fighting one another, rather than play a game of cricket." And he lengthened his stride, oblivious to the pattering feet of Miss Seeton as she hurried to keep up with him, oblivious to Brinton's laboured breathing. The aural evidence of escalating strife obliterated all else . . .

They turned in through the gateway and saw a crowd of angry, white-flannelled men gesticulating and arguing in the immediate neighbourhood of the pavilion. A crowd of interested spectators—among whom, Delphick was relieved to note, Annabelle Leigh was numbered—stood watching, listening, and from time to time moving to join in. There were raised voices; and shouts; and gestures, varying in intensity and meaning. Tempers, it seemed, were growing short.

"Plummergen against Murreystone," deduced Delphick, with a quick look at the faces of the combatants. "But what in heaven's name can they be squabbling about now? I'd have thought you were right, Chris—that they'd finally made it up—but this looks more like civil war than the original!"

"Sounds like it, too," growled Brinton, glaring about him for Foxon, Potter, or anyone else who could be trusted to explain. "Sir George doesn't look too happy, either. You'd expect the umpires to stay neutral."

"I think," ventured Miss Seeton, "that it is the Murreystone umpire with whom Sir George appears to be vexed. He has, you know, a most expressive face—Sir George, that is, and not just because it is rather flushed, at present. And a vocabulary," she added, with a twinkle, "to match, in moments of stress, which I believe we must consider this to—"

Her last words were drowned out in one final explosion of wrath from Sir George, followed by a roar of approval from Plummergen. Murreystone yelled back, and tried to move away—possibly in order to end the argument. Plummergen hands caught at Murreystone sleeves. Loud voices grew even louder.

Very Young Crabbe erupted from the throng and made his scuttling escape, unnoticed by Murreystone. He glanced back at the pavilion, hesitated, and continued to run in the opposite direction:

Directly into the paths of Delphick, Brinton, and an astonished Miss Seeton.

"Hold hard, Crabbe!" Delphick put out a hand. "What's the big hurry?"

"They Murreystone buggers," explained Very Young Crabbe, panting. "Want me to drive 'em back on the coach, they do—soon as they saw me, that was it. Stumps to be drawn at six sharp as previously agreed, and never mind streakers having punch-ups in the pavilion, or burglars being chased by bus, or cars getting smashed up and down The Street. I might've known as Jack'd be the canny one, taking all they wrecks to the garage and leaving me—hell's bells, they've seen I've gone! Well, now I'm going!"

And, brandishing a set of keys in his hand, he fled.

"Well!" Brinton glared at the onrush of Murreystone as it came running towards him, and folded his arms. "Of all the dirty tricks—stop! All of you—not one step nearer!"

Murreystone stopped, recognising Wrath in the personage of a superintendent of police. Bob Ranger, though a mere sergeant,

came thundering to stand at Brinton's side; Delphick, familiar to
some as a Scotland Yard man, stood grimly by his colleague surveying the insurgents as Sir George and Admiral Leighton hurried
to support the forces of law and order.

"Stand right where you are!" bellowed Brinton, rejoicing in the
chance to release some of the blood pressure he'd had to hold in
check for most of the afternoon. "That bus goes nowhere until the
innings is over—stumps or no stumps! So get back to your places,
you horrible shower, or I'll have the lot of you nicked for obstruc-
tion!"

Bob scored the necessary three runs off the second ball of the
over, which he smote mightily, for six.

Very Young Crabbe was coaxed out of hiding to drive the
losing team back to Murreystone, with Bob assisting Potter and
Foxon—who'd come back from Ashford just in time to see the
end of the match—to ride shotgun. The bus returned to Plummergen in safety, and they trooped off to join their friends
in the George and Dragon.

Miss Seeton, whose tender heart was troubled for Nigel, had
accepted Lady Colveden's kind invitation to supper and was
trying to take the young man's mind off his woes by asking
him exactly what all the fuss had been about. Nigel, who'd
been depressed to learn what a poor judge of character he was,
decided he must cultivate discrimination, and wisdom, and fair-
mindedness from now on: and this would be as good a time as any
to begin.

"Murreystone," he said grimly, "are a load of double-crossing,
narrow-minded, two-faced cheats!"

"Nigel," warned his mother, spooning vegetables. Nigel
shrugged, and sighed.

"Oh, well. You can't blame them, I suppose, though I'd be sorry
if I thought I'd play the same sort of trick in a similar situation. *Not*
the way you and Dad brought me up." He glanced towards the top
of the table, and the empty seat where his father usually sat. But Sir
George, with his new friend Admiral Leighton, hero of the match,
was, like most of Plummergen's menfolk, in the pub. Young Mr.
Colveden somehow hadn't felt like joining them.

"Murreystone just weren't playing the game, Miss Seeton. Downright sneaky of the beggars, when you remember it was because of Plummergen all their things weren't pinched from the pavilion—well, mostly it was." For the first time since the truth about Annabelle Leigh had been made known, Nigel managed a faint grin. "I suppose you could argue that if their idiot streaker hadn't been so slow to get dressed that the burglars bumped into him, they might just have got away with it—but he was, and they did. And they didn't, thanks to Bob raising the alarm"—he grinned again, rather more cheerfully—"and leading Plummergen to the rescue—but catch Murreystone admitting it! They insisted on sticking to the original agreement, you see— stumps to be drawn at six o'clock, and no argument. Which would have meant Bob wouldn't have had his chance to score the winning runs . . ."

But, thanks to Superintendent Brinton and the others, they had; and he had. Which is why everyone was drinking his health just half a mile down the Road, in the George and Dragon. Nigel didn't bear a grudge for having been run out: these things happened. Good for Bob—he was a decent chap.

A lucky one, too, with a wife like Anne . .

And maybe other people could be lucky, in the end. One woman might have pulled the wool over his eyes—the utter cheek of leaving that *Anyone's* article in her bicycle pannier for him to find— her strange response when she found out his father was a magistrate (he could kick himself for not having wondered why) . . . but that didn't mean they were all like the same, did it? Everyone was different . . .

Nigel glanced at his mother, then at Miss Seeton, and found himself smiling. Women didn't come much more different than those two. He spooned more potatoes and began to chuckle.

"If you wanted to, Miss Seeton, I suppose you could say the way they tried to behave simply wasn't cricket . . ."

And, as his audience chuckled with him, he began to wonder whether it would seem terribly rude if, once supper was over, he nipped off down to the George, and his friends, and a few pints, instead of staying at home for coffee.

# HAMILTON CRANE

**Hamilton Crane** is the pseudonym of Sarah Jill Mason, who was born in England (Bishop's Stortford), went to university in Scotland (St. Andrews), and lived for a year in New Zealand (Rotorua) before returning to settle only twelve miles from where she started. She now lives about twenty miles outside London with a tame welding engineer husband and two (reasonably) tame Schipperke dogs. Under her real name, she is currently working on a new mystery series starring Detective Superintendent Trewley and Detective Sergeant Stone of the Allingham police force.